THE DEATH TRADE

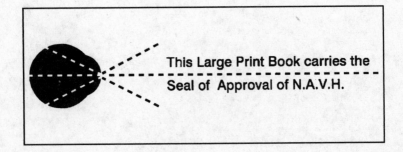

This Large Print Book carries the
Seal of Approval of N.A.V.H.

THE DEATH TRADE

JACK HIGGINS

THORNDIKE PRESS
A part of Gale, Cengage Learning

GALE
CENGAGE Learning®

Detroit • New York • San Francisco • New Haven, Conn • Waterville, Maine • London

LIBRARY OF CONGRESS CATALOGING-IN-PUBLICATION DATA

Higgins, Jack, 1929-
    The death trade / by Jack Higgins. — Large print edition.
        pages ; cm. — (Thorndike Press large print core)
    ISBN 978-1-4104-6393-7 (hardcover) — ISBN 1-4104-6393-1 (hardcover) 1.
    Large type books. I. Title.
    PR6058.I343D43 2014
    823'.914—dc23   2013040434

Published in 2014 by arrangement with G. P. Putnam's Sons, a member of Penguin Group (USA) LLC, a Penguin Random House Company

Printed in the United States of America
1 2 3 4 5 6 7 18 17 16 15 14

IN MEMORY OF MY DEAR FRIEND
David Coleman

Above all things, cherish life while you can, for death is serious business.

SUFI SAYING

····

HELL ON EARTH
HOULA
SYRIA

····

1

The man who called himself Ali LeBlanc surfaced from a deep sleep to cries of anguish, screams, gunfire, exploding grenades, and the roaring of many engines. It was the stuff of nightmare, but rising from the bed above the little café and moving to the window, he saw that this was no dream.

The previous evening he had left Tehran on the night plane to Iraq using his Iranian passport. His shabby canvas bag had a false bottom containing three passports, and he had chosen the French one for the flight from Baghdad to Aleppo. At an extortionate price, he had obtained a hire car to take him to Homs, and from there he intended to cross the border and proceed to Beirut. Its population of two million, its multiplicity of races and religions, would swallow him up. His Lebanese passport in the name of Ali LeBlanc indicated that he was of mixed French-Lebanese parentage, and a doctor, which was true enough, although he had not practiced for some years.

He wore a dark suit showing signs of wear. He was sixty-four years old and seemed older, his eyes tired, his white hair uncut. Age had caught up with him, as well as the strain of traveling in the war-torn country, and he had stopped to rest at the café in the small town of Houla. As he stood by the window, the door opened and the café owner, Hassan, rushed in, beside himself with rage.

"Stay back from sight. It's a butcher's shop out there."

LeBlanc peered carefully from behind the curtain and was horrified by what he saw. Automobiles of every type, and light trucks with machine guns attached, crisscrossed each other, shooting at anyone who moved. Across the square, men and young boys were being lined up against any available wall and machine-gunned. Even the mosque was being used for that purpose. Women were being dragged inside by the hair, their assailants in semi-military uniforms, looking more like brigands than soldiers.

LeBlanc said, "Who are they?"

"They belong to an organized gang culture a bit like the Mafia used to be in Sicily. Throat cutters to a man, they think nothing of killing children, the women after they've been raped. They're supposed to be militia. The regular army tolerates them and lets them do the dirty work, which suits the government down to the ground." Hassan's face was wild.

"So what happens now?" LeBlanc asked.

"The doors are bolted, I've paid my protection. My wife and two daughters are locked in the cellar." He shrugged. "There's not much more I can do. Come down to the kitchen. With what's going on out there, you won't have much of an appetite, but there's coffee and several stronger things under the counter."

LeBlanc glanced out of the window. The shooting had abated considerably. Most of the vehicles had roared away, the men in them laughing and shouting to each other, with only the odd shot in the distance. "No one moaning in pain, not a sound out there," LeBlanc said.

"The bastards take pleasure in finishing everyone off," Hassan told him, leading the way downstairs and into the kitchen.

There was an eerie quiet, the aroma of good coffee from an electric percolator, an old AK-47 assault rifle lying on the table. Hassan went into the café and returned with a bottle of Courvoisier cognac, LeBlanc put

13

his bag on the table and picked up the rifle as Hassan got the bottle open.

"May Allah forgive me." He raised it to his mouth. At the same moment, the outside door was kicked aside and a brute of a man, bearded, long hair bound by a bandanna, slipped in. He was carrying a Mac 10 machine pistol.

"Drop it or I'll drop you," he told Le-Blanc, who placed the AK-47 on the table at once.

"Of course," he said.

The man reached for the bottle. "Cognac, eh? Are we celebrating something your old friend Hamid should know about?" He poured some into his mouth. "Good stuff. Seems a shame to keep it all for ourselves. Why don't you let your wife and daughters out of the cellar so they can join the party."

"No, damn you, I will not do it," Hassan said violently.

Hamid raised the Mac, and LeBlanc cried, "No need for that! I have money, see?" He unzipped the bag, reached into the false bottom, produced a wad of currency, and dropped it on the table. "A thousand American dollars."

Hamid was mesmerized and reached out to examine the money for himself. "Where did you get this?"

"Tehran," LeBlanc told him. "And there's more. Just let us go."

"Show me," Hamid ordered.

LeBlanc scrabbled in the bottom of the bag, but instead of pulling out more money, he produced a Russian Makarov fitted with a silencer and shot Hamid between the eyes, fragmenting the back of his skull and hurling him outside into the street through the open door. A dull thud was the only sound.

It was darker now, starting to rain on the dead, and Hassan kicked Hamid's body. "Bastard," he said, picked up the corpse by its long hair, and dragged it out to where the rest of the bodies lay.

He turned to LeBlanc, who had followed, and grabbed him in a huge embrace. "How can I repay you?"

"That your wife and daughters are safe from harm is thanks enough. It was fortunate I had the pistol. Normally I wouldn't have such a thing, but it seemed prudent when I started my journey. These are bad times, and more to come, I think."

"Then go with a blessing from me," Hassan said. "Now I must join my family." He returned to the café and closed the door.

When LeBlanc checked the yard at the rear, he found the Citroën intact. He found a water tap and washed away the blood that

15

had splashed across his face as Hamid's skull exploded, using a scarf he found in the car, then checked the contents of the bag. A little blood he had missed on his left hand smeared the Iranian passport, and that gave him an idea. What if his Iranian passport, his true identity, turned up on one of the victims in the street, a body so damaged it could not be identified? He got in the Citroën and drove across the square to the mosque.

The piles of bodies were truly shocking, and there were many badly damaged faces. As the rain increased, he knelt beside one old man, smashed beyond recognition, his white hair soaked in blood. He felt in the man's inside pockets, removed a couple of letters and an identity card, smeared the Iranian passport with the dead man's blood, and put it in the pocket. He said a short prayer, returned to the Citroën, and started on the road toward Homs, passing many refugees and a small group of United Nations observers in their blue helmets.

Several hours later, he left the Citroën in Homs and found a taxi driver willing to deliver him to Wadi Khalid on the border with Lebanon, walking through on foot, armed with his Lebanese passport, where he bypassed a crowd of Syrian refugees.

16

The commander of the border post examined his passport and said, "See anything of the troubles in your journey, Doctor?"

"I'm afraid so. I passed through Houla. A dreadful sight."

"It must be good to be home after such an experience."

"Yes, indeed." Ali LeBlanc passed through and took one of the waiting taxis.

The approach to Beirut an hour later was astonishingly beautiful: the hot sunshine, the vivid blue of the sky and sea, the harbor crowded with ships, the whiteness of the houses jumbled together as they lifted in untidy terraces, climbing the hill of the old quarter together.

He left the taxi by the harbor wall and crossed through the open-air cafés, crowded with people of every race and color and religion and so very different from what he had come from. He climbed quickly through narrow cobbled alleys, turned into Rue Rivoli, and came to a building several stories high that was painted a vivid blue. Not surprisingly, a sign by the door said "Maison Bleue," and he rang the bell.

The woman who answered was someone he knew. Sixty-five, of mixed blood, she was handsome enough, and wore a black silk robe and a white chador, the obligatory

17

head scarf for Muslim women. There was astonishment on her face.

"Is that you, Doctor? How long since we have seen you?"

"Five years. How are you, Bibi?"

"All the better for seeing you."

"And the apartment? Everything in order?"

"Of course. Your arrangements here have never failed."

And everything was indeed in order: the cool white-painted hall, the ancient lift that took them five floors up, the penthouse apartment with its huge living room, the terrace with the blue-and-white-striped awning and the view over the city and the crowded harbor and away out to sea. He dropped his bag on the coffee table, took off his soiled jacket, and dumped it on the floor. She moved to pick it up.

"You look terrible, *chéri,*" she told him, and there was a certain tenderness in her voice. "I think you have come from a bad place."

"From hell on earth. I would not have believed such evil could exist if I had not witnessed it with my own eyes." He hesitated, then: "I killed a man for the first time in my life."

She said calmly, "A bad man?"

18

"No, a truly *evil* man. A murderer of women and children."

"Good," she said. "God has already forgiven you. Sit down and rest. I'll bring you a coffee with something in it perhaps, run you a bath, and see what's available in the wardrobe. What you're wearing will go out with the trash tomorrow."

He sat on the couch by the coffee table, opened the bag and explored the false bottom, taking out further packets of dollars, the Makarov pistol, and a small electronic notebook of the kind that could only be opened by a code word. All these things he placed on the table, and last of all, he produced a mobile phone that looked like any other but definitely was not. It had unlimited range, a battery that never needed charging. With the press of a button, it was impossible to trace, and he did that now and entered the code of the person who had provided him the phone. She answered immediately, sounding breathless.

"You didn't block your location," she said. "I can see you're in Beirut. Did you mean to do that?"

"No, I was careless," he replied. "I didn't expect to have to use the phone you gave me in Paris so soon. Where are you?"

"London, Hyde Park. So tell me, what's

happening?"

"I've done it. I've left Iran, left the nuclear facility. The nuclear bomb they've had me working on — in theory, it's ready to produce, but they'd still need me to supervise the construction. I couldn't stay any longer. I fled to Beirut, and I'm using an alias. They'll come after me when they find there's nothing on the computers."

"You tried to wipe your research?" she said. "But they can still find it. There's nothing that can't be recovered these days."

"I know, but it'll slow them down. And I never put the most important data on the computer in the first place. All my calculations were worked out on paper and then destroyed."

"But what about your mother and daughter? Your masters put them under house arrest to ensure your obedience."

He was silent for a long moment. "No more. After Vahidi and I flew back from Paris, he disappeared. When he didn't rejoin me at the nuclear facility, I asked questions, but nobody would tell me anything. Then I got an anonymous phone call. Apparently, he was driving them to an appointment when their car was hit. My mother, my daughter, they're dead. Vahidi's in a military hospital in serious condition."

"Oh my God," she said. "Oh, I'm so very, very sorry. That's terrible. And you mean to tell me the authorities are putting a lid on it? How stupid. They can't keep that up for long. I wonder what they'll do."

"I didn't stop to find out. I've been making preparations for years, false passports and money, in the hope that something would come up, although not something as dreadful as this. I left in the middle of the night, but obviously they'll be after me."

"So you haven't left anything at all that could lead to a computer trail?"

"It's all in my head, I told you."

"Which means they're going to try very hard to get ahold of you."

"Then I'll have to see that they don't."

They talked for a few minutes more, then he hung up.

Bibi, who had been standing behind the room screen listening with a frown, a striped towel over her arm, now smiled and entered.

"I've run a bath for you. You'll feel much better after a nice long soak."

He smiled. "You're right."

"I always am." She ushered him into the bathroom, then came out again, closing the door.

A fantastic story. She'd always liked Ali LeBlanc. He was a decent man who'd

21

looked after her well over the years, but what she'd overheard was too good to keep to herself, and there might even be money in it.

But who should she tell? The Army of God charity on the waterfront was a front for al-Qaeda, everybody knew that. There was the Café Marco next door. Its owner, Omar Kerim, was a genial thief interested only in money; his underlings were constantly stealing it for him all over Beirut. She knew him well, had once worked for him.

She made her decision, went into the kitchen, found a large linen shopping bag, and called, "I'm just going out to the market. I'll be back soon."

She stepped into the lift and went down, while in the bath, head raised and slightly turned, Ali LeBlanc slept.

■ ■ ■ ■

Two Weeks
Earlier
Nantucket
London

■ ■ ■ ■

2

The wind roared as waves crashed in on the shore of the Nantucket beach but failed to drown the sound of the helicopter as it landed up at the house.

Former President Jack Cazalet said to his Secret Service man, Dalton, "Have General Ferguson brought straight down."

Dalton nodded, cell phone to his ear, and Cazalet turned to meet the demands of his cherished flatcoat, Murchison. He picked up another stick to toss into the sea, and it was instantly retrieved and dropped at his feet as the jeep braked and Major General Charles Ferguson emerged.

"The salt is bad for his skin, Mr. President, he'll need a good hosing. I've said that a few times over the years." He held out his hand.

"So you have, old friend," Cazalet told him. "Which can only mean that Murchison is getting a bit long in the tooth. You can cut out the title, by the way — there can only be one Mr. President."

"Who offered me the use of his helicopter when he heard I was coming to New York, and suggested I drop in and see you on the way. I'm supposed to offer an opinion or two on the Middle East to some UN select committee or other."

"Will the President be there, too?"

"No, he's on his way to the UK to spend a couple of days at the Prime Minister's country retreat at Chequers. Then on to Berlin, Brussels, perhaps Paris."

"Oh, the times I've spent at Chequers." Cazalet laughed. "I used to love that place. I've been asked to put in an appearance at the UN myself — but I imagine you knew that."

"Yes, I can't deny it," Ferguson said.

"I expected nothing less from the commander of the British Prime Minister's private army. Isn't that what they still call you people in the death trade?" He smiled. "You'll stay the night, of course, and accept a lift in my helicopter to New York tomorrow?"

"That's more than kind," Ferguson said.

Lightning flickered on the horizon, thunder rumbled, it started to pour with rain. "Another stormy night," said Cazalet. "Let's

26

get up to the house for the comforts of a decent drink, a log fire, and the turkey dinner Mrs. Boulder has been slaving over all afternoon."

"That's the best offer I've had in a very long time," Ferguson said.

"In you get, then." Cazalet smiled. "Let's see if we can reach the point where I've flattered you sufficiently that you can tell me why you've really come to see me."

The dinner was everything Cazalet had promised. The coffee and port were served, Murchison steamed on the rug in front of the fire, and Dalton sat at the end of the small bar by the archway to the kitchen at his usual state of readiness.

"Well, it's an interesting situation," Ferguson said. "It concerns a man named Simon Husseini. He was born in Iran to a French mother, his father an Iranian doctor who died of cancer years ago. Husseini followed in his father's footsteps, and his work on medical isotopes has saved thousands of lives."

"Good for him," Cazalet said.

"Yes. But as one of the world's great experts in the field of uranium enrichment, his masters insisted that he extend his research into nuclear weapons research."

"And he agreed?"

"No choice. He's a widower, but his ancient mother is still alive and living with his forty-year-old daughter, who's an invalid. They're under house arrest in Tehran."

Cazalet was not smiling now. "The suffering some people have to go through. So how do things stand?"

"Very badly. The word is he could be close to making a nuclear bomb, and, worse, one that is cheap and four times as effective as anything else on the planet."

Dalton looked startled, and Cazalet said, "God in heaven. How sound is this information? Is there real substance to it, or is it just bogeymen stuff put out by the Iranians to frighten the pants off us?"

"That's what we've got to establish," Ferguson said. "One of our people has a connection with Husseini, very tenuous at best, but it provides the hope, rather slight at the moment, I admit, of my people touching base with him."

"Then make it happen right this instant, General, before the whole damn world blows up in our faces."

Ferguson nodded. "I thought you'd say that, sir. In fact, as we've been talking, I've already changed my mind about this trip. The UN committee is just going to have to get on without me. As soon as we get to New York tomorrow, I'm heading straight back to London."

"Very sensible," Cazalet said. "And since it'll be an early start, I think we'd better close the shop and go to bed. But not before you tell me about this connection of yours. . . ."

At the Holland Park safe house in London, Roper sat in his wheelchair in the computer room, drinking tea and smoking a cigarette, when Ferguson, wearing pajamas and a bathrobe, called him on Skype.

"There you are," he said. "What time have you got?"

"It's four o'clock in the morning in London, people tucked up in their beds, the sane ones anyway."

Ferguson said, "I'm at Jack Cazalet's beach house on Nantucket. It sounds like the storm of the century's outside trying to get in."

"That must be interesting. How is the great man?"

"Not best pleased at the news I bore about Husseini. At least, he wants us to get moving on it right away. Some of the people I've talked to seem not to want to believe it could even happen. I get an idea that's even the way the CIA sees it."

Roper said, "I can't blame them, in a way. The possibilities are horrendous. No sensible person would want to face the kind of future that would bring. Did you tell him about —"

"Yes. I mentioned Husseini's history as an academic ten years ago, when he was a professor at London University."

"Where he met a certain Rabbi Nathan Gideon and his granddaughter, a young second lieutenant out of the Military Academy at Sandhurst named Sara Gideon. Who now works for us."

"Correct. And I've actually figured out how we can use her. Did you know that Husseini is due in Paris this Friday to receive the Legion of Honor?"

"No, I didn't. That's a surprise, that he's being allowed out of Iran," Roper said. "But maybe not. His work on medical isotopes has saved a great many lives, his mother is French — from the Iranian government's point of view, the signal it sends letting him accept the award is: Look what nice people we are."

"Except that they've got his mother and daughter in Tehran under threat and they know Husseini's not the kind of man to let anything happen to them. He's totally trapped," Ferguson pointed out. "But still, there might be an opening. That's why I'm arranging for Sara to be on the guest list at the Élysée Palace. She'll stay at the Ritz, which is where Husseini will be."

"Together with his minders," Roper said.

"Of course. But I'm betting there might not be as many of them as we might think. With his mother and daughter held hostage, there's no need. We have an asset at the Ritz named Henri Laval. He told me that when Husseini visited a year ago to lecture at the Sorbonne, he had only one man with him, a Wali Vahidi, who stayed with him in a two-bedroom suite."

"Do I look him up or have you already done that?" Roper asked.

"Wali Vahidi, thirty years a policeman of one kind or another. He's been Husseini's bodyguard for eight years, sees to his every need, more like a valet, but I'd be wary of taking that too much for granted. He saw plenty of action in the war with Iraq and survived being wounded. He holds a captain's rank in the military police, so he can look after himself."

"What does Sara think of all this?"

"I haven't told her yet," Ferguson said. "I left a message to say I'd be back for breakfast on Thursday morning, and that you and

I would like to call in at ten-thirty. It would be interesting to get her grandfather's input, too, since he knew Husseini so well. You could also check with Colonel Claude Duval to see what kind of security French Intelligence is putting on Friday night at the Élysée Palace. He's in London at the moment."

"Is that all?" Roper asked.

"You have something to contribute?"

"Yes, I think she needs backup. What do you think of sending Daniel Holley with her? Though we'd have to find out where he is — in Algiers or deep in the Sahara, for all I know."

Ferguson said, "No. Those two enjoy what people of a romantic turn of mind describe as a relationship, and I don't want anything getting in the way of this serious business. I agree she should have backup, though."

"So what's the answer?"

"To send Dillon with her, of course. Good night, Giles, I'm going back to bed for another hour or so," and he switched off.

At six-thirty, Roper phoned Claude Duval, who was annoyed and showed it. "Whoever you are, it's too early and I don't want to know."

"It's Roper, you miserable wretch. Did

she say no last night, whoever she was?"

"Something like that." Duval laughed. "What in hell do you want, Giles?"

"The Legion of Honor award to Simon Husseini at the Élysée Palace on Friday night. Will you be attending?"

"Should I?" Duval's tone of voice had changed.

"Sara Gideon will be there with Dillon."

Duval was completely alert now. "What for?"

"Ten years ago, he was a friend of her grandfather, the famous Rabbi Nathan Gideon. Sara was just out of the military academy and met Husseini. Now she just wants to say hello to him if she gets a chance."

"And I'm supposed to believe that, *mon ami*?"

"Of course. Do you seriously expect her to persuade him not to return to Iran?"

"Of course not. He'd never leave his mother and daughter behind."

"So Sara and Sean can turn up?"

"Yes, of course they can come, and what's more, I'll go myself, if only for the pleasure of meeting the divine Sara again."

"You're a diamond, Claude. I'd kiss you on both cheeks if you were close enough."

"Like hell you will." Duval laughed.

"You're definitely up to something, Giles, and I'll find out if it's the last thing I do."

Tony Doyle, back from military court duty at the Ministry of Defence on Thursday morning, didn't bother to change out of his uniform. He helped Roper and his wheelchair into the back of the van using the hydraulic lift, and they were turning into the drive of Highfield Court exactly at ten-thirty, to find Ferguson's Daimler parked in the drive, the chauffeur at the wheel. The front door opened and Mrs. Cohen appeared.

"Major Roper, how are you?" she asked, for they had become good friends.

"All the better for seeing you, Sadie," he said as the two men eased the wheelchair into the hall.

"They're waiting for you in the study," she said, opening the large mahogany door. "In you go. They're on the coffee, but I know you like a decent cup of tea, so I'll go and get you one."

Roper felt the usual conscious pleasure on entering the beautiful Victorian library with the crowded bookshelves, the paneled walls and Turkish carpets, the welcoming fire.

Nathan Gideon was a wise man and looked it. He had a gray fringe of beard,

34

white hair topped by a black velvet yarmulke, and he wore an old velvet smoking jacket that Roper had seen many times. He seemed to have stepped in from another age entirely.

He shook Roper's hand. "You look well, Giles."

"No, I don't. As usual, you are far too kind," Roper told him. "We both know I'll never look anything like well again."

"My dear boy, feeling sorry for ourselves, are we?"

"Of course." Roper produced some of his special painkillers and crunched them.

Sara, who had been sitting opposite Ferguson by the fire, stood up, poured a whiskey, and brought it to him.

"Wash them down, Giles." She kissed him on the head and turned back to her seat.

She was wearing a one-piece flying suit and boots. Roper said, "I must say you look terribly dashing in that gear."

"That's nice of you," she said. "I just passed my practical navigation test doing a takeoff while it was still dark. I can't tell you how wonderful it is as dawn breaks. I'm grateful you arranged for me to learn to fly with the Army Air Corps, General."

"I believe in people extending themselves," Ferguson told her. "Maybe it's to your advantage, but who knows when it could suit my purposes, too." He turned to Roper. "Nathan and Sara and I were just discussing Husseini."

"So what's your opinion?" Roper asked the rabbi.

"Simon is a fine doctor. His interest in matters nuclear fascinated him because of the medical possibilities, and that was what led him to his pioneering work on medical isotopes. He's spoken of the awesome powers generated by nuclear energy as the Breath of Allah, which must surely have endeared him to Islamic opinion."

"I'm sure it did," Ferguson agreed.

"However, further studies showed how quickly it could be turned into a weapons-grade material, which was exactly what his masters were hoping for, and, as you know, it was impossible for him to argue because they had his family," Nathan Gideon said.

"The fact that they're allowing him to venture into the outside world only proves how serious the threats must be to his mother and daughter," Sara put in.

"You're dealing with a regime that doesn't stop at stoning a woman to death," Roper pointed out.

Ferguson said, "Have you spoken to Claude Duval?"

"Yes, I have, he's on our side and intends to be there himself. But let's get clear now what we're expecting to come out of this." He turned to Sara. "The ball is in your court."

She sat there, looking intense and troubled. "I always remember Simon as a lovely man. I'd just like to hear him tell me out of his own lips what *he* would like done to solve this situation. I have a horrible feeling that not much *can* be done and we'll be at a stalemate, but I'd still like to try."

"And so you shall," Ferguson told her. "And it's of vital importance that you do, because if he really has made progress beyond the theoretical in his nuclear experiments, it's essential that we get our hands on his results before Iran does."

"But what if he doesn't agree? What if he's faced with something so terrible that he'd rather nobody had it at all?" Sara asked.

Ferguson said calmly, "It'd be too late. He could destroy his case notes, all records of his findings, and it would do him little good. A scientist discovers what already exists. Eventually, someone else would follow in Husseini's footsteps."

She took a deep breath and said sadly, "I suppose you're right."

"I'm afraid I usually am, Captain." Ferguson got up. "I'm sure you'd agree, Nathan."

The rabbi, looking rather troubled, nodded. "I'm afraid so."

Ferguson said, "Thank you for your input. We'll get on. We've much to do, and in limited time." He kissed Sara on the cheek. "I can see this is getting to you, but be of good heart. There's a solution to everything, I've always found. We'll see you at Holland Park early this evening, Dillon and the Salters and we three. Maggie will produce one of her special meals and we'll discuss the future. It's been very useful, Rabbi, my sincere thanks."

Roper was already moving out in his wheelchair, and Ferguson followed him.

It was just after six that evening when the taxi dropped Sara at Holland Park. It always reminded her of a nursing home or something similar, although the razor wire, high walls, and numerous cameras indicated a different agenda. She didn't have to do anything except wait to be identified. The Judas Gate in the massive front entrance clicked open, she stepped inside, and it closed behind her. She crossed the courtyard to the front door, went in and made her way to the computer room, where she found Roper in his wheelchair in front of the screens. She removed her military trench coat.

"Where is everybody?" she asked.

"The boss is in his office, the Salters haven't turned up yet, and the music wafting through from the dining room is Dillon on the piano. It pains me to say it, but the wretch is really quite good."

"No, he isn't, he's damn good," Sara called as she went out along the corridor and turned into the dining room.

Dillon, at the piano, was just finishing "Blue Moon" while Maggie Hall was laying a table for dinner.

"Don't exaggerate, Sara," he said. "I play acceptable barroom piano, that's all."

"Don't you be stupid," Maggie Hall said. "You're better than that and you know it, so why pretend?"

She moved off to the kitchen. Dillon said, "There you go, she should be my agent. What would you like?"

"What about 'A Foggy Day in London Town'?"

"Why not?"

He started to play, and she listened and said, "Could you up the tempo?"

He did, attacking it hard, and she started to sing, surfing the rhythm, her voice lifting, and Maggie Hall emerged from the kitchen and stood there, staring. The music soared and came to an end. Maggie clapped vigorously and called, "Right on."

Dillon was astonished. "Where the hell did that come from?"

"I learned to play guitar at twelve and I loved singing, but just for me. I don't advertise."

"Well, you should. Any cocktail bar I've ever been in would snap you up."

Clapping broke out from behind, Sara turned and found the Salters standing in the doorway.

"Marvelous," Harry Salter said. "I'd give you a booking any time for my restaurant."

"Harry's Place, Sara," Billy told her. "You haven't been yet, very classy. We'll take you."

"Some other time." Ferguson appeared behind them. "But not now. There's work to be done. Back to Roper, if you please."

For half an hour, Roper ran a compilation of film featuring Simon Husseini, mostly garnered from news reports. It finished, and Ferguson said, "Well, there you are. That's our man."

"Looks a decent enough chap to me," Billy observed.

Harry said, "Do I take it we can be certain

40

he's not out to blow up the bleeding world, then?"

"He's a decent man who's in a very bad situation and doesn't know what to do about it."

"The way I see it, there's not much he can do," Dillon said.

"I've got film of an Élysée Palace ceremony coming up," Roper said. "Just for information."

They saw a place crowded with people, many of them in uniform or ecclesiastical wear, palace guards in full uniform, a glittering scene, sparkling chandeliers. People who were to be decorated sat near the front and went forward in turn for the President of France to pin on the insignia of the Legion of Honor or whatever. Finally, Roper switched off.

"So there you are," Ferguson said. "What do you think?"

"An awful lot of people," Sara said. "Difficult to make contact with our man."

"Or perhaps the crowded situation would make it easier. There's a buffet, champagne. It would depend on how long you wanted to be in contact with him. Perhaps a few snatched moments is all you could expect."

That was Ferguson, and Dillon said, "There might be an opportunity at the hotel. We'll just have to see."

"Perhaps Duval could be useful there," Ferguson said.

"He's a sly fox, that one." Dillon grinned. "So he may have a useful idea or two. How are we going to Paris?"

"The Gulfstream from Farley Field. My asset is at the Ritz, an aging waiter named Henri Laval. He knows the hotel backward. Can be very useful. You'll be given his mobile number."

"Well, if his help would lead us to a meeting of some sort with Husseini, it will be more than welcome."

"Excellent," Ferguson said. "Now we'll eat and I'll tell you what else I'm planning for the future."

Maggie Hall had excelled herself. Onion soup, poached salmon, Jersey new potatoes and salad, a choice of cheese or strawberries, backed up by Laurent-Perrier champagne.

"You've been too nice to us entirely," Dillon said as coffee and tea arrived. "So what's this about future plans?" he asked Ferguson.

"*AQ.* Two letters only, but we all know they stand for 'al-Qaeda.' Osama may be dead, but in a worldwide sense he lives on and is as potent as ever. His jihadist message appeals to people in every country and from all levels of society. He made them think they were fighting for a just cause, doing something worthwhile with their lives. The purity of terror excuses all guilt from the message. That also has great appeal. Take the Army of God organization. It's a perfectly legitimate charity, dedicated to the welfare of Muslims in many countries. Right here in London, it operates from an old Methodist chapel in Pound Street, and its welfare work is first class."

"And we know from past experience," Dillon said, "that certain areas of its activity are directly linked to al-Qaeda."

"Which would shock many wealthy Muslim businessmen, people so rich that we can count them as being beyond reproach, who provide considerable financial support, based on the fact that the charity promotes interfaith involvement with Christians and Jews and sources at a government level."

"Which would seem to me to muddy the waters nicely," Sara put in.

"Where is this leading?" Dillon asked.

"Many in al-Qaeda's hierarchy have been assassinated in Pakistan and elsewhere by Reaper drones and similar weapons. But sometimes a different approach is needed.

Because of his knowledge of shipping in the Mediterranean, Daniel Holley has been able to give me names of tramp steamers and rust buckets delivering arms of every description on behalf of al-Qaeda."

Sara nodded. "So you want us to —"

"Board some of them at night, drop a few blocks of Semtex into the hold, and sink them. We've done it before. Many times over the years, haven't we, Billy?"

"You're right," Billy said. "A few times, Dillon and me. Twice in Beirut." He turned to Dillon. "Get the diving suits out again."

Harry said, "I'm not sure that's wise, my son; you've been damaged enough in your time. Professor Bellamy would like you to take it easy."

"That was over a year ago." Billy nodded to Dillon. "You up for it?"

"I wouldn't be asking you to pair up with Dillon," Ferguson said. "I was considering you and Holley when he's available." Before Billy or anyone was able to say anything, he carried on. "I was thinking of Sara and Dillon teaming up for something else. In fact, having seen you in action together earlier at the piano, I think it's an excellent idea. But we'll get to that later. We'll have some more champagne now."

Maggie had been standing at the back,

already opening a fresh bottle. She poured it into glasses and went around with the tray.

Ferguson said, "I must say you all seem rather subdued. Why don't you give us a suitable toast, Sean?"

"You're too kind," Dillon told him. "Considering what you've just discussed, I'd say something appropriate would be: We, who could be about to die, salute you."

3

Ferguson left first, then the Salters. Roper retired to the computer room and Dillon decided to use the sauna. Sara chose the quiet of the library and sat checking everything she could find on Husseini. She spent an hour in this way, then returned to the computer room, where she found Roper at the screens.

"Still here?" he said.

She explained what she'd been doing, and he nodded approvingly. "Nothing like being prepared."

"I thought I knew him, but there was a lot I didn't," she said. "What are you up to?"

"Same thing, in a way. Having a look at his Iranian masters."

"That's interesting," she said. "Can I see?"

"Of course you can. I'll put them up in sequence. There's the President. There's the Council of Guardians, which enjoys a lot of influence."

"Who's that man?"

"Well, according to their official release in Paris, they seem to be expecting a few people from London to be joining them. This chap, Emza Khan, is one of the businessmen who support the Army of God charity."

"Can he be trusted?" Sara asked. "Or is there an al-Qaeda connection?"

"I'm famous for not trusting anyone," Roper said, "but I tend to think Khan's on our side. He's a billionaire, the chairman of Cyrus Holdings, which is responsible for Iran's oil and gas interests and many other things. The headquarters is in London. He'll be seventy next birthday."

Khan stared grimly at Sara from the screen, the once powerful body straining to get out of the excellent suit. Sara said, "He looks like he likes to have his own way and normally gets it. Who's the bearded thing in the black suit behind him? That's a hell of a scar bisecting the left side of his face."

"His name is Rasoul Rahim, Khan's bodyguard and thug. Reputedly, he kills people for him whenever necessary."

"Of course he does." Dillon appeared, wearing a toweling robe. "He'll drop in on the Ritz like a lead weight. On the other hand, one sliding stamp of the foot down-

47

ward will dislodge the kneecap of even a seventeen-stone rugby player. Remember that, girl dear, if you're trying your aikido on him."

"And you say Khan's on *our* side?" said Sara.

"You can't always choose your friends," said Roper.

Another image appeared on-screen, a laughing young man, black tie loose, quite obviously drunk, his arms around a couple of women, the three of them looking the worse for wear.

"And who's this, the pride of the nightclub circuit?" Dillon demanded. "What about his Muslim principles?"

"Gone out of the window where the drink is concerned," Roper told him. "That's the son, Yousef. Educated at Harrow, where he twice almost got the heave-ho. Several court appearances for drink driving, brawling. Twice accused of rape by different girls who changed their minds and wouldn't continue to give evidence. He's twenty-six."

"Obviously bought off by Daddy," Sara said. "The girls."

"What would you expect?" Roper added. "Can you stand another?"

"Do we have to?" Dillon inquired.

"Well, you have to travel hopefully," Roper

said. "And if you do, sometimes you get a surprise."

A picture appeared of a man in some sort of army summer uniform, medals making a brave show. He was of medium height, with a bronze aquiline face, black hair, a peaked cap in his hands. His gaze was direct and somber, but to Sara's disquiet she found him rather attractive.

"Lieutenant Colonel Declan Rashid," Roper said. "Military attaché at the Iranian Embassy at 16 Princes Gate right here in good old London town. You know what Muslims are like about family being so important. He's some sort of third or fourth cousin of the Khans."

"Well, that's hardly his fault," Sara said.

Dillon cut in, "But where in the hell did he get the Irish name?"

"His mother was a strong-willed young Irish doctor from Cork named Rosaleen Collins, and his father couldn't deny her anything, which explains where the name Declan comes in. The Rashids weren't Iranians, they were from Oman originally, Bedouins."

"Which means they're warriors," Dillon said.

"Certainly as far as his father, Hassan Rashid, was concerned. He rose to brigadier general in the Iranian Army. Remember, they were at war with Iraq for eight years."

"Why do I sense the worst coming?" Dillon asked.

"Because it did. He was killed in nineteen eighty-six, and unfortunately his wife was with him. She'd visited behind the lines, they went for a spin in a spotter plane and were shot down."

Sara said, "So how old was Declan?"

"Sixteen, and an only child. His mother hadn't been able to have any more children."

"It must have been hell for him."

"It was," Roper said. "I've got the photo to prove it."

The boy in the photo wore desert combat fatigues and the red beret of a paratrooper, a pistol strapped to his right knee, an AK-47 assault rifle crooked in his left arm. The eyes were haunting in the young face, the cheeks hollow.

Sara took a deep breath. "What happened?"

"He was at school here in London at St. Paul's, flew back to Iran right away, but missed the funeral. After that, he simply joined the queue of peasant boys at the recruiting office, of which there were many, joined up, and kept his head down to avoid the search for him. There was another two years of war, during which he jumped five times into 'action' without having been trained for it. It was during the second year that Emza Khan traced him and he was promoted to the officers corps. He was an acting captain at the end of the war and all of eighteen. He's forty-two now and unmarried."

There was silence after that for the moment. Dillon said, "Well, all I can say is it must be the Irish in him. Having said that, I'd buy him a drink anytime."

Sara said, "A remarkable story, and you've gone to a lot of trouble telling us. Is there a reason?"

"The handout from the London Embassy's press office covers the award of the Legion of Honor to Simon Husseini and makes the point that Emza Khan, Chairman of Cyrus, will be visiting to support him."

"Is Khan's son going?"

"I shouldn't imagine so, with his track record. They wouldn't want any more scandal. However, the military attaché from Princes Gate, Lieutenant Colonel Declan Rashid, respected war hero, will be in attendance, all staying at the Ritz."

"It will be just like old home week," Dillon put in.

"But isn't this going to be rather obvious?" Sara asked. "Our presence there?"

Dillon said, "There isn't an embassy in London that doesn't know about Charles Ferguson's motley crew. They know who we are and we know who they are. The real work in our line of business is finding out what everyone else is up to, and that includes our friends. Take Claude Duval. A strong right arm to us, but France will always come first."

"I suppose you're right, although it does get complicated on occasion," Sara said.

"It's a damn sight better than Afghanistan, and you've got the permanent limp to prove it. So content yourself. If you don't mind waiting till I change, you can drop me off at my place on the way home. We'll share a cab. You've had too much to drink."

She laughed out loud. "You've got the cheek of the devil, Sean Dillon."

"It's been said before." He grinned. "But think of the pleasure it gives you helping out a poor ould fella like me." He was gone before she could reply.

Emza Khan had purchased the apartment on top of a tower in Park Lane because it was within walking distance of the Dorchester and it pleased him to have all of the amenities of one of the world's great hotels so close to hand. As time went on, he'd fallen in love with the rural sweep of Hyde Park. Finally, the city by night captivated him, the lights stretching into the darkness as if stars had come down from heaven to please him.

Just now he was sitting by the open sliding windows to the terrace, drinking a Virgin Mary, not that he was averse to adding vodka to it if he wished. As chairman of Cyrus Holdings and incredibly wealthy, he was only lacking in life where family was concerned. Two sons killed in the war with Iraq, a third, Yousef, a libertine and drunk who disgraced himself with whores and refused to take anything seriously. Which left Khan with only Declan Rashid, a remote cousin of the family clan, but a man who would make any father proud, except for one thing — careful discussion with the colonel had indicated that he had not been moved by the words of Osama bin Laden, had not warmed to him at all.

This was a pity and a complete reversal of what had happened to Emza Khan, whose conversion had been quite genuine after hearing Osama speak for the first time. He had immediately contacted the right people, made it clear that he believed in the great man completely, and was soon serving him as required. After Osama's murder, which was how Khan saw it, he had placed himself at the disposal of those carrying on the holy work of their deceased leader via the Army of God. Following instructions, Khan had declared his opposition to al-Qaeda in newspaper and television interviews, and so now that was the public perception of him, and by everyone around him, including Declan Rashid. It would have been absurd, after all, to have believed otherwise, and al-Qaeda was hardly popular with the Iranian government.

He was involved right now with extremely important work concerning the delivery of arms to various places in the Mediter-ranean. He had thought of involving Yousef in it, but hesitated, concerned at the conse-quences if failure occurred. That al-Qaeda could be unforgiving in such circumstances was a known fact.

Rasoul Rahim came in from the kitchen, a green barman's apron over his black suit, his beard perfectly trimmed, the scar vivid on the left cheek.

"You still look like an undertaker in spite of that ridiculous apron," Khan told him.

Rasoul didn't even smile. "How may I

serve you?"

"As Yousef is taking his time about getting here, I can only fear the worst. We'll give him another half hour, then you must go and search his usual haunts in Shepherd Market. In the meantime, mix me a Bloody Mary, and don't forget the colonel intends to drop by on his way home from the embassy with the schedule for the Paris trip."

Rasoul nodded and returned to the kitchen.

Dillon and Sara, sharing a cab on their way to their respective homes, were driving along Curzon Street when Dillon told the driver to turn into Shepherd Market and drop them at the Blue Angel.

"It's a piano bar," he informed Sara. "One of the best in London, with one of the greatest players in the business."

"You rogue, Sean." She shook her head. "You intended this all the time."

"Me darling Sara, do I look that sort of a guy?"

"Absolutely," she told him.

At the same moment, Declan Rashid was turning into the underground garage at Emza Khan's building. As he got out,

55

George, the night porter, joined him.

"I think you should know that young Yousef's on the loose, Colonel."

Declan said, "Is he bad?"

"Drunk as a lord, sir. I refused to give him his car keys and he tried to punch me. Then he said he didn't need the car because he'd find what he wanted in Shepherd Market. He said he'd get me sacked."

"Good work, George, and hang on to those keys. Don't worry about your job, I'll see to it."

He was back in the car in seconds and reversing. It was only a matter of a few hundred yards through empty streets and he turned into Shepherd Market, parked, and saw Yousef at once in the middle of a cobbled alley approaching the Blue Angel, swaying drunkenly. He called his name as Yousef got the door open, and ran to join him, arriving just after him. As he entered, Declan was immediately aware of a woman singing.

Earlier, Dillon and Sara had been greeted by the sound of a great driving piano backed by a trio. Most people had faded away at the lateness of the hour, just a couple of dozen aficionados left. Dillon was welcomed at once by the gray-haired black piano player, who called to them.

"Hey, Dillon, my man, get up here. Who have you got there, old buddy?"

"My very special date. A captain in the British Army."

The pianist leaned over, still playing, and kissed her on the cheek.

"That can't be right. This rascal is IRA. Those guys never retire. Once in, never out, ain't that so, Dillon?"

Dillon said to Sara, "Jacko St. Clair, off a boat from New Orleans."

"That's true, honey, only it was about thirty years ago. Are you for real? Is it true what he says?"

"I'm afraid so," she told him.

Dillon cut in, "She's got a great voice, Jacko."

"You mean she sings with you? Some of that cocktail bar stuff?"

"Tell the barman that, for this time only, we'll do it for free."

Jacko got up. "Be my guest."

Dillon sat down, nodded at the trio, and smiled at Sara. "Show them what you've got, I'll do the intro strong, just so you get used to it." He turned to the trio. "You get that, guys? Then we'll do it again with her joining in. Just remember, Sara, the hero of Abusan can do anything."

His hands moved into the driving rhythm of Cole Porter's "Night and Day," and as Sara swept in powerfully, people in the audience started to clap. The outside door swung open with a crash. Yousef Khan stumbled, fell on his knees, and then turned and grabbed at Declan Rashid, pulling himself up.

"What's going on, and why is that silly bitch making such a row?"

Declan said, "Remember your manners. We're leaving now."

Yousef slapped him in the face, snarling, "You stupid Bedu peasant, why don't you stumble out of here and find some goats to milk?"

Sara, who had stopped singing, moved close to him, followed by Dillon. "The only one getting out of here is you, you piece of camel dung," she told Yousef in Farsi.

He pulled away from Declan and tried to grab her. Immediately, a Colt .25 was in her right hand and rammed up under his chin. A warrant card was produced from her left pocket and held high for the audience to see.

"Do I have to arrest him, Colonel, or can you persuade him to go? I'm an officer of the Security Services."

Rasoul appeared in the open doorway, the

ugly scarred face intimidating. "What's going on?"

Declan ignored him and said to her, "I'm sorry for this trouble."

"Not as much as he is," she said. "I believe he's wet himself."

"Damn you, whore." Yousef's drunken rage boiled over and he struggled to get at her.

Declan pulled him around and shook him. "Control yourself, fool." Yousef spat in his face and Declan hit him very hard, a short and sharp punch, catching him as Yousef's eyes rolled and he started to slide.

Rasoul was outraged. "How dare you do that? His father shall hear of it."

"I'm frightened to death," Declan told him and shoved Yousef into the big man's arms. "Get him out of here, put him in my car, and wait for me."

Rasoul hesitated, then pulled Yousef up over his right shoulder, and Declan turned to Sara and Dillon. "You are a remarkable lady. I won't forget you."

"Or we you, Colonel. That's a mean right hand you've got there," Dillon told him. He grinned at Sara. "Ferguson ought to hire him."

"Your lesson may even do that young man some good," Sara said.

"But you don't think it will?" He smiled. "I would agree with you completely, which is very sad for his family. But I must go. His father will be waiting impatiently to hear how badly he's behaved this time. A habit, I fear."

He left, the door closed, and Sara turned to Dillon. "Let's do it again. I don't like disappointing such a good audience."

"Right on, honey," Jacko called. "And I do believe the barman is offering a free drink to everyone who stays."

"That clinches it." She turned and went to where the band was arranging itself, as the audience settled and Dillon eased behind the piano. He was smiling crookedly as he looked at her.

"What's that smile for?" she said as she picked up her mike.

"I enjoyed seeing you in action." He shook his head. "No wonder they gave you the Military Cross. Now let's get down to business."

His hands slammed into the keys, fingers searching as he launched into that driving rhythm for the second time that night.

They went up in the elevator to Emza Khan's apartment, Declan Rashid leading the way, Rasoul with Yousef draped around him. Emza Khan was sitting in a winged chair by the terrace window reading the *Financial Times.* He tossed it to one side and jumped to his feet.

"What is it, what happened?" He was totally dismayed.

"Ask the colonel," Rasoul said angrily. "The one who beat him."

"Is this true?" Khan demanded.

Declan had two main obligations in his life. One was to his country and its army, in which he had served so gallantly. The other was to the head of his extended family, which meant kissing the hand of Emza Khan and, by tradition, obeying him in all things. The truth was that his Irish half was finding it extremely difficult to follow such a path.

He said to Khan, "Listen to this creature's lies if you must, but Yousef behaved like a drunken sot, tried to attack a young woman who turned out to be an army officer. She had to draw a weapon on him, I took appropriate action and knocked him out. If you want to call in Dr. Aziz to check him over, that's your privilege."

Khan turned to Rasoul. "Get Aziz now. No more arguments, and take Yousef to his bedroom." Which Rasoul did. Khan carried on, "It is most unfortunate, the drinking.

It's a sickness, a known fact. I had great hopes for him." He shook his head sadly. "He was such a lovely boy. I was hoping to take him to Paris. What do you think?"

"God help the chambermaids at the Ritz if you do. I've other things on my mind, like finding out who these people we were involved with tonight are. A name was mentioned, Ferguson. If he's who I think he is, we need to know. I'll borrow your office and computer to link into the embassy."

"Help yourself to what you need," Khan said. "We'll speak later. I must check on Yousef."

He went out.

As the cab turned a corner, Sara leaned against Dillon, eyes closed, and they stayed that way as she murmured, "Are we there? I need my bed."

"So I can see. Can you remember what happened?"

Her eyes opened. "Sean, for your personal information, I like a drink, but never get drunk. So, yes, I remember everything, however improbable it appeared at the time."

"Colonel Declan Rashid and a rotten young bastard called Yousef Khan, do you recall them?"

"Of course I do, and the colonel was far more interesting. Why do you ask?"

He got the door open for her. "I just wanted to remind you he's the enemy."

She got out. "He joined the paratroopers at sixteen and jumped into action five times without any training. Why would anyone do that?"

"Perhaps he had a death wish." Dillon smiled bleakly, followed her, and paid the driver, who drove away.

Sara turned, found herself facing not her own front door but the Judas Gate in the entrance to Holland Park. Dillon opened it for her, pressing a button on his Codex.

"What's going on, Sean?" she demanded.

"Oh, I need to bring Roper up to date on what happened, and we're not all that far from your place. You could have a steam for a while in the spa, even stay in the guest wing, or I can drop you home when I've spoken to Roper."

She sighed. "All right."

They crossed the courtyard and opened the front door, but were surprised to hear Ferguson's voice echoing from the computer room.

"I wonder what he's doing here," Dillon said. "Do you want to face him?"

"No, thanks, the steam room sounds fine."

"Okay, off you go. I'll handle it."

She vanished along the corridor into the shadows, and Dillon stood at the door of the computer room, listening, and then went in.

"Holy Mother, and me thinking you'd wrapped up for the night."

"Oh, we never close," Roper told him.

Ferguson said, "I went home to get some essential papers. I'm due at the Cabinet Office first thing in the morning to brief the Prime Minister on Simon Husseini. I thought I'd come back here and use one of the guest rooms so I'd get an early start."

"So what's your story?" Roper asked. "If you have one at all."

"Oh, I certainly do," Dillon said. "Though there are aspects of it that may not get your seal of approval."

"That sounds sinister," Ferguson said. "Better get it over with and tell us the worst."

He was smiling when he said that, but not when Dillon was finished. "That's incredible. We were only discussing the Iranians earlier and then they go and turn up in the flesh."

"Carl Jung called it synchronicity," Dillon told him. "Events that have a coincidence in time, so that it's understandable to imagine some deeper meaning involved."

"Nonsense," Ferguson told him. "Pure co-incidence. Emza Khan lives in Park Lane just up the road from Shepherd Market, where his son is a well-known drunk in local bars and clubs. The fact that Declan Rashid turns up, obviously trying to clean up the mess Yousef Khan has created for his father, should surprise no one."

"Well, let's put it down to the romantic in me," Dillon said.

"Nothing romantic about it. Things got very much out of hand, and that Captain Sara Gideon drew her pistol in a public place is to be deplored. The Iranians will be taking a close interest in what we are doing, which was the last thing I wanted."

"Or was it?"

Ferguson frowned. "And what's that supposed to mean?"

"That you're a master of guile and wickedness, always stirring the pot."

Ferguson wasn't in the least put out, just smiled cheerfully. "Of course I am, and one never knows what's going to bubble up to the surface. Take Paris and Simon Husseini. Anything could happen, the possibilities are endless." He swallowed the last of his whiskey, got up. "Must get some sleep. See you at breakfast."

Roper said, "What do you think he's up to?"

"I haven't the slightest idea," Dillon said. "When I do, I'll let you know."

He moved to the door, and Roper said, "Are you staying?"

"I don't think so. Sara's downstairs having a steam. She preferred not to face Ferguson at this stage."

"I don't blame her."

"I'll join her and take her home in the Mini when she's ready."

He went out quickly, leaving Roper to his screens.

At Park Lane, Declan Rashid, a slight smile on his face, read the computer report on Ferguson and company that the printer had ejected. When he was finished, he made another copy and went in search of Khan and found him in the sitting room, talking to Dr. Aziz, a small cheerful Indian with skin like brown parchment.

"I've given him a shot of morphine, which will keep him sleeping for eight to ten hours. Nothing broken, but he'll have a bad bruise," Aziz said.

"That was me," Declan told him.

"Quite a punch, Colonel." Aziz smiled.

"Which he richly deserved," Declan told him.

"I'm sure you're right. Drink will be the death of him." He turned to Khan. "But I'm tired of telling you that. I'll call again in the morning."

"I'm very grateful," Khan said. "Anything he needs. I've got to go to Paris for three days, and I'll need Rasoul with me. Can you arrange a nurse?"

"No problem."

"I think the male variety would be advisable in the circumstances," Declan Rashid said and turned to Khan. "I mean it for the best, naturally."

"Of course," Khan said. "See to it as you think fit, Doctor. Show the doctor out, Rasoul."

Rasoul, who had been glowering in the background, did as he was told, and Declan joined Khan over by the great windows and offered the report.

"No, we'll have a martini," Khan told him, moving toward the bar area. "You can read it to me."

Which Declan did as Khan mixed the cocktails, listening as Rasoul, standing against the wall beside the kitchen door, took it all in, too. Declan finished, and Khan passed him the vodka martini.

"What extraordinary people," he said. "Even the woman is beyond belief. Owner, in effect, of the Gideon Bank, and with this amazing war record." He sipped his drink. "The fact that her parents died in a Hamas bus bombing would indicate to me that she is hardly likely to warm to Arabs in general."

Rasoul, listing intently, couldn't help jumping in. "Do not forget that she is a Jew and not worthy of serious consideration."

"Don't be stupid," Declan told him. "Her exploits in Afghanistan speak for themselves. When the Taliban ambushed that convoy at Abusan, she was as good as any man behind that heavy machine gun. Three special forces men to protect her, two of whom died, the third wounded, and she was wounded herself and left with a permanent limp. Forty-two dead Taliban when they counted the corpses."

"Which leads me to ask whose side you are on in the struggle for Islamism in the world today. A Taliban should be looked on as your brother. There is only one God and Osama is his Prophet, or do you renounce that, too?" Rasoul demanded.

There was a moment of complete stillness, horror on Khan's face at the dreadful slip of the tongue, and sudden desperation on Rasoul's as he realized what he had said.

Declan smiled gently. "An error on your part, I'm sure, but the Prophet, whose name be praised, is merciful and will forgive a sinner."

Khan exploded with rage at Rasoul's slip, for any reference to Osama bin Laden, particularly when it involved Declan, was the last thing he and his masters needed.

He shouted, "What nonsense are you talking? Get out of my sight."

Rasoul bowed his head. Forgive me." He turned and hurried away into the kitchen.

Emza Khan said, "A stupid fool, but I keep him on because of his ability to handle Yousef, you know that."

"Of course I do, so no need to apologize," Declan told him. "I'm leaving now. I'll see you tomorrow, and then Paris next stop. I'll brief you on the plane in the morning about Husseini."

"I look forward to it, it should be fun," Khan said. "Particularly the whores."

"I'm sure they're waiting for you in eager anticipation," Declan Rashid said with considerable irony. "I'll say good night."

While waiting for the lift, he considered what had happened. In rage, anything Rasoul said was likely to be the truth, for he was that sort of person, so what did his slip of the tongue mean? And Emza Khan's angry dressing-down of Rasoul had been a little over the top, or had it? Declan shook his head. Any suggestion that Khan could treat the memory of Osama bin Laden seriously was patently absurd. Making money had been the ruling obsession in his life. He was hardly likely to change now, not with the government and the Council of Guardians to contend with in Tehran. The last thing *they* wanted getting its hands on power was al-Qaeda.

He dismissed it from his mind and a few minutes later was driving his car out of the underground garage, joining the two-o'clock-in-the-morning traffic and thinking, somewhat to his surprise, of Sara Gideon.

Emza Khan read the details about Ferguson and his people that Declan had provided. When he was finished, he thought about it for a while. Charles Ferguson and his people had been a considerable nuisance to al-Qaeda, foiling many carefully planned enterprises over the past few years, and Dillon was something else again, murdering many of their best people. Now there was the Jewish woman of untold wealth, which offended him. How many decent Muslim men had she killed? She deserved to die, and so did her friends.

So he went to his study, fed the report Declan had given him through the coded transcriber, punched a button and sent it on its way to room 13 at Pound Street Methodist Chapel, now the headquarters of the Army of God charity, where it was received by Ali Saif, an Egyptian with an English grandmother, which under familial law granted him a United Kingdom passport.

Saif was senior lecturer in archaeology at London University. Specializing in the four-hundred-year occupation of Britain by the Romans was his passion. Involvement with the Army of God and belief in the gospel of Osama bin Laden was his religion, which in itself contained enough excitement for any man.

His study room was packed with three state-of-the-art computers, a transcriber, and various other gadgets, no expense spared, for one thing al-Qaeda was not short of was money.

He sat behind a Victorian desk in a swing chair, twenty-five years of age and already a Ph.D. He wore a khaki summer suit, tinted horn-rimmed glasses that suited his aquiline face, and long black hair that almost reached his shoulders. Just now he was drinking coffee and smoking a cigarette, leaning back in his chair, looking at two computer screens. One showed Declan Rashid's background list of Ferguson's people. Based on this, he had used his skill to pull out the original information, which was now on his second screen, pictures of all the protagonists included.

And what an interesting lot they were, particularly Sean Dillon, the man who'd tried to blow up the British War Cabinet during the Gulf War and almost succeeded. A top IRA enforcer for many years, who ended up in the hands of Serbs and was saved by Ferguson from execution on the understanding that he would serve under him as a member of the Prime Minister's private security squad.

Dillon's score was remarkable. He seemed to have killed anybody and everybody, without fear or favor. One week an assassination, the next, flying some old turboprop plane loaded with medical drugs for children into a war zone.

Some guilt there perhaps, but the important fact was they had all been a considerable nuisance for some years to al-Qaeda. Obviously, punishment was what Emza Khan wanted, and considering the size of his contribution to the war chest, he was entitled to see it duly administered.

As regards the trip to Paris, he would alert the right people there, but obviously what Khan was seeking here in London was something more immediate and certainly more final. The Army of God had assets employed in hospitals, every level of local government, theaters, cinemas, restaurants, and bars. It took Ali Saif only seconds to find one working as a cleaner at the Blue Angel, a Yemeni who had witnessed the fracas and seen Dillon and Sara eventually leave in a cab with a Pakistani driver.

Within fifteen minutes, Ali Saif was in touch with that man and had established that he had dropped Sara Gideon and Dillon at what Saif knew was the Holland Park safe house. They could well be staying the night, but the possibility that they might not was too tantalizing to ignore, so he turned again to his computers.

The man he called was propped up on a bed in a warehouse development by the Thames. He wore shabby jeans and jacket, was unshaven, and had black tousled hair. He was smoking a cigarette and reading the *Times* newspaper.

The Egyptian's voice rang out. "Abu, this is Saif. I have something for you, most urgent. The information coming your way now, facts and photos. The man is immensely dangerous, the woman is a decorated veteran of the war in Afghanistan. I'd advise taking Farouk on this one, but whatever you do, do it now. There's a big pay packet waiting, *very* big."

Abu swung his legs to the floor, went to the computer where the text and photos were still printing. He had a quick look at Dillon and Sara and made a call on his mobile.

The answering voice said, "Get lost, I'm in bed." There was the murmur of a woman's voice.

"Abu here, Farouk, kick the bitch out. I have a hit for AQ, man and woman, big, big money. Fifteen minutes. Long enough to get here from your apartment. If you're not here, I'll go alone using the London cab, but I'd rather leave that to you. You may be a stupid sod because your mother dropped you on your head or something, but you're a genius at handling anything with four wheels. I'll be backup on the Montesa."

The famous Spanish dirt bikes had been specially created to aid farmers and shepherds in the high country of the Pyrenees, and could do half a mile an hour over rough ground and considerably faster if need be. It had a stripped-down look and Abu was

besotted with his and refused to ride anything else.

He didn't wait for a reply from Farouk,
but pulled on heavy biker's boots, unlocked
the outside door, went into a small study,
operated an old-fashioned safe, and took
out two Glocks, a couple of boxes of ammunition, and two silencers, sat down at
the desk, and loaded the weapons expertly.
Then he removed his denim jacket, opened
the wardrobe, and produced two lightweight
bulletproof vests. He pulled one on quickly,
then took down a black leather biker's jacket
and zipped it up.

Moments later, footsteps thundered up
the stairs outside, the door crashed open,
and Farouk stumbled in, the twin of Abu in
appearance and dress except for his shaven
head.

"So there you are," Abu said. "Daft bastard. In bed with a tart again. Get your vest
on and check those two photos and the
details. When we get to this Holland Park
place, we simply sit and wait for them to
come out. Dillon's car is a ten-year-old
souped-up Mini, color Ferrari red."

Farouk said, "Nobody could be as good
as this Dillon. I mean, he's a small guy and
around fifty years of age. As for the woman,
it's got to be a joke?"

75

"Ali Saif is from Cairo, like you and me, and if he says Dillon is hell on wheels, he is. As for the woman, even if you hate the Brits, they don't award the Military Cross lightly. Now, stuff that Glock in your pocket, don't forget your silencer, and let's go and do this."

4

It started to rain at about three-thirty, when Dillon and Sara looked in on Roper. "So there you are," he said. "Was that nice?"

"Perfect," Sara told him. "What about the general?"

"All quiet since he went to bed." Roper lit one of his eternal cigarettes and poured himself a whiskey shot.

"Excellent idea," Dillon said. "I'll drop Sara off at her place and see you tomorrow, to finalize the trip."

"Two-thirty from Farley Field, the Gulfstream to waft you off to Paris and the joys of the Ritz. What a way to earn a living."

"I know, Giles, and so kind of you to remind us how lucky we are," Sara told him.

"Let's hope your luck lasts when you leave. My security cameras outside have noted a London black cab that pulled up and parked amongst the plane trees halfway down the street about twenty minutes ago.

It's still there. There it is, on screen three."

"He could be early for a pickup in one of those Victorian villas on the other side of the road," Sara said, and at that moment Farouk got out of the cab in spite of the pouring rain and relieved himself into the bushes.

Roper went in for a close-up. "A large young man in grubby denims and kicking boots, the kind who only shaves his skull, never his face. What's he doing out there?"

Dillon shrugged. "He *could* be a hard-rock laborer on some building site. But let's go and see. Is that all right with you, girl?"

"Absolutely," Sara said and led the way out.

They stood in the porch for a moment, the rain bouncing from the flagstone of the courtyard. "God help us, but it's like Belfast on a wet Saturday night. Even an umbrella won't do you much good. Let's see what's in the cloakroom."

There was an ample choice hanging from the pegs in there, and Sara selected a khaki anorak and jungle hat to go with it that was so soft, it crushed in the hand. Dillon helped himself to a military trench coat and an old black trilby hat.

"Will I do?" he asked.

"If you want to look like a French gangster

in one of those old Jean Gabin movies."

He smiled wickedly. "But that's exactly what I was hoping for."

He took her arm and they ran through the rain to the Mini.

Abu was in a small car park outside a burger bar on the main road, one of several bikers and truck drivers. He and Farouk had a highly sophisticated device in the left ear that allowed them to communicate with each other, and it was Farouk who used it first.

"The main gate is moving, so I'm getting out of here now. I'll pull in on the main road.

"Excellent, and I'll be on your tail unless it turns out to be a false alarm. Remember to switch on your For Hire lights so you look nice and normal."

Roper picked up the cab on his security camera the moment it moved and called Dillon on his radio. "You've got traffic, Sean, take care."

On the main road, Farouk had pulled in to the curb, switching his For Hire lights on, and was immediately approached by a middle-aged couple. He turned them away, saying he was booked, and the Mini flashed by a moment later. He allowed three or four cars to pass before pulling out, and Abu did the same thing so that he hung well back, relying on Farouk to give him a running commentary as to where their quarry was going.

Meanwhile, Dillon, handling the Mini carefully in the pouring rain, had Roper on the line.

"He's definitely on your tail, Sean. What do you intend to do about it? Are you sure the cab is the only vehicle you have to contend with?"

"It's all your security cameras noted. A few cars, the odd van or truck behind, is all. It's early morning, remember."

"What about Sara?"

"Just now she's reloading her Colt .25."

"Never mind that. What's going to happen to her?"

"Well, I can't take her home to Mayfair, because gunfire at this hour in the morning would certainly disturb the neighbors."

"You could drop her off at the Dorchester?"

"Get real, Giles," Sara told him. "I'm going where Sean is, so no arguments."

"I'll come back to you on that," Dillon told him. "Just now, I want to try some heavy driving. I'll leave the radio on so you can monitor."

Sara said, "Are we aiming for your place?"

"Let's say the general direction, then I'm going to divert down to the Thames. There are some decaying warehouses on Butler's Wharf. A couple of cobbled streets, a few alleys, and the warehouses waiting to be knocked down. With development money being in short supply these days, everything is locked up. I often do my early-morning run down there, and I know it well."

"So what are you suggesting?"

"Bottom of the hill is the big gate into the yard of an old warehouse. It's been smashed open by someone so you could drive inside."

"And why would you do that?"

"Because if someone was pursuing you at speed and you swerved into that yard, the only way the cab would have to go would be straight along the wharf. As that collapsed halfway along two years ago, they'd go straight over the end to drop forty foot into the Thames."

"My God," she said. "And that's the best you have to offer? You must be crazy."

"That's what everyone says, so let's get on with it. Driving should be fun, don't you agree? I've had this little beauty for years

81

and it's been supercharged, which gives you quite a turn of speed, so let's do it, shall we?"

He dropped a gear, slammed his foot down, and the engine roared as he swerved out of the tail of traffic and took off. Farouk was caught napping, but only for a moment, then smiled in delight.

"You want to play games, do you? Well, let's see what you've got," and he pulled out of what traffic there was and roared after Dillon, leaving Abu far behind.

Belted in tightly, Sara braced herself with both hands as they swung off the High Street into a network of mean lanes and run-down houses, with lights still on in some of them, Dillon working the wheel and the brake pedal expertly, sliding on cobbles slippery in the rain.

Farouk, on his tail, was enjoying himself, because this bastard was as good as anyone he had ever raced against and that was meat and drink to him. He drove as he hadn't driven for years, and Abu, far behind because he'd been totally caught out, was shouting loud in Farouk's ear, demanding answers.

"He's broken away," Farouk told him. "We're headed down to the Thames. It looks like he's trying to shake me off in the warren above Butler's Wharf. I don't know what he's playing at, but he's a hell of a driver."

"But what would he be trying to do down there?" Abu called.

"I haven't the slightest idea," Farouk replied.

"Well, take care. This guy is special, I told you."

Dillon turned into Butler Walk and slowed, the narrow alley dropping steeply, just the odd streetlight still working, the warehouse below. What was left of the wharf jutted out into the river, lights sparkling on the other side, a couple of tugs moving toward the estuary, lights on.

Farouk roared in behind him, Dillon glanced sideways at Sara, who braced herself, a fierce look on her face, and nodded. He stamped hard, gunning the engine, and they plunged down, gathering momentum. At the head of the wharf was a single light, and it seemed to rush toward them.

Farouk followed, giving it everything he had, teeth bared as he shouted, "I've got you, you bastard."

The lamp and the light were suddenly larger, but it illuminated the entrance to the warehouse on the left, the two wooden gates standing half open, and Dillon stamped on the brake pedal, jerked the hand brake, spinning the Mini around to slide in through the entrance, bouncing the gates and sliding to a halt.

Farouk, desperately trying to brake too late, hurtled along the wharf and over the edge and plunged down into the Thames. Dillon slid from behind the wheel, ran out of the yard onto the wharf, but there was only darkness down there, and he turned and went back to see how Sara was doing.

From the top of the alley, Abu had witnessed what had happened and was filled with rage. He had tried to impress on Farouk how dangerous Dillon was, but his friend wouldn't listen. Now he was dead. There was only vengeance left, and with Allah's blessing, Abu intended to have it. He switched off the motor, eased the hand brake, and sitting astride, freewheeled down the alley.

Dillon, returning to the yard, discovered Sara struggling with her seat belt, which had jammed because of the impact the Mini had suffered when bouncing the half-open gates aside. She'd lowered the window, and he leaned down.

"Are you okay?"

"I will be when I've cut myself out." She

was struggling in the confined space, trying to find the flick-knife in her right boot, when suddenly the Montesa swerved silently into the yard at a surprising speed.

"Behind you, Sean," she cried.

The Montesa slid sideways, and as Dillon turned, Abu swung his arm in a powerful blow that had him on his knees. Abu let the bike fall, kicked Dillon in the body, turned and wrenched the Mini door open.

"Get out, bitch," he said, drawing his Glock. "I want you to watch. My name is Abu, and mark it well."

Dillon had raised himself to one knee, his right hand under his jacket feeling for the Walther against his back.

Abu said, "There is only one God and Osama is his Prophet."

Sara found the flick-knife, sprang the blade, slicing the seat belt in a second, reached out of the open door and stabbed Abu in the back of the leg, withdrew the razor-sharp blade, and stabbed at the base of his right buttock before tumbling out against him.

He howled in agony, kicking at her, discharging the Glock twice into the ground. Dillon's hand swung up and he shot him in the center of his forehead, hurling him back against the Mini. He slid to the ground and sat there, eyes open.

Sara said, "I wonder what he's staring at?"

"Who knows?" Dillon said. "Eternity, if there is anything out there." He closed Abu's eyes. "You're a remarkable woman, and you saved my life."

She lifted her hands. "Look at them, Sean, not even the hint of a shake. Would you say that was normal?"

"What it indicates is that you're a warrior of the Old Testament Sword of the Lord–and–Gideon variety, and thank heaven for it."

The rain became heavy and driving, and Dillon took her hand and they ran to the shelter of a deep doorway, where Sara said, "It's as if something's trying to wash it all away, the blood, everything. What happens now? Nobody seems to be interested."

"They wouldn't be," Dillon said. "Not in what's happening in a wasteland like this, a mile away from the main road and civilization."

He produced his silver cigarette case, put one in his mouth. Sara said, "Give me one."

"You don't smoke."

"Now and then." She snapped her fingers. "Come on!"

She took the one he offered, his Zippo flared, and she inhaled without coughing.

"When did all this start?" he demanded.

"Afghanistan," she said. "A godsend on occasions."

"I can see where it would be," he told her. "So enjoy, while I speak to Roper."

Which he did, hurrying across to another doorway and calling in, giving Roper a swift and accurate account of events.

Sara was sitting on a ledge in the corner of the doorway when he went back. "Teague and the disposal team will be here in half an hour. You'll just have to hang on. Would you like another cigarette?"

"Why not." He gave her one, and she said, "Our own private undertaker."

"Abu will be six pounds of gray ash about two hours from now."

"And how long has Ferguson been getting away with this?"

"Since Ireland and the Troubles. He was annoyed by really bad guys evading punishment because of human rights lawyers and the like. So, in a sense, we stopped taking prisoners. It saves a hell of a lot of court time. You don't approve, do you?"

"Don't be too sure about that. Afghanistan was a cruel taskmaster. Perhaps it dulled the senses. Exposure to the butchery of children, innocent civilians, made one indifferent to the lives of those who had murdered them. If anything, a quick bullet seemed too easy for them."

"Had anything happened to make you feel that?"

"Six months before the fuss at Abusan when they gave me an MC, I was on a similar gig with three brigade reconnaissance guys. We touched on a village called Mira and came under fire from the Taliban. We poured it in, they gave up. We found fourteen dead, mainly children. It looked like two families, with four young women who appeared to have been raped."

"And the Taliban?"

"They stood there, hands on heads, impassive and unconcerned as I passed along the line, Glock in hand. I reached the last one, and he smiled and pursed his lips as if to kiss me, so I shot him between the eyes and worked my way backward, taking out all four."

It was quiet there in the rain, and Dillon said softly, "And what did your three companions do?"

"There wasn't much they could do, it had happened so quickly. They swore to keep their mouths shut, not that it mattered. BRF duties are some of the most dangerous in the army. They were dead, one by one, over the next four months."

"Which leaves you alone with your guilty secret?"

"Not quite, Sean, now that I've told you."

Dillon put an arm around her shoulders. "I'm glad you did, girl, perhaps I can help carry your burden."

"But there *is* no burden," she said. "Those men deserved what they got. I don't feel the slightest guilt in the matter, so what does that say about me?"

Dillon actually laughed. "God save us, Sara, I can't help you there, being in the same boat." He passed her the pack of cigarettes. "Have another if you want, I'm going to check out the Mini."

His clothes were completely soaked now, and Abu had slumped onto his side. Dillon pulled the body away from the car and laid the corpse out on its back.

He crossed himself and, remembering Abu's final words, murmured, "You'll know all about it now, son."

He turned to the Mini and inspected it as best he could. The passenger door required a bang to close it, but the fact that the gates standing half open had bounced out of the way on the Mini's passage into the yard meant there was little damage. The lights still worked, and he found that he could drive it around the yard. As he was doing that, a large black van coasted in silently and four men in black overalls got out.

"Good to see you in one piece, Mr. Dillon," the man in charge said. "No injuries, I trust?"

Dillon shook hands. "I'm in perfect working order, and so is Captain Gideon, Mr. Teague."

"A pleasure to see you, ma'am," Teague said as Sara approached.

Two of his colleagues were already easing Abu into a black body bag, the third had righted the Montesa and was wheeling it to the rear of the van.

"No problem with the bike, we'll dispose of it, but I'd be obliged if you would show me what happened with the London cab."

Which Dillon did, Sara following them. They stood on the broken end of the wharf, and Teague shone a powerful torch. "Forty feet down and possibly a depth of thirty feet. Remember, the Thames is fiercely tidal, so the wreck of the cab could be swept away. No exchange of fire?"

"Absolutely not," Dillon told him.

"So if it ever was examined — say, by the river police — it would pass as a very unfortunate accident."

"Which you could say it was, in a manner of speaking," Dillon told him.

"So that's what we'll leave it as." Teague turned to Sara. "What a world we live in, ma'am. So pleased you're in one piece. The Mini being usable, Mr. Dillon, I presume you'll be driving back to Holland Park?"

Dillon turned to Sara. "Would you rather go home?"

"I think that would be a good idea. I've got to face them sometime, put on a show of normality." She held out her hand to Teague. "I'm sure we'll meet again, but I hope it's later rather than sooner."

She went to the Mini, and Teague said, "A remarkable lady."

"You can say that again. That al-Qaeda assassin had me in his sights, and she took him on with a spring blade. Saved my life."

"So you owe her, and big-time. Always remember that, my friend." Teague shook hands, went to the van where the others waited, got in, and was driven away.

Dillon went to the Mini, where he found Sara behind the wheel. He slipped into the passenger seat. His only comment was "When you drop a gear and put your foot down hard, there's a huge power surge. It's the supercharger."

"Thanks, I'll bear that in mind," she told him, switched on, and drove away. He selected a CD and music drifted out. Fred

Astaire. As the intro played, Sara joined in, singing softly: *"There may be trouble ahead / But while there's music and moonlight and love and romance / Let's face the music and dance."*

"Great lyrics," Dillon said.

"A lesson for everybody." She hummed along and never said another word until they reached South Audley Street and Highfield Court, where she drove into the drive. Dillon got out as she moved halfway to the house and turned. "Night bless, Sean, it's been a sincere sensation. See you later."

"Take it easy," he said, got behind the wheel, and reversed out of the drive.

The front door opened to her, and Sadie, wrapped in a dressing gown, stood to one side as Sara entered and closed the door behind her. "It must be four o'clock in the morning, and you've been drinking, I can smell it."

"And singing in a piano bar." Sara made for the stairs. "Is Granddad all right?"

"Went to his bed hours ago. Honestly, Sara, I don't know what's to become of you."

"That's easy, Sadie, I'm going to Paris, so let me get to my bed and a few hours' sleep while I can."

By now at the top of the stairs, she got the

door of her room open, kicked off her boots, flung herself on the bed, still in her clothes, and was instantly asleep.

At Holland Park, Dillon found Ferguson in a dressing gown and sitting with Roper, being served tea and bacon sandwiches by Sergeant Tony Doyle, who greeted Dillon cheerfully before anyone else could.

"I expect you might fancy the same, Mr. Dillon."

"Tony, you've got it exactly right," Dillon told him. "But I think I've earned a Bushmills first."

Roper passed him the bottle. "Help yourself."

"And then I'd like an explanation." Ferguson was annoyed, and it showed. "What in the hell have you been getting up to now? And what were you doing involving Captain Gideon?"

"You can rein in your horses right there, Charles. You had retired for the night, I was due to run Sara home, Giles here noticed a suspicious London cab hanging around. It could have been something or nothing, but ended up very much a something."

"In what way precisely?"

"A man called Abu informed me that there is only one God and Osama is his

Prophet. He had his Glock on me, and I was on my knees at the time."

Ferguson frowned. "Al-Qaeda was behind this?"

"I should say so," Dillon told him. "Sara saved me by stabbing Abu a couple of times, giving me the chance to shoot him. I'd managed to attract his backup man into taking a dive off the local wharf into the Thames, so you could argue that a fine time was enjoyed by one and all."

"Including Sara Gideon." There was a small and quizzical smile on Roper's face, a query: "Is she okay?"

"Absolutely," Dillon said. "I've just delivered her to Highfield, where I imagine she's gone straight to bed."

"Which doesn't surprise me at all, having heard all that," Ferguson said. "So, al-Qaeda on our backs again, gentlemen. Rather unexpected, I'd have thought."

"But they haven't put anything our way for some time," Roper said. "So why now?"

"Maybe they've got wind of your interest in those Mediterranean rust buckets, Charles," Dillon said. "That would certainly add a new dimension to things. There's really nothing else that would interest them as regards our present activities."

"Oh, I don't know about that," Roper told

him. "This Simon Husseini business. Al-Qaeda would be happy to know why we are so interested in him."

"So would I," Dillon said. "But not now. I'm going to bed in the guest wing to get some sleep while the going's good."

He departed, and Roper said, "Well, there you are, General. I wouldn't mind knowing what Paris is all about, but I expect you'll tell us in your own good time."

"Well, we certainly aren't going to try to snatch him," Ferguson told him. "That's not on the agenda at all, because of his mother and daughter."

"Which only leaves trying to turn him?"

"Leave it, Major, I'm not prepared to discuss it. I'm going back to bed, which seems the fashionable thing to do."

He went out, and Roper smiled. *So that was it? Trying to bring Husseini on our side.* Someone should have told Ferguson the Cold War is over. The tactics it had bred wouldn't work anymore, but the old boy was stubborn. Better to leave him to find out for himself.

Ali Saif, at his desk in his room at Pound Street, had been in the extraordinary position of being able to follow most of the events that had taken place, from Dillon and Sara's departure at Holland Park to the final bloodbath of Butler's Wharf. The earpieces Farouk and Abu wore were the reason, for they were so sophisticated that Ali Saif had a ringside seat to everything via his incredible receiving equipment.

He was part of the action at all times, heard Farouk's howl of dismay as he went off the end of Butler's Wharf and a great deal of what transpired in the courtyard of the warehouse between Abu, Dillon, and Sara.

To him, the most shocking thing of all was Abu telling Dillon that there was one God and Osama was his Prophet, making it clear to Dillon, and through him Ferguson, that the real enemy in this affair was al-Qaeda. Very stupid of Abu to do that, but to be charitable, one should not speak ill of the dead.

But the arrival of Teague and the disposal team and what he heard of them, until they bagged Abu, really shocked him. The sheer ruthlessness of these people showed Ferguson's organization in a new light to him. He had never cared for the Iranian, a loudmouthed bully who preferred to get bad news sooner rather than later, so Ali Saif decided to give it to him in spite of the time.

In his bedroom at Park Lane, Emza Khan,

rudely awakened, snarled into the phone, "Who in the hell is it at this hour?"

"It's Ali Saif. You said you'd like to be kept informed. I'm afraid we've had problems."

"Of what kind?" Khan said.

So Ali Saif told him.

When he was finished, Khan exploded with rage. "This is not acceptable. What Ferguson and his people are doing is appalling, and what's more, they seem to get away with it on a regular basis. Can't al-Qaeda do something to stop them?"

"I'm sure we can, given time. All this new information gives us insight on the way they operate. We'll come up with a plan of action while you're away in Paris."

"Along with Ferguson, the woman Gideon, and Dillon. Are you telling me you can't deal with them *in* Paris? Is not al-Qaeda as powerful there as here?"

"Oh yes," Ali Saif told him. "Very much so."

"Then speak to the right people, do something about it. Paris is full of narrow alleys and dark corners. Try and damage the woman, I should like to see *her* suffer, at the very least."

"At your command," Ali told him. "We will see what can be done."

97

"See that you do. Another woman, perhaps, who could get close to her. Do you have such a person?"

"Yes, if she's available."

"Who is she, what's her name?"

Saif was trapped, afraid to argue. "Fatima Le Bon."

"Excellent, I like the sound of that. So she lives in Paris? What's her address, phone number? Be quick, you idiot. I want to go back to sleep."

With great reluctance but a certain amount of fear, Saif told him, "She's true to the Cause."

"She'd better be. It would be a pity to have to send Rasoul to visit her and have a quiet word. Good night," and Khan slammed down the phone.

Ali Saif poured coffee, then produced a bottle of cognac from a drawer and poured a generous measure into a cut-glass tumbler. *What fools these mortals be.* That was Shakespeare, a man who had words to cover every situation, and Khan was a fool in spite of his wealth. Ali Saif was not a religious man, but al-Qaeda had supplied him with the right kind of action, a battle of wits, a great and wonderful game, and he had enjoyed every minute of it.

He produced a coded mobile and dialed a number in Paris. It was answered quite quickly. "Osama," he said.

"Is risen" was the reply in French, and it was a woman's voice. "Who are you seeking?"

"Fatima Le Bon, for Ali Saif," he replied in English.

She answered in the same language. "You've got a nerve, you Egyptian pig. I ended up in police hands again after that last drug bust. I thought I was going down for five years."

"Which you didn't," he said. "Discharged with a clean bill of health. Now, who do you think made that possible?"

"Okay," she said. "So AQ had a hand in it."

"Exactly, because we have sympathizers everywhere. I notice you've still held on to that special mobile phone I gave you last time when I was over. That's good, and it proves you're a good Muslim girl who believes in Osama."

"A bad Muslim girl who's French Algerian, didn't understand what Osama was talking about, and was bewildered when you turned up at that night court with a lawyer when I was charged with slashing that disgusting pimp Louis Le Croix's cheek."

"A charge which was thrown out of court when your lawyer presented evidence that the knife was Le Croix's, who was sentenced to five years, which he richly deserved for a litany of foul deeds, particularly where women were concerned."

"The evidence against him was false, and I've been paying you off ever since."

"Nonsense, you enjoy the game, just like me, especially when it's filth like Le Croix who meet a bad end."

"Screw you, Saif. So what is it this time?"

"There's a lady in London giving us a problem."

"By us, you mean al-Qaeda?"

"Of course. She's staying at the Ritz."

"And you'd like her damaged? Does this mean permanently?"

"Fatima, we are at war with the world. She is a soldier on the other side, which makes her fair game because she *is* our enemy. Her name is Captain Sara Gideon."

"You know what? Something tells me you fancy her."

"I admire her, certainly." He took a deep breath. "She's a British Army officer, an Afghanistan veteran, one of the few to be decorated. She now works for an intelligence outfit run by a General Ferguson. Her partner is a Sean Dillon, once an IRA enforcer, and make no mistake, they're good. They've just seen off permanently two of my best hit men. She and Dillon will be at the Ritz tomorrow."

Fatima laughed out loud. "And you expect poor little me to take that lot on?"

"Fatima, my love, not me, but the man I work for, who shall remain nameless, insists on some sort of revenge and suggests that Paris is just the place for it. He's told me to try and damage the woman, as he would like to see her suffer."

"Now I understand you," Fatima told him. "You're like the students who joined the Red Brigade years ago, went round blowing things up and assassinating people, just for the thrill of it." She laughed out loud again. "Your chickens have come home to roost, Saif, because if you don't do your duty by al-Qaeda, they'll hang you out to dry and there's nowhere you'll be able to hide. They're great throat-cutters, an Arab tradition."

She was absolutely right, of course, and he said, "So what's the answer?"

"There's nowhere for me to hide, either."

"Particularly as Khan has your address, the bastard insisted."

"So I'll just have to get on with it. Tell me everything about their reason for being here in Paris, the whole story. At least that will mean I'll be prepared for anything that comes along."

PARIS

5

The Gulfstream lifted off at Farley Field at 2:30 that afternoon bound for Charles de Gaulle Airport. Sara and Dillon held conference on board together, Roper on Skype on the large screen with Ferguson.

"Any thoughts about last night's events?" Ferguson asked.

"I've thought about it," Roper said, "but can't see that it has any relevance to our Paris trip. One of the hit men made the al-Qaeda connection clear. This was all about revenge, and they were waiting outside Holland Park to exact it for the many times in the past when we've done al-Qaeda great harm. It was only last year we foiled the plot to blow up the President on his visit to Parliament and managed to dispose of Mullah Ali Selim, one of their biggest operators in London."

"I agree."

"As far as they're concerned, we're targets

for life because of past misdeeds," Dillon said. "But in Paris, it's a great day for Iran, their scientist receiving the Legion of Honor. The last thing al-Qaeda would want to do is rock *that* particular boat."

Sara said, "What do you *really* expect, General? We've already accepted that Husseini will never leave his mother and daughter in the lurch, it isn't in his nature. So what can I offer him, or to be practical, what could Britain offer him?"

"Besides the joys of London, Oxford, and Cambridge? Freedom to continue his research. The government's ready and willing to provide him with an experimental nuclear facility right here."

"But how could this happy circumstance be achieved?"

"It would take time and careful planning, but I believe the SAS could handle it."

"Giving Britain sole access to a nuclear bomb of a power way beyond anything existing," Sara pointed out.

"My thoughts exactly. It could lead to a whole new era of peace of a kind we haven't known in many years."

"You think so?" Sara said. "What if Husseini has other ideas once you break him out? What if he prefers Harvard or Yale to Oxford or Cambridge? Would he be free to make his own choice?"

Ferguson sighed heavily. "You really are being very difficult."

"But am I right in my conclusions? Have the SAS spirit Simon Husseini, his mother and daughter out of Tehran, fly them to some safe house in England, and, hey presto, we're going to be a great little country again, a power in the world, and all down to Simon Husseini's spanking new nuclear bomb."

Roper laughed out loud on the screen. "Brilliant, Sara, well done."

Dillon clapped hands. "I couldn't put it better myself."

"Shut up, the lot of you, and be practical," Ferguson told them. "There are an awful lot of bad people out there who would love to get their hands on what we think Husseini may have developed. Are you seriously telling me you wouldn't prefer Britain to control it in partnership with our friends in Washington? Can you think of anyone better?"

It was Sara who gave him an answer before either Roper or Dillon could. "You don't get the point, General, which is, what if Husseini didn't want *anyone* to have it?"

"Nonsense," Ferguson said. "What's done can't be undone, the genie's escaped from the bottle and can't be shoved back inside. Husseini could burn his research records and blow his brains out, but sooner or later, someone would come along to untangle the puzzle again."

"Fair enough," Sara said. "Give me a chance to get close enough to Husseini and I'll put it to him exactly as you have to me."

"And you think he'll go for it?" Roper asked her.

"Not the man I knew as a guest in my grandfather's house," Sara said. "But who knows? Life has been hard on him, and I expect his responsibility for his mother and daughter weighs heavily."

"If he says no to what is the only offer of help that's going, he'll find the future grim indeed," Ferguson said. "His mother's eighty-six and can't expect to last much longer, but his daughter's forty and, in spite of her poor health, could last at least twenty years. There's no chance at all of the poor blighter doing a runner. So all he can expect from his future is to live and die in Tehran."

Roper cut in, "We'll see about that. I've had Claude Duval on from Charles de Gaulle, where he's waiting to greet you. I've booked you a large suite on the fourth floor, because Husseini always takes a two-bedroom suite on that floor. It was a matter of luck, they had a cancellation."

"And the others?" Dillon inquired.

"Our friends from Iran are on the fifth. Emza Khan and his so-called valet, this Rasoul Rahim, are also in a two-bedroom suite."

"Valet, my backside," Dillon said. "Rasoul is all bully boy — Khan's minder, I'd say. What about the colonel?"

"Next door to them."

"And Husseini? Is he in Paris yet?"

"According to Duval, they arrived last night, Wali Vahidi in charge as usual."

"I found Vahidi's file interesting," Sara said. "Have you got his photo there?"

"Of course."

Around fifty with a bushy mustache, Wali Vahidi looked like somebody's uncle, solid and dependable. "It would seem the Husseinis are the only family he's got," Sara commented.

"You could be right." Ferguson nodded. "He's Husseini's bodyguard, that's true, but also his protector. That bears thought. Anyway, it's time for us to let you get on with it. I've every confidence in you. Keep in touch."

"Take care," Roper called. "And watch your backs."

■ ■ ■ ■

At Charles de Gaulle, the Gulfstream taxied toward a secluded part of the airport reserved for flights of an official nature. It was raining and Colonel Claude Duval stood outside the private entrance into the VIP concourse, wearing a navy blue trench coat, holding a large umbrella. Porters in waterproofs had rushed to recover the luggage from the Gulfstream, and Sara and Dillon, each with an umbrella held up against the driving rain, joined him.

"*Bonne chance,* dear friends," Duval said. "For some reason, this brings back the memory of many funerals I have attended."

"The rain" — Sara ducked into the porch and closed her umbrella — "and these things always seem to go together."

He kissed her on both cheeks. "Sara, I can only say you have been worth waiting for."

Dillon shook his hand. "Now then, Claude, don't let your mad passion run away with you. Where are we going?"

"A private room, a light lunch, a little champagne to celebrate seeing you two again."

"Why, Claude," Sara said. "You certainly know how to keep a girl happy."

110

"No, Sara, my darling, I know how to keep *both* of you happy, and when you are happy enough, I expect you to tell me exactly what you are doing here and why."

He took them to a small, luxurious private bar. A handsome young waiter resplendent in a white jacket greeted them, the young woman behind the bar wore the same kind of jacket.

"This is only used for the most important of VIPs," Claude told them. "And Jules and Julie are completely at your service. . . . I should point out that they are also officers of the DGSE, so you can speak fully."

The two young agents smiled, Claude nodded, Julie opened a bottle of Dom Perignon behind the bar, and Jules brought three glasses on a tray.

Dillon said, "Well, here we are again. Confusion to the enemy." He raised his glass in a toast. *"Vive la France."* Sara and Duval joined him. Dillon sipped a little, then emptied the glass. "Pure magic, God bless the monks who invented Dom Perignon. I'll have another."

Jules obliged, topped the others up, too, and Duval said, "Have I been Mister Nice Guy for long enough? Can we sit down and discuss what's going on?"

"Fair enough," Dillon said.

He and Sara sat together on a couch, a glass table between them and Claude, who said, "To start with, the news on the grapevine is that you had a brush with an al-Qaeda hit squad down by the Thames."

Dillon turned to Sara. "Terrible, isn't it, the way these rumors circulate. Would you be knowing anything about that?"

"Don't waste my time, Sean," said Duval. "Two dead. I congratulate you, and you, Sara, but does it mean al-Qaeda is likely to carry this further, and in Paris? I need to know."

Sara took over. "Of course you do, so shut up, Sean." She carried on. "As I understand it, even before my time, Ferguson's people have been a thorn in al-Qaeda's side. They have a lot of scores to settle with us. We think the hit squad hanging around Holland Park last night were on the prowl for anyone who came out, and it had nothing to do with what we're here for."

Dillon joined in. "It's a big day for Husseini and Iran. Al-Qaeda wouldn't want any trouble with Tehran just now."

"Well, let's hope that some stupid individual doesn't jump the gun." Duval held up his empty glass for more. "So, as they say at passport control, what is the purpose of your visit?"

"Sweet Jesus, Claude," Dillon said. "It's stretching it more than a little to expect us to tell you that."

It was then that Sara shocked them. "Dillon, enough of this subterfuge. We use it all the time in our business, and I for one am sick of it, in spite of what my superiors say."

"What are you suggesting?" Dillon asked her.

"That we take a chance on Claude being a decent human being who knows the difference between right and wrong, and come right out with exactly what we're doing here."

Claude was astonished. "So, you want to stand the whole system on its head?"

"Why not a little honesty for a change?" Sara asked him. "It's common knowledge that Iran wants a nuclear bomb and that Simon Husseini is working on it, with his mother and daughter held under house arrest to make sure he behaves himself."

"I know all this, and it's a bastard," Claude said.

"Husseini is also an old friend of my grandfather and me, so I intend to meet him and find out if he'd be interested in a future in England, if we could get him and the two women out."

"And how would you do that?"

"The SAS might be able to arrange it," Dillon put in.

"Never," Claude said. "Impossible."

"That's what they said about Osama bin Laden."

Sara pointed out, "And look what happened there. Put it this way: As an old friend of Husseini, I'd like to see if he's happy. If he says he is, then that's it as far as I'm concerned."

"Though there are people," Dillon said, "who would rather put a bullet in his head than leave him working for his country. Anyway, Claude, how do you feel about this?"

"Oh, Sara has answered me. I think I'll go the rebel route myself — any way I can help your enterprise, I will."

"That's wonderful," she said. "You're a star."

"There's a little more to it than that. I greeted Husseini when his plane arrived last night and liked him at once. His bodyguard, this Wali Vahidi, isn't a bad guy, just an old-fashioned copper."

"So what are you getting at?" Dillon asked.

"That I much prefer you all over our Iranian friends who flew in before you.

114

Emza Khan is a loud-voiced toad, and Rasoul Rahim should be in the nearest cell."

"And Colonel Declan Rashid?" Sara asked.

"I'd read of his exploits with admiration, and was even more impressed on meeting him." Duval shrugged. "The only problem is that he keeps such bad company."

"Well, he doesn't have much choice," Sara said.

Duval carried on. "Husseini is guarded by Vahidi at the hotel at all times, his phone calls monitored. At the Palace, you'll be on line with twenty foreign observers privileged to be presented by me, because I'm doing the whole line. Husseini's certain to recognize you, but smart enough to keep quiet." He passed her a small square of paper. "You don't salute, so give him that when you shake hands. It says you are staying at the Ritz and will be in touch."

"A masterstroke," Dillon told him. "But what about Vahidi?"

"We'll arrange to spike whatever he drinks. There's an old hand in the room-service section who has worked for Ferguson for years — but also for me."

"That's very convenient," Sara said.

"Isn't it?" Claude Duval laughed. "But now we eat!"

■ ■ ■ ■

In his suite on the fourth floor of the Ritz, Simon Husseini sat at a Bechstein grand piano, feeling his way into the final fifteen minutes of George Gershwin's *Rhapsody in Blue,* trying to remember it since he didn't have the music. The melody soared, thrilling Husseini as it always did. He was oblivious to everything, including the ring of the telephone, which Wali Vahidi hurried from his bedroom to answer.

He talked through the music, holding out the phone. "He wants us upstairs."

"He'll have to wait," Husseini shouted.

Vahidi shrugged, spoke into the phone, then put it down. Husseini moved into the final crescendo and came to the end.

He was pleased with himself, and smiling. "You know, Vahidi, I can sometimes be rather good, I think."

"You can be very good, but I doubt whether it will be appreciated. Khan slammed down the phone."

"Did he indeed?" Husseini said, and there was a thunderous knock on the door.

"Here we go." Vahidi went and opened it.

Emza Khan marched in, obviously in a rage, followed by Rasoul and Rashid, who

116

wasn't in uniform and wore a tan suit, white shirt, and striped tie.

"I can see you've decided to be your usual awkward self," Khan told Husseini. "It's outrageous that I am forced to come to you, and not you to me. You're getting above yourself again. I shouldn't have to remind you of your position and that of your mother and daughter."

"And I shouldn't have to remind you of how crucially important to the state I am. Can you do what I do?"

Rasoul said, "How dare you?" He took a threatening step. Declan Rashid grabbed him by the scruff of the neck and sent him staggering.

Husseini and Khan still confronted each other. "Is there any man in Iran who can do what I do?" said Husseini.

"Damn you to hell," Emza Khan told him. "My day will come." He turned to Declan. "Fill him in on what's expected of him tonight. I want everything to run smoothly. Everybody will be watching on television. Try to make this idiot see sense."

He crossed to the door, opened it, and Rasoul ran after him. Husseini smiled at Declan Rashid. "I enjoyed that."

"I'm sure you did," Declan said. "I'd try not to make a habit of it if I were you. He really is very powerful."

Wali Vahidi was also smiling, if only slightly. "We have a bar and kitchen next door. May I get you a drink or perhaps coffee?"

"Coffee would be fine," Declan said and moved to the piano, where Husseini had started into "St. Louis Blues."

"You play well. Jazz as well as the classics."

"Oh, that's the French side of me. I got it from my mother. The music has always been a great solace to me, helps keep me sane."

"I'm sorry for your situation," Declan said. "I really am. Your mother and daughter —"

Husseini cut him off. "I know you are, because you're a decent man, but never let me hear you say that again. If the wrong person heard, it could be the end of you. Oh, Wali Vahidi is reasonable enough, but Rasoul is foul and Emza Khan is not used to people disagreeing with him."

Vahidi entered with coffee on a tray and served it on a low table. They sat down, and he poured.

Declan said, "Tehran sees what's happening tonight as a statement about Iran itself to the rest of the world."

Husseini was immediately irritable. "I'm

sorry, but I can't make it happen the way they would like. I wish it wasn't so damned important."

"Well, it is." Declan took a packet from his breast pocket and unfolded it. "This is the official observers list. There'll be over two hundred attachés from embassies all over Paris showing interest in you."

"For one reason only. Because I got famous for work on medical isotopes and parleyed it into the nuclear field and they all want to know how."

"That's true," Declan agreed. "And I won't deny that a lot of these people have been brought in from their countries because of you."

"Like the USA, Germany, the Russian Federation, and, of course, the United Kingdom. Their intelligence desks will all be empty for the great occasion."

"I hear what you say, and there is a certain amount of truth there, but the London end of things isn't busy. Perhaps they're no longer concerned in matters nuclear. They've sent two observers from the Ministry of Defence, that's all. A Sean Dillon and a Captain Sara Gideon."

Simon Husseini's cup was being topped up by Vahidi when Sara's name was spoken, and he knew immediately that it had to be that young officer from ten years ago, just out of Sandhurst and gifted at languages.

He picked up the cup and drank his coffee slowly, giving Declan Rashid time to make a comment if he wished, but he did not, and Husseini realized that could only be because there was no comment to make. His Iranian handlers had failed to make a connection between him and Sara. Could there be any significance to her presence? Only one thing was obvious. She was there because he was. He refused to believe anything else.

Declan said, "She was decorated in Afghanistan."

"Good heavens," Husseini replied. "That *is* rather unusual for a young woman, isn't it?" He turned to Vahidi, who waited by the door. "I think we'll go down to the health club. I could have a steam bath and prepare myself for tonight."

Declan said, "A sound idea. I'll let you get on with it." He moved to the door, Vahidi opened it, and he went out.

"You're joining me?" Husseini asked the bodyguard.

"Of course," Vahidi said. "Remember, we must be ready to leave at five."

Henri Laval was in his sixties, his white hair

perfectly groomed, his uniform impeccable. As a senior room-service waiter for many years, he prided himself on knowing what his guests wanted before they knew themselves. He was astute and cunning and made a great deal of money, and yet seated in the rear of Duval's Citroën while the colonel talked and the driver ignored him, he felt his palms sweat.

"So, report anything and everything to do with the Iranian party to me, and also to Ferguson's people. Your avaricious soul will adore Captain Gideon — she's not just a pretty face, she owns a bank. Now, get out of here and remember what mobile phones are for."

"You may rely on me, Colonel," Laval told him. "I'll not let you down."

He scrambled out into the heavy rain, cursing as he put up his umbrella. Why couldn't they leave him alone? He was fine at just doing his job and pleasing people. The *flics,* the police, were bad enough. The passing of a few banknotes always helped there, but you didn't argue with the French Secret Service, the dreaded DGSE. They were a law unto themselves, those people, not that he could do much about it.

He'd already had a brush with the Iranians earlier, a luggage problem. Emza Khan had bellowed at him and Rasoul had thrown him out, and it was obvious the kind of man he was. He'd delivered a bottle of complimentary champagne to the Husseini suite, but Vahidi had taken it at the door. Which left Ferguson's people. As he went down the side street toward one of the service entrances, he moved to the narrow pavement to avoid being splashed, but the driver showed consideration and slowed. It was a small Fiat van with a canvas roof, and a panel on the side read "The Flower Bower." Fatima Le Bon wound down the window and looked out.

"Henri, my lovely, how goes it?"

He peered from under his umbrella, frowning, and then smiled in recognition. "Fatima, it's you. What's this, finished working the streets at last? Did the *flics* get too much for you?"

"They surely did," she said. "So now I'm in the flower-delivery business, and it suits me just fine."

An embroidered patch said "The Flower Bower" in gold on one side of her blue jacket, and the top buttons on the blue blouse she was wearing were undone enough for Henri to see her cleavage. He warmed to her instantly, reached in and took her hand.

"It's good to see old friends. Perhaps we could have a drink one night at Marco's bar around the corner."

"I'd love that, Henri." She squeezed his hand. "I could be seeing a lot of you now I'm doing this job."

"Perhaps later," he said and took a card from his wallet. "That's mine. Just show it to anyone who queries you and tell them to call me. Say you're attached to my staff."

"I'll do that," she said. "You're the best, Henri."

She watched him go up to the service entrance and enter, and then she drove away. It had been a lucky meeting. It'd be the easiest thing in the world to get him on his knees begging for it. She drove away down another side street, parked and sat under the canopy of a bar, had a brandy and coffee, and smoked a cigarette.

The flower gambit was something she'd used before, and it worked well. In the old days, when money was good, she'd been sensible enough to buy an apartment down by the Seine at one of the places where barges were permanently moored and people lived on them. It was nice down there, especially at night, with Notre Dame floodlit not too far away.

Her apartment had a garage in which she

kept the Fiat for general use, clipping the side panel in place when she was working the flower scam. If you wore some uniform and were attractive, you melted into the hubbub of a great hotel, especially if you were clasping a large bunch of flowers obviously intended for delivery. It worked in elevators, on corridors.

In addition, since her computer skills allowed her to extract names of individual guests and their room numbers, a nice bouquet covered your back nicely on the odd occasion that someone stopped you.

So far, so good. Now it was into battle again. She paid her bill, returned to the Fiat, got in, and drove back toward the hotel.

Dillon was reading *Le Monde* and catching up on world news while Sara got ready for the evening at the Élysée Palace. When the door buzzed, he got up, went to answer it, and found Fatima standing there with a beautiful bunch of red roses.

She smiled, and spoke in English. "So sorry to bother you. I hope I've got it right. Flowers for Captain Sara Gideon."

Dillon gave her his best smile. "You'll have to make do with me, *chérie*. The woman of the house is at the other end of the suite in her room, preparing for an evening out."

"No, she isn't, Sean. Who is it?" Sara cried.

"Flowers for you?" he called back to her.

A moment later, Sara came in from her bedroom in full uniform and walked toward them, smiling. "Can I help?"

Fatima took in the uniform and the medal ribbons, glanced at the lethal-looking man beside her, and suddenly was unsure of herself. She was aware of the Walther in her waistband under the blue jacket, digging into the small of her back.

"Are those for me? How lovely. Who are they from?" Sara asked.

"I don't know," Fatima told her. "The card just says 'Sincere good wishes.' "

She held them out and Sara took them. "That's very kind of you."

"Not at all," Fatima replied. It was still possible, of course — but Dillon was right there, and there was something about Sara that Fatima hadn't expected. So she smiled again. "Have a lovely evening," she said, turned and walked away.

Dillon said, "Nice-looking lady."

"I had noticed," Sara said. "But to more important matters. How are we going to handle it if we bump into the Iranians tonight?"

"You've met Declan Rashid and that slob

Rasoul. The only fresh face is Emza Khan, but you've seen his photo. They know who we are, but they may not know about your connection with Husseini. Just ignore them." Dillon shrugged and smiled wickedly. "Unless bumping into the handsome Declan gives you a problem."

"You think so?" Sara asked. "Actually, my only problem is you, Sean. I'm going to put my flowers in water and you can clear off and get yourself ready. Wear the blue suit, with a white shirt and the Brigade of Guards tie. That way, nobody could ever believe you were the pride of the IRA."

6

Fatima returned to her flat, made coffee, had another brandy, and sat there by the window, looking down the sloping cobbled alley toward the River Seine, considering what had happened. It wasn't Saif she was worried about, for she had known him long enough to understand the complexity of the man, knew already that he would accept any explanation for her failure that she would offer. But, in spite of his joking manner, he was trapped by how far he had been drawn into the dark doings of al-Qaeda. There was a price to be paid for that, and to a lesser degree the same thing applied to her.

Any reluctance to phone him was swept away by the fact that her mobile sounded at that very moment, and there he was.

"I thought I'd call and see how things are going," he said.

Fatima took a deep breath, swallowed

hard, and told him.

When she had finished, he said, "You've got enormous guts to tell me that. I understand, but the boss man in our organization won't. I don't just mean a loudmouth like Emza Khan, I mean the top brass here in Europe, and there's even an order higher than them."

"I can see that those kind of people might not understand."

"Why should they? You were close enough to pull out your Walther at point-blank range and blow Sara Gideon away. You had a good chance to dispose of Sean Dillon, too, before he managed to draw the weapon he was undoubtedly carrying."

"I know, Saif," she said. "I just froze. There was this strong young woman with medals any man would be proud to wear. To have pulled the trigger would have been . . . wrong somehow. I don't know how to explain it."

Saif laughed so much that there were tears in his eyes. "My God, Fatima, you're so right, and you're not being ridiculous at all. What are we? We kill people in the name of our cause, and is that enough? I don't think so anymore. It's a can of worms, not only for me but for you."

"And is there no way out for us?"

"None whatsoever. Al-Qaeda infects the world like a plague and there's no place to hide. We'd simply be hunted down. So, keep your mouth shut and I'll keep mine. I won't mention a word to Emza Khan, but I'm afraid we must continue to follow our original orders. Do you understand me? Look upon it as an assassination, which sounds more respectable. After all, we *are* fighting a war."

"I'll try to remember that."

"Well, good luck to you, and good luck to me also," Saif said and switched off.

The assembly at the Élysée Palace was as fascinating as you'd expect: palace guards to rival London's Household Cavalry, uniforms of many nations on display, beautifully turned-out women, well-dressed men, chandeliers sparkling, and a military band playing.

"You've got to give it to the French," Dillon told her. "They certainly do this kind of thing with style."

"And panache," Sara said. "I always expect King Louis the Fourteenth to enter with a fanfare of trumpets."

"Oh, that will happen quite soon," Dillon said. "Except that it'll be the President, not

129

the Sun King."

There were people standing at the back of the hall, music, laughter, and lots of conversation. In front of the crowd where the aisle down through the rows of crowded chairs began, Claude Duval stood in full uniform to marshal the line of observers. He saw Dillon and Sara and beckoned.

"Off you go," Dillon told her. "Best of luck."

The crowd parted to let her through, and people noted her good looks, her uniform and medals. Duval, very serious, very military, placed her about halfway in line and one of his aides led them to the front of the audience facing the platform in front of an empty row.

Duval waited at a side door on the right. The music of the band ended with a flourish and a voice over the loudspeaker echoed, "Please rise to welcome Dr. Simon Husseini."

Everyone stood and applauded as Husseini entered. Of medium height, he wore a black suit and college tie but looked older than his mid-sixties, mainly because his white hair was too long. There was a kind of melancholy to him, and his smile seemed strained as he waved to the crowd. He and Duval spoke together, and then a voice echoed from the loudspeaker again.

"Please be seated."

The band played music softly and Husseini and Duval started along the line of observers, not all of whom were in uniform. Sara's stomach was hollow, her throat was dry, and she tried to swallow to moisten it, aware of the voices as they approached, speaking in French, of course, and then the moment came.

"*Capitaine* Sara Gideon," Duval said.

He was standing slightly back from Husseini's left shoulder, his face calm, giving nothing away, but Husseini knew her, of course, it was in the eyes, she could tell that instantly. The slight smile was no more than was required and he shook her hand, aware as he did so of the folded slip.

"I'm enchanted to meet you, *Capitaine,*" he said in French. "Your medals pay homage to your extraordinary bravery."

"A privilege to meet you, Doctor," she replied in the same language.

"No, *Capitaine,* the privilege is mine." He passed on, Duval nodded and followed.

What came afterward meant little to her, for the meeting had had a profound effect, the emotion of seeing him again after so many years. The fanfare sounded, the President entered, several people were called up to receive awards, and then Husseini, and then suddenly, it was all over. People stood up and milled around, some making their way toward the champagne on offer. Duval, passing her, saluted, speaking formally in case they were heard by anyone close.

"So kind of you to come, Captain. We are very grateful." Then he quickly murmured in a quiet voice, "I'll speak to you later."

He turned away and Dillon pushed through, reached her, and smiled. "Did it work, did he recognize you?"

"Oh yes," she said. "I've never been more certain. Where is he now?"

"Behind you," Dillon said, "with our Iranian friends. That gargoyle Rasoul is pushing his way through the crowd, followed by Khan and Husseini. Wali Vahidi and Declan Rashid are bringing up the rear, and doesn't *he* look good in uniform. I think he's got even more medals than you."

"You can't take anything seriously for a moment, can you, Sean?" She turned to see the Iranian group pass by and she was recognized, no doubt about that. Rasoul scowled, Khan glared, and Husseini ignored her. Dillon and Declan smiled, swept a little close by pressure of the crowd.

"Captain Gideon, a pleasure to see you again, and you, Mr. Dillon."

132

"God save the good work, Colonel," Dillon told him, pushing people away. "But, one Irishman to a half Irishman, we do seem to meet up in some funny old places."

"So it would appear." Declan Rashid was laughing, and then was swept away after the others.

"You like him, don't you?" Dillon said.

"I suppose I do." Sara nodded. "He's an easy man to like. A fine soldier, decent, honorable."

"I agree," Dillon said. "There's only one problem. In spite of the difference between him and Rasoul, they're on the same side. Never forget that."

"I'm not likely to if you keep reminding me. I think I know my duty."

"So you could shoot him if necessary?"

She frowned. "You are a bastard, Sean, even on your good days."

"Yes, I worry about that constantly." He gave her his special smile.

"And you can forget the blarney, the Irish charm isn't going to work on this occasion."

"God save us, but you've seen through me at last." He tightened his grip on her, fending people off.

She laughed. "You clown," she said. "Let's get back to the hotel and see what Claude Duval has for us."

■ ■ ■ ■

The small champagne party booked by Emza Khan took place in Husseini's suite. It was all waiting when they returned, and Henri dismissed the staff and served the champagne himself. He was hoping that the party would be of short duration, for downstairs in his office, Fatima was waiting. He had found her in the bar at nearby Marco's when he had gone in for a sandwich and a glass of wine, sitting there in her blue uniform. Temptation had proved too much for Henri, and he now had the prospect of untold delights later.

Duval had assured him that the pill he had provided for Vahidi would dissolve instantly and induce a deep sleep within an hour of its being administered. Vahidi would awake in five hours or so refreshed and unaware of what had happened to him. Henri, offering the tray, managed to leave Vahidi till last, the pill concealed in his right palm, dropped at the correct moment as Vahidi looked left at Emza Khan, who was obviously about to speak.

"To the Islamic Republic of Iran."

"Iran."

"I think that went well," Khan said, holding his glass out for a top-up and turned to Husseini, who had gone to the piano and was sitting down. "I warned you to be sensible, and you were. I suppose we can call that some sort of progress."

"Then you would be wrong." Husseini was playing a little Bach, ice-cold stuff as his fingers rippled over the keys. "Your flight from London was short, mine from Tehran rather long. I'm overtired and bored, and I felt that way all during the ceremony. I wanted it to end as soon as possible, and that's why I behaved myself as the lies floated round me. I wanted to shout out the truth to the world."

"But you can't, can you?" Emza Khan snarled. "Because you know what will happen to your mother and daughter."

"Oh, I know that well enough," Husseini told him. "With ghouls like you lurking in the wings, just wishing for the order to do them harm."

Emza Khan cuffed him. "Learn your place, dog."

Husseini slapped Khan in the face. "You learn yours first. If anything happens to me here, you won't be back in London, you'll be trying to explain your miserable self in front of a government tribunal in Tehran."

Rasoul moved in, pulling his Master to

one side, his right hand slamming the keyboard lid down. Husseini managed to snatch his hands away, and Rasoul drew a Webley revolver from his pocket. Declan moved with astonishing speed, stamped behind Rasoul's right leg, punching him in the kidneys, grabbing him by the collar. Off balance, he fell to the floor.

Declan picked up the weapon and put a foot in Rasoul's back, holding him down. He looked at Khan, his face cold and hard as he said, "If anything happens to Husseini, we will all be held responsible. The consequences will be as bad for you, in spite of all your money, as they will be for me."

There was sudden fear on Khan's face, and he kicked Rasoul. "Control yourself, you animal. On your feet now."

Rasoul heaved himself up, panting. "I'm sorry."

"Take him back to his room," Declan ordered. "I'll speak to him again later."

Khan went, pushing Rasoul in front of him, Declan closing the door behind them. Husseini said, "That was well done. I'll have another glass."

Henri, who had stood beside the champagne bar during the whole fracas, said, "Certainly, sir, what about you gentlemen?"

Vahidi, who was yawning hugely, said, "Oh

no, I've had too much already. You do as you want, I'm for bed." He shambled to his bedroom at the other end of the room, called good night, and went in.

"A night for surprises," Husseini said, and Declan Rashid laughed. "Not really, that's the trouble. I'll see you in the morning."

He left, and Husseini said, "A night to remember."

Henri said, "I've seen it all before, or variations of it, during forty years in the hotel trade. Was there anything else?"

"Could you leave clearing the room until the morning?"

"Yes, I could, but I'd like to check the welfare of the gentleman next door. He didn't seem too good to me."

He didn't wait for Husseini's permission, went and opened Vahidi's door, found the light still on and Vahidi, still wearing his suit, lying on the bed and snoring gently.

Behind him in the doorway, Husseini said, "Is he all right?"

"Oh yes, sir, just one too many."

He switched off the light, and Husseini said, "I'll say good night."

Henri, seizing the moment, said, "Actually, I do have a surprise for you, sir. A young lady desires a word with you and hopes you may remember her. Captain Sara

Gideon."

Husseini was stunned. "Where is she?"

"Just along the corridor. I can call her on the telephone."

"But my bodyguard."

"Is out for about five hours. A sleeping pill in his champagne."

"What desecration." Husseini smiled as he had not smiled in years. "But bring her on, Henri, bring her on."

It was Dillon who answered the house phone in their suite where the two of them had been waiting, hoping against hope. Sara wore jeans, ankle boots, and a heavy sweater that concealed a Glock in the belt holster.

"It's ready and waiting," Dillon told her. "Just a few yards up the corridor. I could come with you?"

"I know you mean well, Sean, but I can handle it."

"Of course you can."

Her smile was radiant. "That's the nicest thing you've ever said to me. You're learning."

He smiled. "Go on, get out of it, go and save the world."

The corridor was quiet as she walked along, paused at the door, took a deep breath, and

138

pressed the buzzer. It was Henri who opened the door.

"Welcome, Captain," he said. "Please come in."

She did and found Husseini standing by the piano. He stared at her, face drawn. "Sara?"

"Yes, it is me, Simon," she said. A huge smile exploded on his face and he stepped close and threw his arms about her.

Henri said, "If you'll excuse me, I'll go below to my room, sir." He produced his card and put it on the coffee table by the door. "That has my mobile number. Call me if you need me, the captain can explain everything."

He let himself out, went down in the lift, and found Fatima lying on the small bed in the corner of his office, sleeping. He'd had enough to drink, nips of champagne, so he opened the large thermos he kept primed with strong black coffee, enjoyed a cup, smoked a Gitane, and studied Fatima and saw that she was quite lovely and that that he admired her much more than he'd realized. Could this be love? A long time coming. She turned to the wall, and he lay down beside her and closed his eyes.

Simon Husseini and Sara sat on the couch,

and he held her hands. "It's wonderful to see you, but what is this all about? Your achievements as a soldier speak for themselves, but who are you really?"

Suddenly, Sara was tired of pretense, because he deserved better. "I'm not employed on the battlefield anymore. I'm a member of the Security Services. My boss is Major General Charles Ferguson and we work personally for the Prime Minister."

"The Prime Minister? My goodness, it's that important, is it? So what do you want?"

"We know about your personal situation, about your mother and daughter. Tomorrow morning, you'll fly back to Tehran, call in on them, then return to your work in the mountains."

"Because I have no choice."

"What if you did? What if we arranged for the SAS to snatch your mother and daughter from their villa, and you from the research unit, and have you on a plane to London before Tehran knew it?"

He laughed. "What a sensation that would be."

"You don't think it's possible?"

"Anything is possible. The prospect of my mother and daughter enjoying the calm of life in Hampstead instead of Tehran would be a vast improvement. But there is also me to consider, and what I want."

"What's troubling you?" she asked.

"My work on medical isotopes led me to great recognition because people from all over the world benefited from the discovery. I called it the Breath of Allah. Now that work has developed into the ability to create a nuclear bomb many times more powerful than anything existing. Is that the Breath of Allah as well? More likely mere mortals misrepresenting Allah's purpose."

"So you still believe in essential goodness?"

"I cling to the thought desperately. I first came across it thirty-five years ago from my tutor in moral philosophy at the Sorbonne, a Greek Orthodox priest and monk called Father John Mikali. Although a Christian, he had no difficulty in comparing essential goodness with the Breath of Allah."

"What happened to him?"

"Still alive at ninety. He lives in the Hospice of St. Anthony as a member of the small community that has served the caravan trail, southwards from Kuwait through Saudi Arabia to the Gulf States and the Empty Quarter, since ancient times."

"How extraordinary," Sara said.

"If anyone had a solution to my problem, it would be he."

"So you turn down the idea *I've* put to you?"

"If it succeeded and I arrived in London, the Prime Minister and your General Ferguson would want to fly me away to some hidden establishment, where I'd have to carry on the same work I've been doing in Iran, in gratitude for spiriting me, my mother, and daughter out of Tehran. This is a false hope. I have no intention of continuing my work. I would turn my back on it. Return to my medical interests, if that were possible."

"I can understand that perfectly," Sara said.

"Have I made life awkward for you? It's not exactly the kind of news Ferguson will want to hear."

"He'll just have to accept it."

"So, end of story?"

"Not you and me privately. In spite of all the things you have said, it's an uncertain world and you've no idea what may happen to you." She took a box from her pocket. "You don't need to look at it now, there are instructions inside."

"What is it?" he asked.

"It's a Codex mobile phone, the same that links all our operatives together. It's totally encrypted. You'll find *my* source number noted for you. Call me anytime, day or night, this year, next year. Promise me you will do this."

He hugged her tightly. "Of course I will. You are a wonderful girl, Sara Gideon."

"Safe flight in the morning," she said. "But I'd better go and get a little sleep myself. We'll be returning to London." She moved to the door. "God bless, Simon."

She opened it, stepped out, was gone.

Earlier, Emza Khan, Rasoul, and Declan Rashid had returned to the suite on the fifth floor, Rasoul obviously drunk and decidedly mutinous.

Emza Khan struck him across the face. "When you disgrace yourself, you disgrace me. Remember that, you fool. Now, get to bed."

Rasoul glared at Declan as he went past toward his bedroom. Declan said, "I'm beginning to think he's proving to be more trouble than he's worth. He's like a human attack dog."

"An excellent description. There are ways in which he earns his keep," Khan told him. "I'm going to bed now. I'll see you in the morning. Let yourself out."

Which Declan did, while in the second bedroom of the next suite, Rasoul was sampling miniatures from the minibar that made him angrier than ever. He lay on the bed, watched television for a while, finally got up, opened his door to the corridor, and went out on the prowl.

Fatima came awake with a start, realized where she was, and discovered Henri lying beside her. She gently eased herself up, opened the door to the small toilet in the corner, stood at the washbasin examining herself in the mirror, then splashed a little water on her face and dabbed it away with the hand towel.

She went out, uncertain what to do, restless and ill at ease. She stood there looking down at Henri. Poor old goat, she thought, what would he think if he knew that his girlfriend carried a Walther and sometimes killed people? In a way, it reminded her of Sara up there on the fourth floor, and she decided to take a look.

The hotel was quiet and still as she listened at Sara's suite, then walked down to Husseini's, where at that moment Sara was saying good night. To Fatima, it was just the sound of voices, so she carried on, turned the corridor and walked into Rasoul, who had opened the door to a storage room for bed linen at the bottom of the stairs.

144

Thoroughly drunk now, he grabbed her with one hand and reached into her shoulder bag with the other, finding some business cards. "Fatima Le Bon," he read. "A Muslim girl on the game. Shocking."

She struck out at him with her right hand while the left scrabbled for the Walther, found it, and dropped it. He glanced down. "What have we got here? I think you've some explaining to do." He started pushing her back into the storeroom and began to ruck up her skirt.

She struggled, not crying out, because the last thing she wanted was trouble. Sara, leaving Husseini's suite to return to her own, became aware of the muffled sounds of struggle. She turned, took a few quick paces to the corner, and saw what was happening.

Rasoul gazed at her stupidly. "What do you want, bitch? Mind your own business."

She pulled out the Glock and struck him across the arm so that he howled, shoving Fatima away from him. Sara rammed the Glock under his chin and was aware of the sound of someone hurriedly descending the stairs.

Declan Rashid, in a black tracksuit, arrived in a rush. He took in the scene with extraordinary calm. "What's been happening?"

Sara stood back and reholstered her Glock. "Assault, battery, intention to rape, take your pick, Colonel. He jumped this lady as she was walking along the corridor."

He picked up the Walther. "And who does this belong to?"

"To me, of course." Fatima took it from him and put it in her shoulder bag. "I'm a *poule,* Colonel, out on the night shift. The weapon is for protection. There are some bad people about."

"As you can see," Sara told him.

"Indeed I can." Declan Rashid turned to Rasoul, who was nursing his arm. "Get upstairs. Your boss is waiting for you and is not pleased."

Rasoul staggered away, and Declan smiled. "As Mr. Dillon said at the Élysée Palace, Captain Gideon, we do seem to meet up in some funny old places."

"We do indeed." She smiled. "But it's been a long night, so I'm going to bed after I've seen Miss Le Bon on her way."

"Of course." He smiled again, then followed Rasoul up the stairs.

The two women went along the corridor to the rear lift. Fatima said, "You needn't come any further. I've got my car down-stairs."

"You're not a *poule,*" Sara said. "You brought me flowers earlier today."

Fatima was suddenly more tired than she had ever been and she said, "Damn you, Sara Gideon, for being so nice, and damn you for saving me from that piece of shit just now." She took the Walther from her shoulder bag. "You know what this was for? To assassinate you and maybe your friend, Dillon, when I delivered the flowers."

Sara, very calm, very controlled, for noth-ing surprised her after what she'd seen in Afghanistan, said, "And who were the flow-ers from?"

Fatima dropped the Walther back in her bag and said wearily, "There is one God and his Prophet is Osama."

Sara shook her head. "That's a large bur-den."

"And a heavy price to pay for having got involved in the Cause in the first place." Fatima pressed the button, stepped in, and turned when the doors opened. "Good-bye, Captain Gideon. I don't expect we'll see each other again."

The doors closed, Sara stood there for a moment thinking about it, then returned to the suite to report to Dillon.

■ ■ ■ ■

At the same time in Emza Khan's suite, Rasoul stood dejectedly, waiting for the ax to fall. Declan told Khan what had happened, and Khan gave Rasoul the habitual backhanded slap in the face, "You can leave him to me, I'll handle it," he told the colonel.

Declan went off to his own suite, thinking of Sara, a mystery her being there and not properly explained at all, and then there was the other woman. Since when did a hotel *poule* carry a Walther? Perhaps time would tell, and he got on the bed without getting undressed and went to sleep.

Next door, Emza Khan was examining Rasoul. "Look at you, you drunken sot. You, who are supposed to care for Yousef with his drink problem. How can I trust you ever again? And all this business with the French prostitute."

"But she was Algerian-French, to judge by her name."

Emza Khan frowned. "Which was?"

"Fatima Le Bon. I saw her business card. She sells flowers."

"But Fatima Le Bon is the name of the al-Qaeda agent who was supposed to see to this Captain Sara Gideon. Something smells of rotten fish here. How come the two women ended together?"

"Will you talk to Saif?" Rasoul asked.

"No, someone rather more important."

He dialed a number, a voice answered. "Why have you called?"

Khan told him, "Is Saif in any way derelict, Master?"

"No. The woman has killed before. It's not Saif's fault she failed this time. We'll take care of it."

"Of course, Master," Khan said hastily. "My only concern is serving our cause and, in that way, my country."

"The leaders of which will hang you high in the middle of Tehran for crows to feast on if they ever discover what their premier businessman is up to."

For Emza Khan, it had become clearer what he had gotten himself into. Genuinely moved by Osama's message, he had offered his services to the right people for romantic reasons. Well-received because of his enormous wealth, he had soon discovered he had to obey orders like anyone else. There was no turning back from his chosen path, which had left him completely at the orders of the Master, a voice that could be coming from anywhere in the world.

"We'll speak of the Petra project when you are back in London. Thanks to a sympathizer on the staff at army headquarters in Tehran, Colonel Rashid will find he has been called back for a few weeks to advise on a training program for new recruits. This will get him out from under your feet for a while."

"I'm grateful for that. He is certainly not an Islamist, and his attitude toward the Gideon woman is questionable."

"I would have thought it obvious: the stirrings of desire. We'll speak again when you're in London."

Khan said, "But what about the Le Bon woman?"

"Leave it to me, we'll take care of it."

"But when?" Khan asked.

"At once, of course." The voice was tinged with irritation. "Good night."

Back in Henri's office, Fatima lay down beside him and fell into a troubled sleep. She finally wakened to discover that well over an hour had elapsed and he was still out to the world. This was no good at all. She got up and left the office, went to where she'd left her Fiat, got in and drove away. She had to go to her apartment. A couple of suitcases, essential things, would be enough, and the biscuit tin with her mad money. Then the open road to wherever. It didn't really matter. She had a despairing feeling that it wouldn't make any difference whatever she chose.

Arriving at her building, Fatima pressed the hand control and the door lifted with the usual eerie creak. For some reason, the light hadn't come on, but she drove in and switched off the engine. Before she could get out, a man who had obviously been in the back of the van since the hotel reared up, hands of such power sliding around her neck that it was broken instantly, her life ending in a matter of seconds.

He got out of the Fiat, the diffused light from a nearby streetlamp helping him. He wore a trench coat and cap, and looked perfectly respectable when he leaned in, eased Fatima into the passenger seat, got behind the wheel, reversed out, and started down the cobbled street toward the lights of the Seine below. Rain drifted across the river in a solid curtain, although plenty of lights glowed through it. He moved away from a section with houseboats tied up, drove along to a small dark quay with a slip-way at the end. He paused the Fiat at the top, eased Fatima behind the wheel, switched on the engine again, then reached across her for the umbrella and to release the hand brake and slam the door. The Fiat started to roll and finally veered over the edge toward the end, sliding under the water on its side. The rain increased in force, so he turned up his collar, raised the umbrella, and walked briskly away.

Sara and Dillon reported to Roper because they knew that he'd be available, despite the hour, sitting there in the computer room in front of his screens at Holland Park.

"What do you think, Giles?" Sara asked.

"Fascinating stuff, but I'd say the next step is to speak to Duval."

"Who'll be in bed at this hour," Dillon said.

"So are all sane people, he'll just have to wake up. I'll call him and get back to you."

Duval was his usual grouchy self when he answered Roper's call, but soon livened up at the news of Sara's confrontation and not just at the business with Rasoul. What Fatima had said about her al-Qaeda connection brought him immediately to life.

"I'll get on to it at once. I'll be in touch the moment I have anything."

"Does that apply to the Iranians, too?"

Dillon asked.

"I don't see why not. But let me make one thing clear. I'll bring in full DGSE powers, which supersede any police investigation. We go in hard, Dillon, you know that, possibly harder than any other Western power, and our Parliament usually supports us. So don't call me, I'll call you when I'm ready. Have a good night," he added ironically, and was gone.

"So what about Ferguson?" Sara asked. "He'll raise the roof over this."

"That's Roper's job." Dillon glanced at his watch. "Two-thirty. I think I'll lie on the bed and leave all the action to the French."

"An excellent thought. I'll see you at breakfast."

The following morning, Paris was shrouded in the same heavy driving rain of the night before. No word from Duval, so they ordered breakfast from room service, and they were just finishing when their pilot, Squadron Leader Lacey, called Dillon's mobile.

"It's a foul morning, but there's no reason we can't take off. We'll see you at Charles de Gaulle in an hour and a half."

Dillon had put it on speaker, and Sara called, "Are you sure about that? We're expecting a call from Colonel Duval. For certain reasons, there's a question of permission."

"All I know is we've had this slot booked since yesterday and he's just phoned to say we can use it and he'll meet you there."

"Okay, old son," Dillon said. "We're on our way."

Sara said, "What do you think is going on?"

"Full DGSE powers is heady stuff." Dillon shrugged. "Perhaps the powers that be want to pretend it never happened. We'll soon know."

In the private bar overlooking the runways at Charles de Gaulle, rain driving against the windows, Sara sat close to Dillon as Claude Duval explained what had happened to Fatima Le Bon.

"God help us, but the bastards were on to her quick," Dillon said.

"My dear Sean, there's a problem here," Duval said. "Within forty minutes of our retrieving the body, she was on a slab at the Santé Morgue undergoing a postmortem. Her neck was broken, she'd drunk a great deal of wine. To the rest of the world, she careered down the hill, exited on the slipway, and drove into the river."

Dillon said, "Claude, she admitted being

a member of al-Qaeda, under orders to assassinate Sara. Why would she say that if it wasn't true?"

"There's no mention of anything like that on her police record. Prostitution, drug offenses, yes, but never a hint of anything more serious." Claude looked at Sara. "You understand our dilemma. The Iranian party, down there in the corner waiting for their plane, disclaim any involvement with al-Qaeda, and that is official government policy anyway. None of them left the hotel last night after the business with you, Sara, we've established that. Husseini and his bodyguard have already left for Tehran."

Sara turned to Dillon, eyes burning. "Give me a cigarette, and don't tell me you don't have one."

Without a word, he took out his old silver case, gave her one, and his Zippo flared. She inhaled deeply, and then she exploded. "I've never looked at a more obvious setup in my life. She told me she was al-Qaeda and I was her target. God dammit, Claude, she didn't die crashing into the Seine, she was already dead."

She stood up, sending coffee cups flying, wrenched open the glass door leading to the balcony, and stood under the canopy in the heavy rain.

"She's got a point," Dillon said.

Duval shrugged. "More than that, old friend, she's right, but I've a feeling we'll probably never prove it." He got up and shook hands. "Tell Sara I'm sorry."

"I'll see you to your car," Dillon told him.

As they exited through the glass doors into the concourse, Colonel Declan Rashid got up from the table where he had been sitting with his two companions.

"Where are you going?" Emza Khan demanded.

"To speak to the lady."

"No, you will not," Khan told him. "I forbid it."

Declan ignored him. He wasn't in uniform, wore the fawn suit, and the only military thing about him was the trench coat that hung from his shoulders. He opened the door and joined her under the canopy.

"Captain Gideon?"

"Go on, tell me you don't like women smoking. Does the Koran forbid that, too?"

"Probably in a way it does, but I must admit that I am not a religious man. I've seen too many bad things in my life, and I'm sure you know that my mother was Irish."

She took a last quick puff and flicked the cigarette butt into space. "The smokes helped with the stress in Afghanistan. What did Duval say about Fatima?"

"That it'd been suggested that she was involved with al-Qaeda," Declan said.

"I expect that shook up Khan."

"Exactly. If there is one Islamic country where they are not encouraged, it is Iran."

"And what's your attitude?"

"I never bought the Osama message." He smiled slightly. "But why would you believe me?"

"After that little fracas last night when you went away with Rasoul, Fatima told me she'd been sent to the hotel by al-Qaeda to assassinate me. She actually delivered flowers to my suite, but she said she just couldn't do it, then or later, especially after I saved her from that drunken oaf of yours."

He wasn't smiling now. "Not mine, I assure you. Colonel Duval was not as explicit as you have been. He just said there was a possibility that she was al-Qaeda. I assume you told him she had confessed to you?"

"Oh yes."

"Then why did he not mention it to Emza Khan and me?" And then he saw it. "But you knew what she was and did nothing about it, didn't arrest her when she confessed, and I suspect you probably hoped she'd get away. That's the whole point, isn't it? I believe you were giving her a chance to make a run for it. To this DGSE colonel, you present a problem. You don't follow the rules, and that means you can't be trusted. You are a wild card, Captain. I wonder if Charles Ferguson will take kindly to your approach." He looked up. "But here comes Mr. Dillon in a hurry."

Dillon pulled open the door. "There you are. Everything all right? We're ready to go. The luggage is on board."

She retrieved her shoulder bag from the table and shook hands with Declan Rashid. "Good-bye, Colonel, I'll remember what you said."

He smiled gravely, then she turned and started to half run with Dillon. "What was that all about?" Dillon asked her.

"Everything that's happened, the whole business with Fatima, it was news to the Iranians. Claude Duval didn't tell them about her confession to me."

"The ould sod," Dillon said. "Why would he do that?"

"Declan says it's because I'm a wild card and not to be trusted."

"Declan, is it?"

She ignored the remark. "He has no time for Osama, that's for sure."

"So *he* says, but remember what I told

you. He's the enemy."

"Oh, I hear you, Sean, but my God, he's a lovely man," she said.

■ ■ ■ ■

SAHARA
ALGIERS
LONDON

■ ■ ■ ■

7

The five Sand Cruisers were painted in desert camouflage, each with a crew of five or six men, and a general-purpose machine gun mounted in the center. They had been driving in a convoy for three days, following a wearisome trail that seemed as old as time and probably was, their destination Timbuktu.

The lead vehicle paused as the column emerged in a flat valley, and Daniel Holley called a water stop. He stood up beside the driver of the front vehicle and focused his binoculars on the desolation.

He wore a Bedouin cloak of blue called a burnous, the hood hanging behind, and the dark blue turban of a Tuareg, the face veil hooked back. His only concession to modernity was a Glock seventeen-round pistol at his belt, whereas the weapon hanging from his shoulder was a Lee Enfield bolt-action, single-round .303 rifle, standard issue to the British Army in two world wars. The men in all five Sand Cruisers dressed in a similar way, varying only by their choice of weapons, and an air of general menace radiated from them.

There was a murmur from some of the men as they drank, but otherwise silence, and then two riders appeared, spaced well apart, on the rim of a vast sand dune some two hundred yards away. They sat on their horses, surveying the convoy, and a third rider appeared between them.

He held a flag braced against his right foot, the black flag of al-Qaeda. The murmuring stopped in the Sand Cruiser, and there was a total stillness now.

"There is one God and Osama is his Prophet."

The words echoed high above, and Holley dropped his binoculars, slipped the Lee Enfield from his shoulder, and aimed briefly, a perfect snap shot that caused the flag holder to lift from the saddle, drop the flag, and roll over and over down the side of the dune. The other two horses reared, and one of the riders leaned down to pick up the flag and waved it over his head as they rode away.

There was a roar of approval from the men in the Sand Cruisers, and Holley responded to it. "That'll give these Protectors of the Faith people something to think about. So let's get moving."

The engines of the five vehicles roared into life and the convoy moved forward again.

It had all started a few weeks before Dillon and Sara Gideon's eventful visit to Paris. Daniel Holley was at the controls of his Falcon jet, landing at the Algiers airport one late evening, with darkness starting to creep in as he taxied to the private facility.

He cut the engines, aware of the ground staff waiting, but rather more interesting, the black Mercedes and the young man in a tropical suit who leaned against it, smoking a cigarette. His name was Caspar Selim, a major in Army Intelligence at thirty, on secondment to the Foreign Minister's Office.

Holley went down the airstair door and the ground staff brushed past him to secure the aircraft and retrieve his luggage. He approached the major, smiling.

"Caspar, what a surprise. To what do I owe the honor? Are you here to arrest me or what?"

"The foreign minister's golden boy? You've got to be kidding. He wants to see you, it's urgent, and that's all I know."

"Where to, the Foreign Office?"

"No, he's waiting now at your partner's villa."

"Interesting." Holley joined him in the back and, as the Mercedes pulled away, said, "Give me a cigarette."

"I thought you'd stopped."

"So did I, and then I went to Somalia." Holley accepted the offered light. "Thousands of Kenyan troops are massed to attack Kismayu, the only large port that al-Qaeda still controls."

"Sometimes I think you have a death wish, my friend," Caspar Selim observed.

"I know," Holley said. "And one day it will be the end of me, but not this time. I scraped out of Kismayu by the skin of my teeth, but with plenty of information about the city's defenses. The Kenyans were quite happy to get it."

"They'll love you in Nairobi," Caspar said. "But then, I suppose that was the real purpose of the trip all along."

"To improve my business credentials in that fair city?" Holley shrugged. "No harm in that, but I'd also like to think that the information will save lives when the Kenyans launch their attack. Do you know the Roman saying 'Life is short, art long, experiment perilous'?"

166

"What the hell is that pearl of wisdom supposed to mean?"

"I haven't the slightest idea, Caspar. You went to the military academy at Sandhurst. Figure it out for yourself and give me another cigarette."

They found the foreign minister in the huge sitting room of the villa of Holley's partner, Hamid Malik. The minister's chauffeur lurked discreetly at the back of the room, obviously with a gun in his pocket. Malik was uneasy in the great man's presence, as they sipped fresh orange juice laced with champagne, and the relief on his face was palpable when Holley and Caspar Selim entered.

The foreign minister raised his voice, a smile on his face. "Here he is, the hero of the hour. I've had my opposite number on the line from Nairobi, Daniel. Our Kenyan friends are more than grateful to you."

"Well, that's nice to know."

"The information you brought out of Kismayu will make all the difference when the Kenyan Army starts its invasion. We'll drink to it."

Malik was pouring, and Holley said, "Somehow it makes everything seem worthwhile." He turned to Caspar, glass in hand.

"Don't you agree?"

Caspar mouthed *bastard* and then raised his glass. "A wonderful effort."

"I agree," the minister said. "But now to business. Algiers has been good to you, Daniel, I'm sure you would agree. Twenty-five years ago, you turned up from Ireland with a price on your head, to be trained as a soldier of the IRA at the camp at Shabwa, deep in the desert, kept solvent by the generosity of Colonel Gadhafi."

"Yes, that's true," Daniel said.

"And now here you are, joint owner with Malik of one of the biggest shipping lines out of Algiers, a business founded on your ability to sell arms to every country in the Middle East."

Malik, a businessman to the last, said, "I can assure you, Minister, that our books are completely in order."

"So you perform miracles now?" The foreign minister laughed and turned back to Holley. "Granting you Algerian nationality was one thing, but then I made you a special envoy of my department. That diplomatic passport gets you waved through airports worldwide."

"For which I am immensely grateful," Holley told him.

"Yes, well, now it must be paid for. I have

168

a task for which I believe you are uniquely fitted. Is it true that for some years you have sold arms to Tuareg tribes rebelling in the north of Mali?"

Holley didn't hesitate. "On occasion, I did, but I'm not going to apologize. I thought they had a point."

"I tend to agree, not that it matters. They are just the kind of recruits I have in mind for the task I am going to give you. Timbuktu has been invaded by rebels calling themselves Protectors of the Faith. But they operate under the black flag of al-Qaeda."

"Just how bad is it?" Holley asked.

"Government troops have cleared off; also any police. Timbuktu has been a center of Islamic learning since the sixteenth century. Priceless books and documents, including some of the very rarest copies of the Koran, are there. The invaders are like mindless savages, destroying what they do not understand. They've even ordered locals to stop worshipping at the tombs of saints."

"And those who refuse to obey are slaughtered, I presume?" Holley asked.

"So we understand. Many local people have managed to conceal the treasures in one way or another, but information is scant. It's hopeless to expect help from the UN in these troubled times, but our President has placed this matter in my hands to find a solution. It's one of the worst attacks on Islamic culture for centuries. We must do something." There was a pause. Malik looked hunted at such a prospect, but Holley simply nodded. "So what you're saying is you want me to act completely unofficially, recruit a band of Tuareg bandits, go down to Timbuktu, and save as many of the priceless artifacts as we can?"

The foreign minister nodded. "That sums it up. The Algerian government can't be seen to be using the army or the air force in any way. It might give the wrong impression."

"So I'd have a free hand to take care of it whatever way I want?"

"I'm not even offering to pay you, Daniel. I'm well aware you and Malik are multimillionaires anyway. Look upon it as a good deed in a naughty world." The foreign minister stood up. "Your country will be immensely grateful." He smiled. "Especially if you can achieve our aim with a minimum of publicity."

"Of course, Excellency." Holley shook hands. "Go with God."

"And you, Daniel." The minister turned and went, and Malik hurried after to see him out.

Holley poured himself a whiskey and stepped out onto the terrace to find a full moon, the vast harbor below uniquely beautiful. He stood there, thinking about Timbuktu, and Malik returned, immensely excited.

"Can you do it?"

"I think so. Recruiting the Tuaregs will be no problem at all. They put themselves out as mercenaries these days, and once they've taken the blood money, they're yours. A matter of honor. There are plenty hanging round Algiers, some of the guys whom Colonel Gadhafi recruited. We've got several Sand Cruisers in the holding depot doing nothing. There's no problem tooling them up with the right weaponry. Twenty-five to thirty good men should be enough. They can drive down through the Sahara. I'll go with them."

"So, no helicopter?"

"Terrible sandstorms this time of year. The Dakota will do just fine, and it has lots of room for the rare manuscripts and books we'll be looking for. There's an old airstrip at Fuad ten miles out of Timbuktu, left over from French Foreign Legion days. I'll need another pilot, but Caspar Selim has his wings and he can't say no. The foreign minister won't hear of it."

Malik shook his head. "All you see is another adventure, Daniel. You never change."

"As the foreign minister said, Algeria has been good to me. It's a chance to do something worthwhile in her name, but if al-Qaeda makes this a major campaign the French might have to intervene, and certainly Algerian Special Forces. Time will tell."

A month later, unaware of any of this, Dillon and Sara Gideon found the weather in London just as rain-soaked as the city they'd left, Paris. Billy Salter, waiting for them under an umbrella beside his Alfa Romeo, greeted them cheerfully.

"Taxi, lady?"

"How nice," Sara said as he opened the rear door for her. "Highfield Court, please."

"You'll have to make do with Holland Park," he told her. "Ferguson wants to get straight down to business."

"Sure, and doesn't he always," Dillon said. "How's Harry?"

"Busy with the restaurant. There'll be Roper and the general and we three, but what it's all about, I've no idea."

"And Daniel?" Sara asked. "Still no news?"

"A month now," Billy said, "and not a word. But I wouldn't worry. Anyone who's been sentenced to life imprisonment in Moscow's Lubyanka Prison and yet walks out in five years has got to have a bit of luck on his side. You must know Daniel Holley by now. He's up to his neck in a lot of things we aren't."

"He's right," Dillon said. "The shipping line takes him all over the place, and his arms-dealing must be bigger than it's ever been. It's a sign of the times."

"Come off it, Sean," she said. "Somebody should have told him of a brilliant new invention, the mobile phone. If he's too busy to call, I can only draw my own conclusions," and she folded her arms and sat back in the corner, miserably angry.

"Well, I must say you look better than I thought you would," Ferguson told Sara when she and Dillon joined him and Roper in the computer room.

"It could have been worse," she said. "But I'm sorry about the woman, Fatima."

"You should have reported her confession straightaway, to me or Claude Duval, but I believe you were giving her a chance to get away. That was very wrong. Did I make a mistake in recruiting you?"

173

"That's interesting. Declan Rashid told me that's how you would see it."

"You discussed it with him?"

"Of course. I did tell Claude what she had confessed to me, but he didn't tell Declan and Khan that she was targeting me under direct orders from al-Qaeda." Sara was perfectly calm. "Declan says I'm a wild card and that you won't want to use me again."

"I like the colonel," Dillon cut in. "But if that were true, the general would have sacked *me* years ago."

"And me, come to think of it," Roper said. "By the way, and just for the record, as you seem to have got rather intimate with the colonel, what's his attitude to al-Qaeda? Did you ask?"

"I didn't need to. He told me that he didn't buy the Osama message, but then wondered why I should believe him."

"My goodness, you *did* get close," Ferguson said.

"No cheap cracks, please. That was when I told him Fatima had confessed about her order to assassinate me. It was the first he'd heard about it, since Claude hadn't mentioned the fact, and he wasn't pleased."

"No, he wouldn't be, any more than he'll be pleased at being posted back to Tehran for a while. It's just been announced at the

Iranian Embassy."

Amazing the sudden sense of loss. Sara pulled herself together and said, "So what happens now? Am I returned to unit? If so, that's fine. With my languages and experience, there's still plenty for me to do in Afghanistan."

"And a damn sight more here. To be frank, this relationship with Colonel Declan Rashid may be worth a great deal in the right circumstances," Ferguson said.

Before she could reply, Dillon cut in, "I've said it before, but you have to be one of the most devious bastards of all time."

"I'll second that," Roper said. "So having established that Sara is still a prime mover and shaker round here, can I put a question her way?"

"Of course."

"What did you say to Husseini, Sara?"

"I asked what his attitude would be to an attempt by the SAS to snatch him and his mother and daughter. He said that the idea of them being out of Tehran and living the good life in Hampstead had a certain appeal, but he didn't feel there was much hope of such a venture succeeding. So under the circumstances, he had no option but to accept the current situation."

"Very frustrating," Ferguson said. "I can

see that. What else did he have to say?"

Which was when Sara started to lie. "Oh, he was terribly pleased to see me, wanted to know all about my grandfather. He has a genuine affection for him and follows his academic career online. He's kept quiet about their relationship all those years ago."

"And what did he think about you?"

"Fascinated by my military career, Afghanistan and so forth. I told him I worked for you, no reason not to, and I felt it was necessary to establish my good faith, if that's the right way to put it."

Ferguson nodded. "You've done well."

Billy Salter, who had been sitting beside Dillon, taking it all in, said, "Considering what she and Dillon went through the other night here and then in Paris, I reckon she's been bloody marvelous."

"Yes, you could put it that way," Ferguson said. "Well, let me think about it. In the meantime, there's another matter which'll interest you. Daniel Holley dropped out of sight just about a month ago. Roper said he could be in Algeria or in the depths of the Sahara, and he was closer than he knew. Timbuktu, a center of Islamic leaning for at least five hundred years, is being pillaged by barbarians in the name of al-Qaeda. Rare books, artifacts, manuscripts, an entire culture being destroyed."

Sara said, "But what's Daniel doing down there?"

"We have a short film, shot on the move and pretty rough, but it will give you the idea," Ferguson said.

Roper put it on his largest screen and it was as if they were right there: crowds of people surging through alleyways, smoke, flames, men on horseback galloping around, trucks and the occasional jeep with general-purpose machine guns mounted, and then the Sand Cruisers charging in, Tuaregs standing behind their machine guns and firing.

There was footage of the Dakota at the old airfield at Fuad, trucks drawing up, delivering cargo to the plane. Caspar Selim, in khaki uniform, was supervising the loading. A Tuareg galloped up, dismounted to talk to him, then turned to look into the camera, and it was Daniel Holley.

"Oh my God," Sara said.

"Yes, he does look rather dashing," Ferguson said. "All that's missing are Beau Geste, his two brothers, and the Foreign Legion at Fort Zinderneuf."

Holley was suddenly closer to the camera, smiling and nodding, and then there was a loud explosion and the screen went dark.

Roper said, "Don't get alarmed, that was nothing serious. We've talked to him several times since."

Ferguson said to Sara, "He's calling my office on Skype an hour and a half from now. You can take it first and have a chat. I'll speak to him after."

"I'd like that," she said.

"Good. Now allow me to explain what Holley is doing running this affair. Then we'll see what Maggie Hall has to offer for lunch."

Holley talked to her from the back of a Sand Cruiser, using a highly sophisticated laptop.

"You're looking good," he said. "It was impossible to keep in touch. The Algerians want a low profile on this for obvious reasons. It's lucky that Timbuktu is such a vast distance from the real world, a dot on the horizon of one of the greatest deserts on earth."

"You don't need to apologize," she said.

"It's just that what we are saving is so remarkable. Centuries-old copies of the Koran, manuscripts produced by master painters, precious things of every description. You don't have to be a Muslim to recognize wonderful works of art. These savages we're fighting, the vandals operating

178

under al-Qaeda's leadership, would destroy these amazing things because they don't fit in with their own vision of Islam."

"Well, take care." She tried to sound jolly. "We'd hate to lose you."

"What about you and Dillon? Roper was telling me. The car chase in London, the two al-Qaeda hit men. What was that all about?"

"They just want revenge."

"And Paris and the Ritz?"

"It's the beast stirring, they want payback for past hurts."

"Well, *you* take care."

"Will I see you soon?"

"Not for a while. There's a lot to be done, and UN help is not on offer like it used to be. We'll sort something out."

"Of course we will." There was little hope in her voice. "Ferguson wants a word with you. We'll talk again."

Holley apologized to Ferguson for the fact that he would not be available for the foreseeable future, and Ferguson assured him again that they'd be able to cope. "This work you're doing is of prime importance. Nothing must be allowed to get in the way of that."

Holley clicked off, and Ferguson took out

a file, extracted some papers, went through them, then picked up his desk phone and called Roper.

"Are they still here, Sara, Billy, and Dillon?"

"They decided to have a swim and a steam before they left."

"Excellent. I want to have a word before they go."

"I'll see to it. Anything I can do?"

"There will be. Holley's just made it clear he's not going to be available for some time."

"Which is not unreasonable," Roper said. "This Timbuktu business is pretty important."

"Yes, but his specialized knowledge of the shipping business is what produced the Petra Project. We'll meet in the computer room to discuss where we go from here."

They sat and listened while Ferguson talked. "I know we've discussed this briefly, but let me go back to the beginning. As you know, nobody knows more about the shipping business in the Mediterranean than Daniel Holley. Malik Shipping's fleet contains passenger vessels as well as general cargo, and carries everything from frozen food, automobiles, and farm produce, to military

180

hardware. But there's a second level of the shipping business that's just as important as the first. Old rust buckets, owned by individuals, working a host of small ports from Morocco to Egypt, meeting the needs of local communities. They're known as Petra boats, have been for years."

"Why is that?" Sara asked.

"During the Second World War, North Africa became a pretty lively place. Concrete piers were built in scores of small ports, and a Greek firm called Petra Brothers established basic handling facilities and accommodation."

"Are they still around?" Dillon asked.

"Not for years. These days most of the facilities in each port are owned locally, but things are busier than ever. The Syrian situation, for instance, has produced a lively night trade in arms for the rebels."

"Isn't that good?" Billy said.

"Not if it's al-Qaeda providing the weapons. Their goal is to get a foothold in the movement, with the intention of eventually taking over."

Sara said, "And Daniel believes these Petra boats are involved?"

"Some of them definitely cross into Lebanese and Syrian waters, and there are whispers of arms being landed by night."

"But they may be good guys," Billy said.

"Anything is possible." Ferguson reached for Roper's bottle of scotch, poured a shot, and tossed it down.

"Feel free with my whiskey, why don't you, and tell us what you intend," Roper said.

"Daniel is convinced that al-Qaeda intends to come to power in any future Syria by penetrating the Free Syrian Army. He believes it of crucial importance to recognize that."

"I can see how he would," Roper said.

"He's left me a file listing ships that might be involved. Holley took just over a hundred Petra ships with details of their voyages over the past three months and fed them into a computer. Only twelve of them visited Lebanese waters over three months, and only once or twice — but the *Kantara* out of Oran visited on six occasions. That's twice a month."

There was silence for a moment, then Roper said, "Okay, so you've got me interested. What happens now?"

Ferguson said, "Sean — Billy. Remember your exploits in the Khufra along the Algerian coast?"

"Jesus, who could forget?" Billy said. "I'll remember that till my dying day."

"Don't worry, I'm not asking you to go back. There's a place ninety miles west of Algiers toward Tunisia. It's called Ras Kasar. It's one of the regular small ports on the Petra boats' schedule, and the *Kantara* is due to call in for a couple of days next Friday."

"Are you sure about that?" Dillon asked.

"That's what Daniel's computer says, but I've chosen that particular port for a special reason. There's a hotel there called the Paradise Club, run by a Greek named Andrew Adano. He used to work for me when I was in Army Intelligence in Cairo years ago."

"How long is it since you've spoken to him?" Sara asked.

"Many years, until I found his details on Holley's list of ports and phoned him. He's sound as a bell, so I've no qualms about using him. It's not quite the holiday season, so the hotel is quiet, but there are water sports, diving. The ships don't get in the way. He tells me they drop anchor in the outer harbor. When the season gets going, they even have seaplanes landing."

"It's obviously quite taken your fancy, Charles. When are you going?" Roper asked.

"Still interested?"

"I'm just envious," Roper said. "I don't

183

know if you've noticed the wheelchair, but it does tend to limit things. Have you told Adano what this is all about?"

"No, but I'm open to discussion about it. What's your opinion?"

"How sound is he?"

"Absolutely first class. Backed me, pistol in hand, when we were attacked by three drug-crazy fedayeen in Cairo. Took a bullet in his left thigh."

"Okay, that certainly counts for something. Don't mention al-Qaeda, though, it just might put the fear of God in him. Tell him you suspect the *Kantara* might be carrying drugs."

"That makes sense."

"So does the fact that I'm going to need Billy with me," Dillon said. "If the ships are moved in the outer harbor, we'll only get to inspect the *Kantara* for any sign of arms by swimming underwater."

Sara said, "I'm afraid I wouldn't be much good to you there, Sean. I just haven't had the training."

"One wrong move in the diving game and you're dead, it's as simple as that." Her disappointment showed. "I'll need you anyway. It's always good to have a second pilot."

She looked at him in astonishment, and

Ferguson said, "What was that you said?"

"Lacey and Parry can deliver us to Palma Airport. You have an asset in Majorca, Charles, a Greek called Yanni Christou? I had dealings with him in IRA days. His firm, Trade Winds, rents out some old Eagle floatplanes. I estimate a flight of two hundred miles should have us at Ras Kasar."

Sara said, "But I've never flown a floatplane."

"That's what I like about you," he said. "You didn't say I *can't* fly a floatplane. I'll show you. Trust me. I read the reports when you got your Army Air Corps wings. It said natural pilot."

"There you are," Ferguson said. "Can't argue with that. I'd better go call Adano and get this show on the road."

Emza Khan had returned from Paris to a serious problem. In spite of the supervision of Dr. Aziz and the constant attention of a sixteen-stone male nurse named Hawkins, Yousef had worked his way through two bottles of champagne and one of vodka, then locked Hawkins in the bedroom, descended to the garage, punched the night porter, taken a Mercedes, and driven down toward Shepherd Market, bouncing off several parked cars.

A blood test showed him to be four times over the limit. Dr. Aziz had assumed medical responsibility for him, thus extracting him from a cell, but his future with the courts looked black. For the moment, he was in the Aziz Private Nursing Home a few streets from Park Lane, where Khan sat fuming in his penthouse apartment.

Needing someone to kick, he was not able to resist calling Saif at Pound Street, to take him to task over Fatima, but not to express any regret for her death.

He found Saif sad and subdued, for the Egyptian had been truly shocked to read a small item in *Le Monde* on the recovery of her body from the Seine, a sure sign the DGSE was setting the whole thing up as suicide and thus easily dismissed.

Khan, who had read the same piece online, said, "You should be ashamed to have used a tart for such a task, a common street *poule.* It makes me doubt your ability to serve, Saif, or your worthiness."

Saif replied in an agitated voice, "Why don't you go fuck yourself? She killed four times for the Cause. What have you ever done, you lousy bastard? She was worth ten of you."

Khan was enraged. "Damn you, Saif, you are a walking dead man for saying that. I

186

have the power, make no mistake." He slammed down the receiver.

Ali Saif was not ashamed to cry, to let the tears flow as he sat at his desk. Shortly after that call, he received another. It was the Master, who said, "Are you all right?"

Saif had difficulty choking back the sobs, but finally managed. "I'm sorry, Master, a weakness, she was a good friend."

"Nothing to be ashamed of. I saw the piece in *Le Monde.* I was sure they'd spin it that way. The fortunes of war. She was a soldier and took a soldier's risks, as you and I do. It is a shame that Emza Khan's man was so quick to execute her. An animal, I'm afraid. One would have hoped Khan would have had some control over him. Indeed, Rasoul seems to have had approval for what he did."

Ali Saif was horrified. "That is the truth? But why did he *do* it?"

"Rasoul is a bully and uninterested in the true path of Osama, only in the pursuit of power. He will be dealt with in due course." What he had said about Khan he truly believed, but blaming Rasoul for Fatima's death was a lie for which he made no apology. Everything had a purpose.

They had a rule that all telephone calls must be recorded. The Master said, "Play me the call."

Which Saif did, Emza Khan's harsh and ugly words echoing. There was a strange quiet when it finished.

The Master said calmly, "He is a small man, you are not. Always remember that. Your day will come. Osama blesses you."

Next he called Khan and found him at home, seated by the sliding windows to the terrace, reading the *Times.* Khan was so flustered that he stood.

"Master, what can I do for you?"

"I've seen the results of your Petra plan. So simple in principle — yet it works. The *Kantara* has made six successful deliveries by night in three months. You are to be congratulated. I'll make sure this is known. As I've said before, only an outstanding businessman is capable of this level of planning."

Khan was overwhelmed and could barely speak. "Master — what can I say?"

"I could use a firsthand report, Emza. Someone to take a trip on the boat itself."

"I wish I could do it, but I can't spare the time. My poor efforts for the Cause consume me."

"Indeed, we are so grateful, and so is your country's government. How is your son?

188

There were problems with his health, as I recall?"

The Master, of course, had already been informed of the fix Khan was in with Yousef. Khan hesitated.

"Perhaps a trip round the Mediterranean in the *Kantara* would put roses in his cheeks?"

"What . . . what an excellent idea," Khan said. "Do you think he'd be welcome? I mean, it's a working boat. No passengers."

"We'll soon change that. I admit I've never met Captain Rajavi, but we've spoken many times. After all, I am his employer. I'll see that he calls you. The latest voyage started from Oran a few days ago, but your son could join at any of the ports."

"He'll be absolutely thrilled. Can I send my bodyguard with him, Rasoul?"

"Of course, but send my blessings to Yousef. I hope he has a wonderful time."

"Allah bless you, Master."

"He always does, my friend, every day of my life."

David Rajavi was sitting in the captain's chair of the wheelhouse of the *Kantara* and his bosun, Abu, a Somali, took the wheel. He was enjoying a cigarette and a cup of coffee when his mobile sounded.

189

"Where are you?" the Master asked.

"Just three miles out from a small port called Boukara, east of Algiers, where I intend to drop anchor for the night. What can I do for you?"

"My friends are delighted with what you've achieved. The weapons you landed have reached the right destination."

"That's good to know," Rajavi told him. "But I truly believe it's only the beginning. What can I do for you?"

"You mean, 'What can I do for the Cause?' "

"I would have thought that by now you would know that I regard them as one and the same."

"Excellent. I want you to call Emza. Tell him you'd be happy to have his son, Yousef, and his bodyguard, Rasoul, join you during the next couple of days."

"Oh dear," Rajavi said. "We'll have to padlock the drinks locker. That won't go down well with the kind of crew I run."

"It could be worse," the Master said. "You stop at plenty of ports, there's leave."

"I suppose so, but I don't know how the crew is going to take a spoiled young man like Yousef, a drunk who's only avoided prison for rape because the girls were bought off by Daddy."

"So why not put him to work?" the Master said.

"He'd break an arm or a leg before we knew what was happening, especially if he still had access to booze." Rajavi snorted. "You know what drunks are like."

"Of course," the Master said. "On the other hand, he might do us all a favor and break his neck."

There was silence for a moment, then Rajavi said, "You're serious, aren't you?"

"Let me explain. However unpleasant, Emza Khan is important to our cause because of his billions, his connection with the Iranian government, and the status this gives him in Washington and London. His two sons killed in the war with Iraq is a matter for sorrow, but also pride, as is his relationship with one of Iran's greatest war heroes, Colonel Declan Rashid. The only fly in the ointment is Yousef himself, for rather obvious and disgusting reasons. Our cause could do without him. Do I make myself plain?"

"Very much so," David Rajavi told him.

"Excellent," the Master said. "Call Emza Khan and make the arrangements."

"Consider it done," Rajavi said and, when the Master had gone, lit a cigarette and sat there thinking about it.

191

Abu, the bosun, said, "Trouble, Captain?"

"It could be," Rajavi said. "We've got to pick up a passenger and his minder somewhere during the voyage, and the nearest way I can describe him to you is an alcoholic schoolboy who can't keep his pants buttoned. The problem is what to do with him."

Abu roared with laughter. "It's simple, Captain, throw him overboard."

Rajavi shook his head. "You've no idea how much sense that makes, Abu." He picked up his mobile and called Emza Khan.

At Highfield Court, Sara was in her bedroom busy packing when there was a knock on the door and Sadie Cohen looked in. "Daniel's downstairs on Skype in your granddad's study. The rabbi's out, by the way, and not due back until late."

Sara hurried down the stairs, went into the study, and sat in front of the screen on the large Victorian desk. Daniel, still dressed as a Turareg, stared out at her. There was some faint shooting in the background and a distant explosion. He was unshaven, dirty and sweating, eyes wild.

"Daniel, you look so tired," she said.

"Never mind that," he told her. "Ferguson's just told me about you, Dillon, and

Billy flying off to Ras Kasar tomorrow."

"That's right," she said. "The Petra project."

"Which was my baby." He was thoroughly angry. "The *Kantara* gig, particularly. I've been afraid for weeks that the other side would realize we might get on to them because it's so obvious. Damn Ferguson!"

"That's no way to be, Daniel. Now the proof's there that the *Kantara*'s been up to no good, somebody's got to do something about it, and you're obviously not available."

"Don't rub it in, and if it is al-Qaeda, the crew will be armed to the teeth. It could be a bloodbath. It's crazy sending you into a situation like that."

"But not crazy for Dillon and Billy, only me? That's what it's all about, isn't it." She was cold-bloodedly angry now. "Listen to me, Daniel, I'm a big girl. I don't need somebody to hold my hand. I made my bones in Helmand Province, and I've got the permanent limp and the Military Cross to prove it. So I'm going, and you can't stop me."

He looked quite wild. "Damn you, Sara."

"You take care, Daniel, and I'll take care, that's all I can say. I'm signing off now." She clicked off the screen, turned, and

193

found Sadie standing there looking troubled.

"This work you do, Sara, is it worth it? He loves you so, and he's such a nice man."

"Time for truth, Sadie. This 'nice man' once did five years in the Lubyanka, and carried a gun for the Provisional IRA. So did Sean Dillon, by the way, whom you adore. Do you want to know how many they've killed? Do you know how many dead Taliban I left at Abusan?"

Sadie stood there, a kind of horror on her face, a fist to her mouth, and Sara zipped up her military bag, put an arm around her, and kissed her on the cheek. "It's the life I've chosen, Sadie. Give Granddad my love and tell him I'll be back in a week or two," and she went out.

Harry had driven up from his pub, the Dark Man, with Billy, and they sat in the computer room with Roper, Dillon, and Sara while Ferguson went through what was to happen.

"Since the Gulfstream has diplomatic immunity, you can take your weaponry on board. Yanni Christou will pick you up at Palma. You will have no difficulty transferring your weaponry to the floatplane. Andrew Adano will be handling the usual corrupt system at the Algerian end."

"Diving gear?" Dillon asked.

"Taken care of. Obviously, Adano knows who you are, but I don't see the need to alter your names on this one. You're all mixed up in the holiday trade and looking for fresh venues. Billy is an expert in water sports, Dillon and Sara are more interested in the entertainment side. He'll play the piano a time or two, and Sara will sing a song, just to cover your backs. I'm not suggesting you perform every night."

"That seems to cover everything," Dillon said.

"Take care with the cushion on the front seat on the left in the Gulfstream. If you unzip it, you'll find blocks of Semtex and several tin boxes of pencil timers. I've given you a choice on the timers, various lengths for extreme circumstances. One's a five-hour delay job. Just like the IRA in the old days."

"That's it, then," Dillon said. "The rest depends on the *Kantara.*"

"Absolutely." Ferguson nodded. "I need the Gulfstream back here, so Lacey and Parry will miss the joys of Majorca, which won't please them, but the sooner you're on your way to Ras Kasar, the better. Anything else?"

Sara said, "Daniel isn't very pleased."

There was a troubled silence, and Ferguson said, "When did this happen?"

"He spoke to me on Skype just before I came here."

"He was angry with me?" Ferguson suggested.

"I'm afraid so. He doesn't approve of me being involved."

"That's not surprising," Dillon said.

"So where exactly does that leave you, Captain?" Ferguson asked.

"As far as romance is concerned?" Sara got up and reached for her bag. "A nonstarter, I'm afraid. There's certainly no room for it in our line of work. So if you'll excuse me, gentlemen, it's me for an early night. I think I'm going to have to be on top of my game," and she went out.

At the Aziz Private Nursing Home, the doctor was going through accounts in his office when the door burst open and Emza Khan forced his way past the protesting secretary.

"It's all right," Aziz said and waved her away.

"I've just been up to see him in his room to tell him about this." He dropped a letter on the desk. "He's been ordered to appear at Westminster Magistrates Court on five separate counts next Thursday. This time it could mean prison."

"How did he take it?"

"He seemed genuinely afraid. And sober, for once."

"He would be, we washed him out. So what do you want to do?"

"I have a commercial interest in a cargo boat. The captain's agreed to sign him on as a crew member. I think it might be the best thing for him."

"What does he think about that? Has he agreed to go?"

"Yes. He's afraid of the idea of prison."

"Then just take him. If the police inquire, I'll say he just disappeared. You can say the same thing. They can't prove otherwise."

Emza Khan didn't even say good-bye, the door banged and he was gone.

■ ■ ■ ■

Majorca
Algeria

■ ■ ■ ■

8

The Gulfstream landed at Palma just before noon and taxied to the private planes section where Dillon, peering out, noticed the blue van, and the sign on the side that said *Trade Winds.* Yanni Christou leaned against it, smoking a cigarette, black hair in a ponytail, a bushy mustache on his tanned face. He was sixty years old and yet had the kind of tough look that would make anyone adopt a cautious approach.

Parry opened the airstair door and Dillon led the way down, walking toward Christou, who flung his arms wide. "You bastard, I couldn't believe it." He grabbed Dillon and kissed him on both cheeks.

"I've told you before, why not try shaving if you're going to do that? This is my associate, Billy Salter."

Billy removed his mirror sunglasses and held out his hand and Christou nodded. "Welcome, young one, I don't need to ask

201

what you do for a living."

His gaze took in Sara as she stood at the top of the steps, and he stopped smiling. "God in heaven, you've brought a real woman with you."

"How right you are," Dillon told him as she limped toward them. "Meet Captain Sara Gideon, Yanni. An Afghanistan veteran with the scars to prove it *and* the medals."

Christou kissed her hand. "It saddens me to see you in bad company. The things I could tell you about Dillon would shock you to the core. On the other hand, he did break my nephew Christoff out of a jail where Turkish bastards were holding him on false evidence!"

"Dillon was telling us what a great flyer you are, a Greek Navy pilot in your day?" Sara said in Greek.

"Until I punched my commanding officer in an argument over a woman, and I can't believe you speak Greek."

"Some people have a thing for mathematics, mine is languages. I've taken my wings in the British Army Air Corps, but Dillon tells me I am to be second pilot on one of your Eagles. My problem is I've never flown a floatplane."

Yanni Christou, who had been passing the luggage into the van, paused, and the smile on his face was something to see. "Then it will be my pleasure to show you."

Torina was a small port, the pier stretching out and turning at the end to enclose the harbor. There were fishing boats at anchor, several more drawn up on the beach, a scattering of white houses behind, a cantina café with a large terrace and tables, the awnings and umbrellas being put away for the moment, for this was the off-season and rain and sudden storms were not unknown.

Billy with his orange juice, and Dillon with an ice-cold lager, watched the Eagle come in low over the sea, then drop down parallel to the pier, and Dillon said, "That was close to perfect." The floatplane coasted toward the sands, and he added, "Let's see how she copes with beaching."

It was their second day, for Yanni Christou had lost no time in getting Sara into the air on the afternoon of their arrival and Dillon had had the sense to leave them to it. Sara had taken it very seriously and so had Yanni, and it showed, although there had been a few early belly landings into the sea the first day until darkness had forced them to abandon their efforts.

It had rained during the morning, but not enough to prevent further flying, and the improvement began to show. Now, coasting in toward the beach, she reached for the undercarriage lever and dropped the wheels beneath the floats, as she had done many times that day. Everything worked just right and the Eagle came in with a wave behind it, moved up the ramp, halted, and she switched off.

"What a woman. Let's go and celebrate." Christou opened the cabin door, stepped on the wing, and looked up at the terrace to see Dillon and Billy, whose clapping echoed across the water.

"We're coming up for a glass of wine," Christou called. "Make it something good," and he turned and offered his hand to Sara.

The *Kantara* was moored in the outer harbor of Boukara, and David Rajavi stood at the rail, watching the ship's tender approaching, Abu at the tiller. It carried Rasoul and Yousef and a number of suitcases. Rajavi smiled slightly, then went up the ladder to the captain's cabin behind the wheelhouse, where he started to consult his charts.

Yousef entered. He wore Ray-Bans, an expensive black bomber jacket over a black Armani shirt, and designer jeans. The watch on his left wrist was a gold Rolex. Behind him, Rasoul wore a khaki suit of crumpled linen that made him look overweight.

"Are you Rajavi, the captain of this heap of junk?" Yousef demanded.

"I suppose I am, in a manner of speaking," Rajavi told him. "What can I do for you?"

"You can show us to our cabin," Rasoul growled. "Mr. Khan is tired, and so am I. We've been traveling for eighteen hours straight to get here from London."

"Well, at least you've been doing it privately. I'd have thought that a blessing," Rajavi said. "We're short a first officer this trip, and there are two bunks in his cabin, so you can have it while we sort things out."

"Okay, it will have to do for the moment," Yousef said. "Where is it?"

"Just one thing," Rajavi opened the ship's manifest and held out a pen. "I made it clear to your father we don't take passengers, it's illegal. You'll have to sign on as crew members."

"What the hell's going on here?" Rasoul said, but Yousef was aching for a drink and in no mood to wait any longer.

"Anything you say, Captain. If we could be shown to our cabin and given some help with the luggage, we'll get on with it." He signed with a flourish and passed the pen to

Rasoul, who was looking mutinous. "Do it and let's get out of here."

Rasoul did as he was told, and Rajavi said, "Abu will take a couple of your bags and show you the way. Perhaps you could follow him with the others?"

Which they did, following Abu to where he kicked open a door and led the way into the cabin, one bunk above the other, a washbasin and a toilet in the corner, the aroma from which left something to be desired.

"And this is it?" Rasoul said.

"Unless you'd like to slop in with the other eleven crew members?" Abu said. "Chow is in a couple of hours, the dining saloon is below the main ladder and everyone just pitches in."

He went out, slamming the door, and Rasoul said, "This is terrible, and it stinks in here. We must call your father."

"We'll call nobody," said Yousef, wrestling a suitcase open and revealing several bottles of vodka. "Nothing could be as bad as this, so it can only get better." He unscrewed the cap of the first bottle and swallowed deep. "Allah forgive me, but that's wonderful." He took another long pull, and Rasoul crouched on a stool in the corner and watched him in horror.

By the time the chow gong sounded below, Yousef was drunk out of his mind. "Food," he snarled. "Let's go and get some food."

He threw off Rasoul, who tried to restrain him, shoved him out of the way, and slipped down the ladder to the dining saloon, where stew was being ladled out to a line of men. He staggered up, clutching at people, managed to knock the stew over, and became a target for kicks and punches from everyone.

As Abu picked him up and slapped him, Rajavi appeared and surveyed the mess, Rasoul groveling beside it. "Get him on deck," the captain said. "Plus the luggage. Just save a few clothes, basic stuff. Everything else goes over the side."

They hauled Yousef up to the main deck, Rasoul protesting, stripped him of his finery, looped a rope under his arms, and dropped him over the side, dunking him up and down in the sea until he was half dead.

Rasoul was weeping. "What have you done?"

"Probably saved his life." Rajavi held up a black purse. "His cash, gold Rolex, two mobile phones, and passport. I'll keep them." He turned to Abu. "Wrap the poor sod in blankets and let him sleep. Tomorrow, work clothes and start both of them scrubbing decks."

Rasoul said, "You don't realize how important his father is to al-Qaeda. He will destroy you for this."

"Really?" Rajavi laughed. "He bows to the Master, does he not? Well, so do I, you fool. Now, help get him down to the cabin and do your best for him."

In the café on the terrace, the owner, Anita by name, had discovered a couple of bottles of Veuve Cliquot, a decent French champagne that had been left over from a wedding. She put it in the icebox in the kitchen, while she and Sara fried mackerel and rice, potatoes and onions.

The weather had deteriorated, no blue skies here, but lowering, dark clouds and thunder on the horizon like distant drums, and then the rains came and suddenly everything was fresh and clean and the champagne was all gone.

Yanni Christou had discussed the purpose of their visit in Ras Kasar with Dillon. "I wish you well, all of you, in this affair. If I can help in any way, you know I will." He called to Anita. "You still have a bottle of ouzo. We'll have a shot each for luck."

"Not me," Billy said.

Yanni, who was slightly drunk, said, "I

remember, you don't drink."

"He just kills people, but only when necessary," Dillon said.

"Well, there is no answer to that except go with God, the lot of you."

Things were still wet and gray the following morning, but Christou checked with the weather people at Palma Airport, who assured him that it would improve the closer they got to the Algerian coast. They decided to go for it, Dillon sitting back and letting Sara take off. When they were airborne, she forgot to raise the wheels into the floats and was annoyed with herself when he had to mention it.

"How could I be so stupid?" she said.

"I bet you don't do it again," Dillon told her. "These Eagles were specially developed for use by bush pilots in the far north of Canada, but you'll find they're really sweet to fly, and if your engine conks out, you can always land in the sea."

"Thank you, Sean, that's very comforting."

"Come off it, Sara, you're thoroughly enjoying yourself."

And he was right, she realized that, the rain bouncing off the windscreen, the wipers fighting to keep it clear, the wind outside struggling to get in, the plane rocking, the need to fight to hold it for a while — it was all meat and drink for her.

She turned to glance at Dillon and found him smiling. "You can switch to autopilot for a while if you want."

"Like hell I will." She grinned. "But I'd appreciate a cup of coffee from that thermos."

Emza Khan called the Master in some distress. "I've had a visit from two policemen, an inspector and a sergeant, in search of my son."

"Indeed?" the Master said. "I suppose their rank indicates the importance they attach to this affair. What did you tell them?"

"That the last I saw of him was in the Aziz clinic from which he had disappeared. That I have no idea of his whereabouts and he has not been in touch."

"And that is the way it must stay. You know what Scotland Yard is like. The higher you are, the more they'd enjoy pulling you down, especially because you're a Muslim."

"But I'd be telling the truth, I haven't had a word from him and Rasoul."

"But you do know exactly where they are. May I remind you that mobile phones can be a curse. Unless they're encrypted at both ends, they are the most traceable things in the world. Everything you say is out there in the ether. This is no time for your son, or indeed Captain Rajavi, to be calling you, and I would suggest you leave them to get on with it."

"You really think so?" Khan asked.

"Absolutely. Trust me in this."

"Then I must be guided by you," Khan said with some reluctance and switched off.

The Master called Rajavi on a personal encrypted link and found him in a rainstorm on the bridge wearing foul-weather rig.

"How are you?"

"At the moment, it's raining rather hard."

"And your new crew members?"

"Swabbing the foredeck."

"Well, that must be different for them."

Looking down at Rasoul and Yousef, struggling with large brooms in the pouring rain, soaked to the skin, while Abu, in oilskins, supervised them, a knotted rope in his hand, Rajavi was inclined to agree.

"Who knows, it may be the making of the boy."

"I suppose so," the Master said. "It's all a question of survival, I suppose. I'll be in touch, but don't speak to Khan, that's essential."

■ ■ ■ ■

Two hours out of Majorca and approaching the Algerian coast, the weather had changed, as if high summer had come out to welcome them. Dillon had left ninety percent of the flying to Sara, allowing her to get thoroughly comfortable with the amphibian experience. They drifted into perfection at five thousand feet, in a velvet blue sky, the sea below constantly changing colors from blue to green, and all the reefs and shoals visible.

A tailwind for the past half hour meant they had made better time than Dillon had expected, and as the coast loomed large, he suggested she go down to a thousand feet and take her time, which she did, and Ras Kasar appeared on the port side.

The old Arab town behind the harbor was the usual cascade of buildings climbing up the hillside, but fronting the beach was a pier and the inner harbor, several fishing boats, and what appeared to be a dive center.

"Things look pretty quiet down there," Billy said.

"All these places are the same in the off-season, Billy," Dillon told him. "That would be the Paradise Club just above the beach with the terrace and the tables with a few umbrellas out. No more than half a dozen people sitting there and a man in original British Army shorts and a straw hat gazing up at us, who I suspect is Andrew Adano."

There was no airstrip, only amphibians allowed, so there was also no control tower, just a windsock on a pole, and Sara throttled back, drifted in, and dropped into a perfect landing outside the inner harbor.

Billy nodded his approval. "Bloody marvelous."

She entered the harbor, found a ramp and taxied toward it, dropping the wheels, and ran up onto the ramp, braked, and switched off. The man in the straw hat came down the steps from the hotel.

"Andrew Adano," he called cheerfully. "Welcome to Ras Kasar."

Sara found her room very Arabian, small but comfortable with a private bathroom. She quickly unpacked, then showered, dressed in a cool khaki linen jumpsuit. She opened the door to the terrace, looked over the balcony, and found the others seated under an umbrella.

"Remember me?" she called.

Dillon glanced up. "We've been waiting. Come and have something to eat."

There were onions cooked with roast lamb, rice and peppers, couscous to follow, steam rising from the semolina, and a great bowl of peeled fruits to go with it. Ice-cold Chablis complemented the meal, the French influence on most things Algerian still surviving.

Adano, when talk had touched on diving, admitted to being sixty, but was muscular and fit-looking. "I take care of what business there is in the off-season. When things pick up, I bring in young guys to handle the pressure."

"It sounds good," Dillon said. "So it's the holiday trade, a few fishing boats from the town, and how much shipping?"

"You know the story of the Petra boats. That's about it — one at a time. General cargo, quite a lot of farming machinery, that kind of thing." He poured another glass of wine for Dillon and Sara. "As Ferguson has explained, more than one boat probably delivers arms by night, but the *Kantara* seems a different case entirely."

"What do you think of the al-Qaeda connection?" Sara asked.

"Obviously, bad news. They're devious

bastards, capable of anything." He looked at his watch. "The *Kantara* is due between four and five."

"Good," Dillon said. "Now, since Sara and I are supposed to be checking out the entertainment possibilities at the Paradise Club, we'd appreciate looking at your piano."

"You mean you take it that seriously? I didn't realize." Adano got up and led the way into a coal-dark bar, mirrors behind all the shelves, rows of bottles, the whole place stuffed with cane furniture. A couple of waiters were setting tables for the evening and a barman was on duty. A grand piano sat on a small stage with a set of drums.

Adano said, "One of the waiters can play those, but I'm short a double bass player."

Dillon examined the piano. "Schiedmayer. Very nice. You don't see these on the market much. Lovely tone." He sat down and played a few chords. "It's famous for always staying in tune."

Sara lifted the lid and propped it up. "Come on, Sean, let's be having you."

"How about 'I Get a Kick Out of You'? Does that send you?"

"You're too kind," she said, pulled a stool forward as his hands moved into the intro, sat down, and launched into that first

215

famous line: *I get no kick from champagne,* and now he pushed her at a driving pace. The barman and waiters were mesmerized and three cooks appeared from the kitchen to see what was going on. The entire place was jumping.

It ended on a high, everyone cheered, and Andrew Adano said, "My God, that was marvelous. There's no chance of you being free for the season, I fear?"

"I'm afraid not," Billy told him. "They've got pressing engagements."

"Ah, well, I suppose I'd better take you down to have a look at the boats and the dive center."

There were two thirty-five-foot sport fisherman boats, each with a flying bridge and dozens of air tanks stacked in their holders in the stern. Everything was shipshape and in very well-kept condition.

Billy said, "This is as good as it gets."

"Well, it's got to be these days if you want to get anywhere at all," Adano said. "What qualifications have you got, Billy?"

"Master diver." Billy shrugged. "Same with Dillon. But I've got the paramedic qualifications, too, which he hasn't bothered with. He isn't interested in saving life, only taking it."

"As usual, you exaggerate," Dillon said. "But let's get down to what happens to-night. Where shall we go?"

"Why not upon one of the flying bridges?" Adano said. "You can look to the outer harbor, where the *Kantara* will be lying at anchor, while we talk."

He found some cold lager in the vessel's icebox and orange juice for Billy, and they sat there, drinking and talking.

Dillon said, "What do you think, Sara?"

"If we invade *Kantara,* drop some Semtex in the hold and blow her up, I don't think the Algerian government will be very pleased, especially if it wasn't carrying arms at all."

"A fair point," Dillon said. "So what do you suggest?"

"Someone should board by night and see what's in the hold."

"Easier said than done," Billy put in.

"If you use the underwater approach. But if you look along the pier, you'll see a fast inflatable with a silent running motor. Last year, I passed the handling course on that craft with the Royal Marines. I could take you out there in the dark and wait for you."

Dillon said, "Come to think of it, that would make a lot of sense."

Adano said, "I agree. Let's go and lay

217

claim to the boat while we can."

The *Kantara* approached at four with a triple hoot from its foghorn, but did not immediately drop anchor in the outer harbor. Instead, it eased in beside the end of the long pier, sprang its crane hoist, and swung three farm tractors out onto the pier, where men were waiting to drive them away.

It was slow work, several crew members struggling to handle each one, supervised by Abu the bosun, Captain Rajavi directing from the bridge, a megaphone in one hand. Standing to one side, looking very much the worse for wear in shabby, dirty clothes, were Rasoul and Yousef.

A small crowd of Arabs had gathered, farmers and fishermen, a few hotel workers, a dozen or so residents. Adano, Sara, Dillon, and Billy were there, too, but back a ways — even so, they were spotted. It was Yousef who recognized Sara first, which was surprising because the only time he had seen her in the past was when he was drunk.

He grabbed Rasoul by the arm. "Look who's here. That stupid woman from the Blue Angel in Shepherd Market, the one who stuck a gun in my face."

Not that Rasoul needed to be told who Sara and Dillon were, not after Paris. "Allah preserve us," he said. "What can they be doing here? And that's Dillon with her."

"What do you think it means?" Yousef asked hoarsely.

"It's crazy," Rasoul said. "It doesn't make sense." His face was puzzled. "Unless it's something to do with the *Kantara*. That must be it, the only possible explanation, especially when you remember these people all work for British Intelligence. I must speak to the captain. This could be to our advantage."

Sara hadn't noticed them, but Dillon did, and he grabbed Sara by the hand, started pulling her away, and she said, "What are you doing?"

"I've just seen Rasoul, Emza Khan's minder, and the drunken son, Yousef. I'm hoping Rasoul didn't notice us. He'd be bound to recognize you."

"Trouble?" Adano asked.

Billy said, "What's going on?"

"Sean thinks he's seen Emza Khan's hard man and the drunken son, up there on deck," Sara said. "How were they dressed?"

"Working clothes, just like the other sailors," Dillon told her.

"Emza Khan's a billionaire. Why would his son be there dressed like that?"

They'd reached the steps to the terrace.

Dillon said, "I haven't the slightest idea, but it's them and I want to know what they're doing there."

"But what could they be doing on a boat we suspect of peddling arms for al-Qaeda?" Sara's frustration was starting to rise to the surface. "Emza Khan is notoriously anti-al-Qaeda, as is the government he represents."

Adano joined in. "Maybe they didn't recognize you."

"And if they did?" Dillon asked.

"Then we deal with that when it comes."

"I'll go along with that," Dillon said and turned to Sara and Billy. "As we used to say in Belfast, just make sure you carry a pistol in your pocket."

Rasoul, followed by Yousef, had managed to avoid the bosun and scramble up the ladder to the captain's cabin behind the wheel-house, where Rajavi repelled boarders.

"Get back on deck at once," he called down to Abu. "Pull these fools out of here."

Rasoul clutched at him. "In the sacred name of Osama, Captain, I beg you to listen to both of us, for something strange and mysterious has happened."

He was desperate and it showed, sweat running down his face, all of which Rajavi took in with a kind of resignation.

"If you are wasting my time, I'll have Abu take a knotted rope to you. Get on with it, you fool," and he was smiling.

Which Rasoul did, and very quickly, his story replacing that Rajavi smile with a deep frown. "You're sure about these people being British security agents?"

"A few days ago, I was in Paris with Emza Khan, staying in the same hotel as these people, the Ritz. The woman is a British Army captain in the Intelligence Corps. I need hardly remind you that my employer's position is a delicate one."

Rajavi told him, "Wait here."

He went out. Rasoul went to the door, noted Rajavi walking to Abu on the tween deck, then returned to Yousef. The large black bag that Rajavi had filled with their valuables was lying on the deck, and Rasoul opened it. No point in snatching the gold Rolex or the two mobile phones, but the thick wad of American hundred-dollar bills was tempting. A thousand wouldn't be missed. He counted out ten bills, slipped them in a pocket and closed up the bag again.

"Just keep quiet and go along with me," he said to Yousef.

Rajavi returned. "You two stay here. I'll go to the hotel later to check things out.

Meanwhile, I want you to behave yourselves. If you don't, I'll put you in irons. Back to your cabin now."

They went with a certain excitement. Rasoul explored drawers, found a waterproof plastic bag, and rolled the money up inside.

"What are you doing that for?" Yousef demanded.

"To preserve it from rough treatment or immersion in water, this useful roll of American dollars. It might be the saving of us. For now, we just wait."

The unloading of the tractors had finished, followed by a considerable amount of canned foods and produce. Darkness was very quickly descending, and to Adano's surprise, the *Kantara* didn't retire to the outer harbor, but stayed snug against the end of the pier. They all stood up on the terrace with him, taking turns examining the boat through Adano's night glasses.

Billy appeared, wearing ankle boots, jeans, and a dark sweater, a longshoreman's knitted cap pulled down over his skull. He was also wearing a backpack. He accepted the night glasses from Dillon and took a look.

"A watchman on the stern deck who shouldn't be smoking, but is. Not a soul on the upper decks, and the bridge and wheelhouse in darkness."

He passed the night glasses to Sara, and Dillon said, "What are you up to dressed like that?"

"The original river rat, me, Dillon. There's nothing I don't know about nicking from moored ships. Compared to that, this is a piece of cake." He produced a Walther, cocked it and slipped it into his waistband at the rear and under the sweater. "They'll all be at their evening meal."

"What the hell is this all about?" Dillon demanded.

"You want to know definitely that there's a cargo of arms somewhere on that ship, so I'm going to find out where."

"Now, just a minute," Dillon began, but didn't get any further, because Billy ran away very fast, hugging the side wall of the pier. Dillon watched him go and passed the night glasses to Adano.

Sara said, "Is this just a little bit crazy, or is there method to his madness?"

"He doesn't need to waste time searching," Dillon told her. "Not if he's ruthless enough, and our Billy is certainly that. All he needs to do is to suggest the watchman lead him to the weapons and offer him a bullet in the kneecap if he doesn't. He can do that without warning the rest of the crew, because his Walther is silenced. There he goes."

Billy moved into view under a light, then melted into the dark, and Sara said, "Doesn't anything frighten him?"

"The first time I worked with Billy, we needed to parachute in over a house in Cornwall where Blake Johnson was in mortal danger. Billy volunteered without hesitation, which was quite something, as he'd never had any training. Does that remind you of anyone?"

Billy went up the gangway, shoulders hunched, head down, hands in his pockets, aware of the pungent tobacco smell, aware of the tip of the burning cigarette, and also aware at the last minute, as he approached, that the smoker was a woman who was sitting on the watchman's knee.

Typical of many Algerian women of both French and Arab extraction, the woman spoke English, and she and the watchman were murmuring together in that language.

The man flicked on a torch.

"Who the hell are you?"

Billy struck him across the face. "Shut up or I'll kill both of you, do you understand?"

The watchman said, "Don't hurt her. My

ship comes in here often. She's a regular of mine."

Billy turned to her. "Is that true?"

"I'm just a *poule,* but yes, we are friends."

"Well, if he's a good boy, I'll bring him back to you unharmed. All he needs to do is show me where they stow the arms they're carrying on this ship. My gun is silenced, and if you raise a fuss, then I'd have to kill both of you."

She had a kind of Arab calmness to her, turned to the watchman, and said, "No need for that, is there? You will do as he says?"

"Sure, why not? I've just about had enough of this old tub. And if guys like you are around, I'd imagine our time is short anyway." The watchman held out his hand. "I'll show you on one condition. That I can leave with her."

"My pleasure," Billy told him.

In the tween decks, he showed Billy the sliding bulkhead, which revealed an Aladdin's cave of weaponry. Boxes of rocket-propelled grenades, the ubiquitous AK-47 rifles, plus a supply of general-purpose machine guns, just right for mounting on Land Rovers. Stacks of ammunition, hand grenades, and Stinger missiles completed the picture. Billy told the watchman to wait outside, did what he had to, closed the door and followed him.

It took no more than fifteen minutes and they were back on deck, where the woman was still waiting. "I think we should go now," she said and took the watchman's arm as a door opened in the bowels of the ship and music erupted.

They went hurriedly. Billy paused to let them get ahead and then slipped down the gangplank and started to run back along the side of the pier toward the Paradise Club and his friends on the terrace.

"So what was that all about?" Sara asked Billy when he joined them.

"The watchman had a *poule* on his lap, and she was the one smoking the cigarette. Love won out in the end, he showed me a false hold crammed with arms, and I allowed them to slide off into the sunset." He grinned. "Obviously, not exactly like that — I mean it's dark, but you get the picture."

"I think so," Sara said. "You didn't have to shoot him."

"Which makes a change," Dillon said. "So, except for his absence, no one on the ship is aware of what happened?"

"So it would appear," Billy told him.

"Now we wait and see what happens."

9

Captain David Rajavi looked more than respectable in the summer uniform of a captain in the Merchant Navy. They'd made up a uniform for Abu, the bosun, consisting of a peaked cap in navy blue, a khaki shirt with black tie, and a navy blue pea jacket.

"Yes, very nice," Rajavi said after looking him over. "Your face is still ugly enough to frighten the Devil himself. There isn't too much we can do about that, but on the other hand, it has its advantages."

They were in the captain's cabin, Rasoul and Yousef sitting on two chairs in a corner, and Rajavi said to them, "You just sit tight. I'm going to go face the enemy, see where that gets us. I've an idea that it might be good for us to move on sooner rather than later."

It was Rasoul who answered. "We are in your hands, Captain."

"I'm glad you see it that way." He picked

up the internal phone and called down to the chief engineer. "I'd like you to make ready for *Kantara* to put to sea, Mr. Stagg."

The Scottish burr sounded comforting. "And when would that be, Captain?"

"Within the next hour. I'm going to just pop in at the Paradise Club first."

"In your best uniform, no doubt."

"Of course. We mustn't let the side down. But I want your assurance that if I want a quick departure, I'll get one. Two long blasts on the foghorn as you cast off."

"If that's what you want," the old Scot said, "that's what you'll get."

"Thank you." Rajavi put on his cap and that, plus a certain amount of gold braid, made him look rather handsome and dashing. He led the way down the gangway to where a Land Rover waited. Abu opened the door for him, the captain got in, and the Somali slipped behind the wheel and drove away.

"Park at the bottom of the terrace steps and be ready for a very fast exit."

"What you want, you get, Captain, you know that. So it's to be the woman?"

"I think she could prove to be the key to the whole thing. A mine of information . . . and a very useful hostage."

They were at the bottom of the steps in a

few minutes. Abu had to maneuver skillfully because of a couple of parked motorcycles, but he finally ended up pointing the right way for a quick departure.

"Good man. Here we go." Rajavi started up the steps, climbing toward the sound of piped music, Abu following him, a light duster coat over his left arm.

The bar and dining room was distinctly overstaffed. No more than a dozen hotel guests were scattered around the cane tables, but with half a dozen waiters and three barmen serving them.

Adano, wearing a white tuxedo, was standing at the end of the bar next to the open glass doors leading on to the terrace. Rajavi moved in without hesitation, Abu remaining outside by the steps.

Adano held out a hand. "Captain Rajavi, isn't it? We saw you a couple of times last month."

"Yes indeed," Rajavi said.

Adano made the introductions. "Sara Gideon and Sean Dillon of the Playwright Production Co. We're considering improving our entertainment facilities. Mr. Salter here is interested in developing a diving business."

"How interesting," Rajavi said to Sara.

"You provide acts for cabaret, is that the idea?"

Adano said, "Yes, but actually they do a very good act themselves."

"Indeed? I'd be fascinated to hear them."

There was a slight challenge there, or so it seemed to Adano, who dismissed it by saying to Sara and Dillon, "How about something for Captain Rajavi?"

"Why not?" Sara turned to Dillon. "Do you recall a film called *To Have and Have Not*?"

"Great novel by Ernest Hemingway," Dillon said. "Bogart played a sea captain. His girlfriend in the movie, Lauren Bacall, sang a number called 'How Little We Know.' "

"Would you happen to know it?"

There was a certain skepticism on Rajavi's face, but Dillon said, "For you, anything. I love that movie."

He stepped onstage, sat down, raised the lid, and his fingers felt for the beginning. One of the waiters, a boy of sixteen named Javier, dropped his napkin, ran to the stage, and started to play the drums. Slow and sensual, the music had people mesmerized. When Sara started to sing, there was instant applause.

When she finished, there were cries for her to repeat it, so she did. After that, people

230

made requests, calling out titles, and Sara complied, ending up singing by popular demand "As Time Goes By" from the film *Casablanca.*

But enough was enough. Adano said, "My God, I could fill the place with you two during the season."

Sara smiled and said, "If it were only possible, Andrew," and walked out on the terrace.

Abu was still standing at the top of the steps, the duster coat draped over an arm, and Rajavi went after her, followed by the waiter, Javier, who had played the drums. He offered her a glass of champagne on a tray, which she took, and he retreated to the open glass door and watched her, fascinated.

Rajavi said, "You are a remarkably talented young woman."

Sara said, "I learned to play guitar as a child, and singing came naturally."

"There's more to it than that, Captain Gideon. I think you are a woman of many talents." A foghorn sounded mournfully twice.

She knew instantly what was happening, but in the same moment, he shoved her hard toward Abu, who punched her in the side of the face with such savagery that she was momentarily stunned, then tossed the duster coat over her head. Abu slung her over his left shoulder and went headlong down the steps to the Land Rover, followed by Rajavi.

Javier ran into Adano and the others. "The men from the ship have run off with Miss Gideon."

Billy and Dillon ran through to the terrace, Adano trailing, reached the head of the steps, to see Rajavi vanishing inside the Land Rover after Abu and Sara. The engine started, and the vehicle roared into life and made for the *Kantara,* clearly visible in the lights on the pier.

Billy arrived at the bottom of the steps first, swung a leg over the first motorcycle, and a moment later, it roared into life. Dillon just had time to leap on the pillion and they were away in pursuit. In the distance, they saw the Land Rover stop.

The two men pulled Sara out between them and rushed up the gangway onto the ship, which was just casting off. They dragged her across the deck and mounted to the bridge.

As the ship drifted away from the pier, Billy aimed for the gangway, which was inclined upward. He accelerated and they soared over the rails, landing on the deck and sliding sideways. They kicked free and let the machine skid away. In the darkness, the ship seemed to be lit up like a Christmas tree.

At the upper-deck rail above them, two sailors appeared holding automatic shotguns. Both Dillon's Glock and Billy's Walther fired instantly. Their silencers on, they knocked the sailors back without a sound, their shotguns flying.

Someone called in English above them, "For Christ's sake, keep your heads down."

There was a sudden silence, and Dillon said, "Let's find Sara, they were taking her up to the bridge. I'll cover you as you go up that ladder."

Billy nodded, ran crouching across the deck. Someone glanced over the bridge rail, a porthole to one side. Dillon fired at once, the only sound glass splintering. "If you do that again, I'll kill you," he called. "We've come for the woman. If you don't have her, stay out of it."

It was Rasoul who had peered over. He and Yousef crouched behind the rail while Rajavi and Abu dragged Sara to where the door to the wheelhouse stood wide, brightly lit in the darkness, showing Chief Engineer Stagg at the wheel. "I'll need some help if we're to get out of here," Rajavi said.

Rajavi's arm hugged Sara's neck, who was already regaining her senses as he squeezed and dragged her in to Stagg, followed by Abu, who tied her wrists with twine, and Rasoul and Yousef, out on the rail, heard nothing of the exchange that followed.

"Do I alter to the emergency course, make for Turkish Cyprus, or not?" Stagg asked.

Rajavi nodded to Abu. "We'll do that. You stay and help the chief engineer, I'll go round the ship and rally the troops."

"What about the woman?"

"I'll get those two fools outside to look after her." He dragged her out into the captain's cabin, shoved her into a chair, and called to Rasoul and Yousef, "Get in here!"

They appeared, and he said, "Obviously, this woman is not our friend." He opened a drawer in the desk and produced a revolver. "It's nice and simple and loaded. You just pull the trigger."

"But Dillon and the other man, what happens there?" Rasoul demanded.

"The ship, as you may have noticed, is starting to swing, which means we'll be pointing out to sea very shortly. Dillon and his young friend won't last long on their own." He opened a small door in the corner, which gave entrance to a spiral staircase. "I'll be back soon," he said and disappeared.

"So what are we going to do?" Yousef demanded.

Rasoul was examining the pistol. "Suddenly, everything is different," he said.

Behind them, sitting in the chair Rajavi had thrust her into, Sara reached down with her bound hands to withdraw the flick-knife from the sheath around her right ankle. She pressed the button, and the razor-sharp blade jumped into view, slicing her bonds instantly. She pushed the blade back in and stood, the knife concealed in her hand.

They turned to look at her. "You're not laughing now, bitch," Yousef said and snatched the pistol from Rasoul's hand. "I could put a bullet in you, but then, with a long sea voyage ahead of us, it might be to my taste to put something else into you." He stroked her cheek with the pistol barrel. "Would you like that, eh?"

"You sick bastard," Sara said, springing the flick-knife and ramming it under his chin. His eyes rolled as he dropped the weapon, choked on his own blood, and fell to the floor. She picked up the pistol, and Rasoul, terrified, staggered back, hands raised.

"Please, no, this whole affair has been nothing to do with me. I was at my Master's bidding. I am a simple servant."

"Just shut up." Sara opened the small door in the corner. "Get down there and stay out of the way, or I'll kill you."

Rasoul did, without a moment's hesitation, and Sara flung open the door into the wheelhouse and confronted Stagg and Abu. The Somali reached in his pocket.

"I wouldn't, if I were you. I've still got blood on my hands from Yousef. Put your weapon on the floor, kick it over, then slow this tub right down." They stood there gaping at her, uncertain what to do. "It's time scum like you learned to take women seriously."

That was too much for Abu, who said, "Who do you think you are?"

Sara shot the lobe off his left ear instantly.

Abu grabbed it, howling, blood spurting between his fingers, and Dillon said as he walked in behind her, "That's who she is."

Billy appeared from the darkness. "There's a ship's tender tied to the end of the passenger steps on the port side. Big outboard motor. We can get back with no trouble." He took a handkerchief from his pocket and gave it to Abu. "Here, hold that on it and shut up. I say we go."

"Agreed," Dillon said. "As there hasn't been any sign of Captain Rajavi, I can only conclude he's decided that discretion really is the best part of valor. We'll vacate the premises, although taking the tender with us."

"Never mind, Dad," Billy said to Stagg. "There is one God and his Prophet is Osama."

"Don't give me that kind of crap," Stagg told him. "I'm just a ship's engineer, son."

Rasoul had sat at the top of the spiral staircase, listening through the door. He was certain only of one thing. He had no intention of remaining on the *Kantara.* When all was quiet, he went out and discovered that someone had bolted the wheelhouse door, leaving Stagg and Abu inside. He decided to leave them to Rajavi, but sought out the captain's black bag, remembering that it contained not only a considerable wad of cash and two mobiles, but also his and Yousef's passports. By now familiar with the ship, he located the tender in spite of the darkness and before the others. He burrowed under a pile of tarpaulins in the prow and waited.

Sara, Dillon, and Billy appeared after fifteen minutes. "Let's just get out of here," Sara said. "It's been fraught, to say the least."

"Yousef was a despicable human being

237

and no loss," Dillon told her.

"I wouldn't try telling that to his father if I were you," Sara said impatiently. "Let's get back to some sort of civilization."

The engine rumbled and they were on their way. Swathed in tarpaulins, Rasoul had heard only the murmur of voices, but the sound of the running engine wiped out all conversation.

"Well, there she goes, the *Kantara*," Dillon said. "God knows where she's bound for after this, but I shan't be wishing her well."

"I know where she's going," Sara said. "I heard the chief engineer asking if he should change course to Turkish Cyprus."

"I can see the point of that," Dillon said. "Easy routes across to Turkey, Lebanon, Syria, perfect if you're running in guns by night. I should imagine Ferguson would want us to dispose of her when she gets there."

"Well, he'll have to wait," Billy said. "As far as I'm concerned, I'm hoping our friend Adano has got something good for supper."

"Well, you'll soon see," Dillon said as he sat in the stern, grasping the tiller. "There he is now, standing by the Land Rover with what looks like three or four members of his staff and a few curious locals."

"Do you think there's likely to be any

repercussions from the local police force?" Sara asked.

"Not really," Dillon told her. "This is Algeria. In a place like this, they're usually ten miles down the coast dealing with something else, or pretending they are." They were close in now, and he called, "She's safe and sound, and guess what? We've brought you a present of a ship's tender."

The Land Rover drove them back to the hotel. It was suddenly very quiet on the water, no one around at all. The tarpaulins in the tender heaved, and Rasoul stood up and walked away, vanishing into the shadows beside the pier.

He had money, a passport, and a mobile phone, but the prospect of calling Emza Khan to tell him that his son had been stabbed to death by Captain Sara Gideon was more than he could handle for the moment. Listening to men in the crew on *Kantara* speaking of Ras Kasar, there had been mention of the coastal railway passing only three miles inland. He would make for that, a ticket for Oran, and then a flight to London. His problem was what to do when he eventually reached there, but he pushed that thought away and continued to walk.

■ ■ ■ ■

On the *Kantara,* Rajavi returned to the
captain's cabin with four armed sailors and
was met only with carnage. Yousef lay there
in a pool of blood, and it was a badly damaged Abu who unbolted the door to the
wheelhouse.

Stagg was smoking his pipe at the wheel,
his face remarkably cheerful in the light of
the binnacle. "Ah, there you are," he said.
"Trying to do something about Abu. He
can't stop moaning. I've changed to the
emergency course, so I could do with
somebody to spell me."

Rajavi nodded to one of the men. "Take
the wheel, Selim." He added to Stagg,
"Have you seen what's happened to the
son?"

Stagg went into the cabin with him,
looked down at Yousef, and shook his head.
"The woman will have been responsible for
that. She came in here like a raging maniac
and shot off part of Abu's ear."

"You'll find what you need to patch him
up in the bathroom," Rajavi told him.

"Right, I'll see to it," Stagg said. "But
what about young Yousef?"

"We've got body bags. These guys can put

him in one. We'll hang on till we're another few miles farther out, then he gets the deep six."

"Fine. I'll take charge of that for you," Stagg said. "What are you going to tell his father?"

"I don't know. There's someone else I need to inform first, and anyway, I've got a more immediate problem. The man, Rasoul, doesn't seem to be around." Rajavi frowned. "Just a minute." He quickly searched his desk. "He's gone, dammit."

"How do you know?" Stagg asked.

"The bag with the passports and cash isn't where I left it. Rasoul must have found it and cleared off."

"The Brits left in the ship's tender," Stagg said. "Maybe Rasoul concealed himself on board."

"What does it matter?" Rajavi said. "This whole trip's been bad luck for us. Let's get the hell out of here."

He went up on the top deck, breathing in the good salt air to clear his head, then smoked a cigarette for a while. It was a mess, whichever way you looked at it, but there was no point trying to avoid the inevitable any longer. He stepped back into a doorway as it started to rain and called the Master.

As usual, the reply was instant. "Yes?"

"Rajavi. I have nothing but bad news for you."

"Then tell me."

Rajavi did.

When he was finished, there was a pause, then the Master said, "Well, Ferguson and his people certainly have been busy. So, Yousef is dead, Emza Khan doesn't know, and this man, Rasoul, seems to have disappeared."

"He's certainly not on this ship, Master."

"All right. Tell me, to all intents and purposes, is there any reason the *Kantara* can't go about her ordinary and legitimate business?"

"None at all."

"No one has reason to inspect you for illegal arms?"

"Not that I know of."

"Good. Who else knows about the emergency course for Turkish Cyprus?"

"The chief engineer and the bosun, that's all. And they're entirely reliable."

"All right," the Master said. "You have my blessing. Keep in touch."

Rajavi looked down as a door on the lower deck opened and Abu appeared, his ear heavily bandaged, followed by four seamen carrying Yousef in a black bag on a stretcher. Walking behind them was Conrad Stagg, holding an umbrella.

Abu paused, glanced up, and saw Rajavi. "Permission to carry on, Captain?"

Stagg looked up and Rajavi saw that he held a Bible in his left hand. He called up, "Aren't you going to join us, Captain?"

Rajavi could have made the point that Yousef was a Muslim and a Christian Bible was not the Koran, but what did it matter in the grand scheme of things? All that was important was to do the decent thing, and he went down the steps and joined them on the lower deck.

Rasoul sat in a first-class apartment of the night train to Oran, brooding. He was going to have to speak to Emza Khan at some point but simply couldn't face it. A waiter entered, a tray around his neck, with cups, holding a pot with one hand.

"Coffee, *effendi*?"

"Have you anything stronger?" Rasoul asked.

"It's against regulations."

The lies flowed easily. "I go to Oran to comfort my brother and his wife. Their son has died of cancer, only fourteen years old."

He took out a twenty-dollar bill.

The waiter produced half a bottle of vodka with a Russian label and the transaction took place.

"Allah will reward you for this," Rasoul said. "My relatives will thank you."

"No need for that," the waiter said. "I believe in your money, not the story."

The vodka caught the back of Rasoul's throat and he coughed harshly. When it subsided, he started drinking again, quickly disposing of half the bottle. He felt as if he was floating but so clearheaded. It had been wrong to think as he had done. Emza Khan needed to be told of Yousef's death. It was only right. He found his mobile and punched in the number.

It was midnight. Dr. Aziz was just about to administer an injection when Khan's mobile rang. "Get that for me," he said.

Aziz did, listened, then handed it to him. "Rasoul."

Khan was stunned — neither Yousef nor Rasoul was supposed to call — then prepared his face and held out his hand. "News at last. Allah is merciful!"

Aziz retreated to the sitting room. He was closing the old-fashioned Gladstone bag containing his medical equipment when he

244

heard a howl of agony, and Emza Khan appeared in the bedroom door, clutching the mobile.

"Yousef is dead!" He was holding out the mobile.

Shocked, the Indian took it from him and said, "This is Aziz. Are you sure?"

"Oh yes, murdered by a bitch from hell on the *Kantara*. It was the British Army officer from Paris."

"Where are you now?"

"Algeria on a night train to Oran. I'll be there tomorrow if everything goes smoothly. I'll have more information then. Understand, the whole business must stay confidential, especially the fact that I am alive."

"Of course."

Aziz had never experienced the raw pain that poured out of Khan as the doctor led him back to bed. "My son is dead," he croaked, and appeared to be choking. "What am I going to do?"

Aziz pushed him back onto the bed, primed a syringe with a knockout drug from his bag, and injected it into Khan's left wrist. Khan tried to sit up, and Aziz eased him back. "For several hours, the pain will cease to exist. Your problem and mine, as your doctor, is what to do when you are awake."

Khan gazed at him blankly, then his eyes closed. Aziz left him, let himself out, and went down in the lift to the basement garage. George Hagen, the night porter, was just cleaning the windows of the doctor's Mini Cooper with a chamois leather.

"Cup of tea, Doctor?"

"Not this time, George, I've got to return soon to keep an eye on him." He took out his mobile, walked to the entrance, and called the night sister at the clinic. "I'm on my way. Mr. Khan has just heard that his son passed away in unfortunate circumstances. I've had to knock him out for a few hours."

"Very well, Doctor. Just let us know if there's anything we need to do."

He returned to the Mini Cooper. "Thanks, George, I'll be back."

He drove away, deep in thought. Hagen was deep in thought, too. A Dubliner who had served in the Irish Guards, he had enjoyed a close relationship with Colonel Declan Rashid, who had saved him from being sacked by a drunken Yousef on a number of occasions. This had led to an arrangement between them, for Hagen to call Declan if anything unusual happened in the Khan household.

Hagen had already passed on the news of

Yousef's most recent brush with the law and the way he and Rasoul had dropped out of sight. Having overheard the doctor's conversation at the clinic, it was obvious that he should pass this tragic news on, too. But he was too early, with Rashid in Iran. He'd give it a while yet.

Back in her bedroom at the Paradise Club, Sara stripped, tossed her jumpsuit and underwear into a laundry basket, then stood under the hottest shower she could stand, washing the ship smell from her body, soaking away the tension. When she held up her hands, there still wasn't even a hint of a shake. After what she'd done to Yousef and Abu, how could that be normal? Dillon had said it proved her to be a warrior. She pushed the thought away, went downstairs, and found Dillon and Billy sitting at a corner table on the terrace with Adano.

She sat down, looked out to sea, and the *Kantara* wasn't even a light on the horizon. "So she's fled into the night," Sara said. "And, frankly, I'm starving."

"Taken care of," Adano told her as the waiters arrived. "Smoked salmon, chopped onions, and scrambled eggs. I thought you might enjoy something light after your endeavors."

"Enjoy," Dillon told her, pouring more champagne. "And afterward, we have a surprise for you."

"And what would that be?" she asked.

"Courtesy of Andrew Adano, we're talking to Ferguson and Roper on Skype in an hour."

Roper and Ferguson sat side by side and Adano crowded in with Sara, Dillon, and Billy.

Ferguson said, "First, can I thank you, Andrew, for looking after my people in the way you have? It's deeply appreciated."

"My pleasure, General."

"Now, Sara," Ferguson said. "What happened to this man, Rasoul?"

"He broke down in sheer terror after I'd killed Yousef," Sara said. "So I threw him out of the captain's cabin. He must be somewhere on the ship."

"Was it necessary to kill Yousef?"

"I've never been more certain of anything in my life," she said. "I did the world a favor. He was a walking pustule."

"Perhaps you should have disposed of Rasoul while you were at it," Ferguson told her. "But never mind."

Sara said quickly, "There's a matter I'd like to raise before you go, General."

"And what's that, Captain?"

"We've established beyond doubt that *Kantara* is a tool of al-Qaeda. So why were Yousef and Rasoul on that ship? It raises a question about Emza Khan, doesn't it?"

"It does indeed, and I can assure you, that point will be discussed at Cabinet Office level at Downing Street. Major Roper and I intend to get to the bottom of it as soon as we can. That's all I can say at the moment."

A mobile alarm suddenly sounded, and Billy took out his Codex and checked it. "If I could have a word, General, before you go. I've rather wasted your time listening to you all."

"What on earth are you talking about," Ferguson demanded.

"The Semtex you provided in the Gulf-stream seat and the timers of assorted lengths? I was wearing a backpack when I boarded the *Kantara* and made the watch-man show me where the arms were. I left two blocks of Semtex in the bulkhead."

"Oh my God," Ferguson said. "Tell me."

"A five-hour timer pencil in each one." The Codex beeped again and he held it up. "Wonderful gadgets these. Five hours exactly. I think you'll find that's good night Vienna to the *Kantara.*"

Ferguson turned to Roper, "Could you

249

check on that, Major?"

There was a slight smile on Roper's face. "You're a young bastard, Billy Salter."

"Always have been."

"Damn his eyes, he can't even have a drink on it," Dillon said.

Billy grinned. "No, but my friends can. Sleep well, General." He reached over and switched off.

It was five o'clock London time when George Hagen tried Colonel Declan Rashid on his mobile and found him at his Tehran apartment. Declan was in uniform, ready for a day at the War Office, and was just about to leave.

"I've not got much time, George," he said. "I've a meeting with the minister. Can it wait?"

"I don't think so, Colonel. The thing is, Yousef's dead and Mr. Khan's in a bad way."

Declan was shocked. "When did this happen?"

Hagen told him everything he knew, which wasn't much, concluding with the information that Aziz had returned to the apartment and was there now. Declan said, "You were right to let me know."

He hung up, then phoned the War Office and made his excuses, then called London.

A woman answered who proved to be a nurse, and Declan told her to put Dr. Aziz on the phone.

"Colonel Rashid," Aziz said. "Rasoul told me to keep it all confidential, especially about him still being alive, but obviously that wouldn't apply to you. I've had to drug Emza Khan quite heavily."

"But how did this happen and where? You must know something."

"Yousef was to face several severe driving charges committed while terribly drunk. This time there was a prospect of prison, and then he absconded from my clinic, which made his re-arrest inevitable. To avoid this, Rasoul took him away."

"And the idea was that Emza Khan could say he had no idea where they had gone and be believed? I don't think the police would buy that."

"I can assure you that *I* did, Colonel, I have my license to consider," Aziz said. "I had not the slightest idea where they were until Rasoul called here with his terrible news."

"And why were you there?"

"Emza Khan has been constantly unwell. I was treating him when Rasoul called with the bad news, which he refused to believe and passed the phone to me."

"And what did Rasoul say?"

"I'll never forget it. That they had been on a ship called the *Kantara* and that Yousef had been murdered by a bitch from hell, a British Army officer that he and Emza had met in Paris."

Declan Rashid was thunderstruck. "You are sure of this?" A stupid question, because he knew already that Aziz must have been to have said it.

"Oh yes," Aziz said. "I'll remember it till my dying day."

"Okay, but don't tell Rasoul you've spoken to me. We'll keep this between us." The colonel turned off his mobile, then sat down at his computer.

He had access to a great deal of classified information, and when he inserted *Kantara,* there it was on a list of vessels known to deliver arms by night in Lebanese and Syrian waters, and it was suspected of a link to al-Qaeda. But there was more — news of a ship exploding and going to the bottom off the Cyprus coast. Wreckage had clearly proved it to be the *Kantara.* Swift justice indeed by someone who was obviously anti-al-Qaeda, and it could only mean British Intelligence and Ferguson.

So where did that leave Emza Khan? And what about the involvement of Sara Gideon? Certainly not a bitch from hell, so there was a lot more to the story than that. He went and stood staring out of the window, thinking of her, but also trying to make sense out of a situation that didn't seem to have any sense to it at all.

At that moment, his mobile sounded. It was General Ali ben Levi calling from the War Office. "The minister is expecting you, Colonel, are you aware of that?"

"Profound apologies, General," Declan said. "I'll be there quite quickly."

"I'd advise it, Colonel, it's a matter of grave urgency," ben Levi said. "I've sent a limousine."

"I'm on my way."

Declan got his briefcase, left his apartment, and made for the elevator. Emza Khan, the *Kantara* with al-Qaeda associations, Yousef and Rasoul and Sara Gideon — they were all in his thoughts far too much. What was he getting into here and what could the minister expect of him? At least he'd soon find out.

■ ■ ■ ■

LONDON
IRAN
BEIRUT

■ ■ ■ ■

10

In spite of the early hour, Roper completed an incisive account of the *Kantara* affair and forwarded it to the Cabinet Office, where the Cabinet secretary, Henry Frankel, another night owl, devoured it and forwarded it to the Prime Minister, which led to a command performance for Charles Ferguson at Downing Street at 6:45 a.m. This meant that Ferguson, who had spent the night at Holland Park, was forced to rise at 5:30. He went to the computer room and found Roper roaming world news and drinking tea, the room, as usual, thick with cigarette smoke.

"Ridiculous bloody time for anyone to have to get up," Ferguson said, helping himself to tea. "The Prime Minister must be mad. What is our faithful troops in Algeria's next move?"

"They've already made it," Roper said. "One hour ahead of us. They rose at the crack of dawn, said farewell to Ras Kasar, and are well on the way to Majorca. I've alerted Lacey and Parry, the Gulfstream will be fueled up and ready to go. Allowing for weather, they should be back here late afternoon."

"Excellent. They can get straight on to a thorough examination of Emza Khan's past," Ferguson said. "But I'd better be off. Can't keep the Prime Minister waiting."

Ferguson found Henry Frankel sitting outside the Prime Minister's study, reading a file. He glanced up and smiled. "Roper's account of the *Kantara* affair. Marvelous stuff, the Prime Minister read it twice. You look a little strained, Charles."

"Not my idea of fun, this time in the morning, Henry. I haven't had my breakfast."

"I make no apology, the PM's got an unbelievably full day. Now, let's go in."

Frankel poured coffee for all of them, and the Prime Minister said, "Fascinating report, remarkable performances from Dillon and Sara Gideon. Young Salter's a cheeky sod, discovering the arms like that. He might have told you sooner, but then I suppose his background *is* rather unusual."

"You mean his years as a gangster?" Ferguson said. "That was then, now he's a valued member of the Secret Intelligence Service. And things were happening rather quickly out there. He saved us from having to pursue *Kantara* to Cyprus-Syrian waters to dispose of her."

"So there's no doubt it was *Kantara* which went down?"

"No doubt at all."

"Do you think this might cause a question in the House of Commons?"

"I don't see why. These waters are a war zone, plenty of ships dumping arms at night. The *Kantara* was just another casualty."

The Prime Minister held up Roper's report. "And Dillon, Salter, and Captain Gideon are convinced this Captain Rajavi *was* al-Qaeda?"

"Absolutely," Ferguson said.

"And Yousef and Rasoul went down with the ship?"

"Not Yousef. He died in a hand-to-hand fight with Captain Gideon."

"Good God," the Prime Minister said. "Was that really necessary?"

"The name of the game," Ferguson said. "And Rasoul ran for it."

"Do you think he managed to get to shore?"

"I don't see how. We left in the only available boat, and it was too far to swim."

"So he must have perished with the rest of the crew?"

"I'd say so."

"So what were they doing on the *Kantara*?"

"Yousef was running away from the threat of prison, Rasoul must have been looking after him."

"And where does Emza Khan fit into all this?"

"Yousef disappeared from the clinic where he was receiving treatment. Khan insisted to the police that he had no knowledge of his son's whereabouts."

"How would he explain their presence on an al-Qaeda boat?" the Prime Minister asked.

"I imagine he would blame his man, Rasoul, insist he had no knowledge of Rasoul's links to al-Qaeda. Iran wouldn't touch al-Qaeda with a bargepole, and Khan has always supported that attitude."

"Will they still believe him?"

"I think so," Ferguson said. "Khan's always been very vocal on the matter, a pillar of attack against al-Qaeda. But —"

Henry Frankel cut in, "Yes, but. Didn't somebody say that if you exhausted all sensible and logical explanations to any problem, then the answer had to be the most improbable?"

"Yes, I've heard something like that," the Prime Minister said. "But what are *you* saying?"

"That he lied to the police about not knowing where his son and his servant had gone. That it was no coincidence the *Kantara* was the boat they chose. He's as guilty as sin."

Ferguson smiled. "I completely agree."

The Prime Minister smiled back. "Never cared for him anyway." He leaned across and shook hands. "Now you must excuse me."

In the corridor outside, Henry Frankel grinned and said, "Oh, I did like that." He glanced at his watch. "I've got forty minutes. Toast and marmalade, two boiled eggs, choice of coffee or tea. Can I send you away happy?"

"Just lead the way," Ferguson said and followed him downstairs.

He was in a cheerful mood when he returned to Holland Park and told Roper what had been discussed at Downing Street.

"That's fine," Roper said. "But remember that as far as Tehran is concerned, there are other ways to look at this. That Khan's well-known drunk of a son absconded rather than face the humiliation of a police court makes Emza an object of pity. The fact that his servant, Rasoul, vanished with Yousef could be admired as an example of Arab loyalty."

"Fair enough, but I want to create a real profile of the man. Go through his computer, access his diary. If you dig deep enough, there's bound to be some sort of indication of his nastier side. Where exactly is he now, home?"

"No, the Aziz clinic. He's been diagnosed with insomnia, panic attacks, and bouts of depression."

"My heart bleeds for him. Are the telephones on our side?"

"Oh yes, so we can snoop on the landlines, but what about the mobiles? Our Codex Fours are encrypted. Don't tell me al-Qaeda hasn't got something similar."

"Understood. Meantime, we have assets who are agency nurses. Get one in to keep an eye on him."

In fact, Emza Khan, after a troubled night, had opted for an early breakfast. Afterward, although it was raining, he had borrowed a raincoat and umbrella and was walking in the clinic gardens, hoping to clear his head, when his mobile phone trembled in his pocket. As Roper had surmised, it was encrypted, a present from al-Qaeda.

The Master said, "There are no words to express my sorrow at the loss of your son. All I can say is it was his time."

Emza Khan sobbed for a moment, so great was his emotion. "Bless you, Master, for your kindness, but all I feel is my need for revenge, not only on that whore who murdered him but on Ferguson and all his people."

"And you shall have it, but you must be patient, and above all, you must be strong. I have news. Rasoul will arrive from Oran soon."

Emza Khan said, "Allah is good to me, I can speak with him?"

"No, you may not. In the eyes of the world, he is dead. Everyone thinks he went down on the *Kantara,* and so they will not be searching for him."

"Where will Rasoul go?"

"When he flies in from Oran, Ali Saif will pick him up and take him to the Army of God center in Pound Street, where he can pose as a religious student. Saif will act under my instructions, not yours. You are forbidden even to try to contact Rasoul. Do you understand?"

"I do, Master, but what *are* my orders?"

"Your story is clear. You son absconded to avoid the shame of a possible prison sentence. Rasoul, who had known him since childhood, vanished with him. You have no idea where they have gone, and they haven't been in touch. No one can prove otherwise, so go home, back to your work, and behave normally."

"And Tehran?"

"A family matter, as far as they are concerned. All you will find is sympathy, but only if you keep the true facts to yourself. No one can link you to the *Kantara* except Rasoul."

"And Dr. Aziz," Emza Khan said. "Remember, he was at the penthouse when Rasoul's call came in . . . ?"

"The good doctor will be dealt with."

Emza Khan said, "And what of Colonel Declan Rashid?"

"He is to know nothing. He is no friend to our cause. In fact, I must tell you that a day will come when serious measures will have to be taken against him."

"If that is the will of the council in this

matter, who am I to say no? I am at your orders."

"Good — be strong."

Emza Khan's phone went quiet. He put it in his pocket, took a deep breath, and returned to the clinic.

When the Master phoned Pound Street that afternoon Ali Saif was not prepared for the litany of woe he was about to hear.

He said, "This is incredible. So much bad fortune in such a short time."

"Obviously, I do not expect you to spend any time weeping for Emza Khan or Rasoul, not after what he did to Fatima Le Bon. But personal considerations must be cast aside for the good of our cause."

Saif managed the right answer. "As always, I am at your command."

"So you will meet Rasoul when he arrives at Heathrow and bring him to Pound Street. I shall phone at three o'clock and give him his orders. If you leave now, you should be back in time to take my call."

"Of course, Master." Saif got to his feet and went out of the door on the run.

At Heathrow, Rasoul met up with Saif with no difficulty. With his wad of dollars, he had purchased fresh clothes at Oran's airport, a bag and a light raincoat for London's March weather. Several days' growth of beard had been taken care of by a visit to the barber. So, in spite of his scarred face, he looked respectable enough.

Remembering Fatima, Ali Saif was conscious of a burning hate for the man, but he stayed calm. "A good flight?" he asked as they drove away.

"What do you think, you stupid Egyptian pig?" Rasoul said. "I can't wait to get to the penthouse."

"Well, you will have to. We're going to the Army of God at Pound Street."

Rasoul exploded. "Who says so?"

"The Master." Saif was enjoying himself, swinging through the traffic and rain. "He's just put Emza Khan in his place, and he's waiting to do it to you."

"Now, look here . . ." Rasoul was beginning to bluster, but tailed off.

"That's better," Saif said. "Go carefully. He's not used to people who say no."

A point that the Master himself made over the phone.

"I don't like you or your arrogant and bullying ways," he told Rasoul. "Your behavior on *Kantara* left much to be desired."

"Not true, Master, I was protective of

Yousef in every way," Rasoul said.

"I was in constant telephone communication with Captain Rajavi, who told me different. You will obey Ali Saif, because his orders are my orders. If he has reason to put your name to the Brotherhood, scores of believers out there on the street would be happy to cut your throat in the name of Osama."

Rasoul almost had a bowel movement. He was a thug and a bully, but also, as Sara had found on the *Kantara,* a coward.

His voice rose in panic. "Master, there is no need for this."

"I am sure there isn't," the Master told him. "Now, give the phone to Saif and go and wait for him."

Rasoul did exactly as he was told. Saif said, "What are your orders?"

"Put him in one of the students' rooms, they're private and comfortable enough."

"I would remind you that students work for their keep."

"The idea of Rasoul in the kitchen is certainly amusing, but we have the Aziz problem to take care of. I'm afraid the doctor has to go. Unfortunately for him, he knows too much. Sooner rather than later, I think."

"So you would prefer Rasoul to handle it?"

"It would give him something to do. Not the knife, a broken neck, I think. Have him take Aziz's credit cards and mobile phone. A simple mugging."

"His clinic in Mayfair — he has to walk through the garden to get to his car."

"What could be better," the Master said. "I'll leave it in your capable hands."

Saif sat there thinking about it, then became aware of Rasoul still waiting in the corner. He stood, hands folded, for once a look of resignation on his face.

Saif said, "I'd almost forgotten about you."

Rasoul said, "What happens now?"

"I'll show you to your room, explain our system. You'll be a religious student who performs light duties when required. The Master thought you might find that rather boring, so he's come up with a special task for you."

"And what would that be?" Rasoul asked.

So Ali Saif told him, not that it needed much explaining, Rasoul obviously being so familiar with Aziz and his comings and goings. "Think you can handle that?" Saif asked.

Rasoul's face didn't even flicker. "A piece of cake," he said and went out.

■ ■ ■ ■

It was bad March weather and early-evening
dark when Aziz finished visiting his patients,
accompanied by a nursing sister. He ended
up in the entrance hall of the clinic, where
his Burberry, umbrella, and briefcase
waited. As he dressed, the sister opened the
front door, revealing rain bouncing on the
steps.

"Not fit for man nor beast, Sister," he
said, putting up his umbrella.

"I know and I'll be following soon. Good
night, Doctor."

Rasoul, in the shadows of a summer
house, had seen Aziz clearly in the lights of
the front-door porch, waited until the doctor passed, then went after him. Aziz hurried toward the balustrade overlooking the
carpark, the steps going down, a camera on
a stand to one side, though Rasoul had put
that out of action.

"A moment, Doctor," he called.

Aziz glanced back and paused. "Oh, it's
you, Rasoul, so you're back. What's up? Is
something wrong with Emza Khan?"

"No, Doctor, only with you."

Rasoul grabbed him, spinning him
around, and as Aziz dropped the briefcase,

slipped his left arm around to throttle, while the right hand grabbed the chin, jerking sideways with an audible click, breaking the neck. Aziz died instantly. Rasoul eased him down, felt for the wallet, found it and the mobile phone in a breast pocket, turned, and hurried away.

It was little more than five minutes later that the nursing sister finished her shift and, on her way to her car, discovered Aziz lying there. A tour in the Army Medical Corps in Afghanistan had inured her to such situations. A quick check established that Aziz was dead, and she went hurrying back to the clinic to alert security.

Saif emptied the wallet and counted. "One hundred and twenty pounds, a driver's license, and three credit cards."

"And this." Rasoul took a mobile phone from his pocket and pushed it across.

"Well done, thou good and faithful servant," Saif told him.

"What's that supposed to mean?" Rasoul asked.

"It's from the Christian Bible, I was being ironic. You wouldn't understand." He pushed the money, the cards, and the mobile together. "So this is the measure of a man's life, brought to an end by you. Does that ever worry you?"

"Not in the slightest. I was doing what the big man wanted."

"And I can tell you now how to really please him. This Billy Salter, who sank the *Kantara*, lives with his uncle, Harry Salter, in their pub, the Dark Man by the Thames at Wapping. If you wanted to make your bones with the Master, the death of Salter would definitely help. You still have that Walther I gave you in your pocket, don't you?"

Rasoul nodded, turned, and went out.

The apparent mugging and murder of Aziz was mentioned on the evening crime statistics from Scotland Yard. Roper saw it and reported it to Ferguson, who was going out to dinner.

"Could it be just be an opportunist mugging that went too far?"

"If so, it'd be an awfully big coincidence. Especially since his neck was broken by an expert."

"Well, that takes care of that. If you find out any more, let me know."

Roper called Dillon, too. There was music and voices. "Where are you?" Roper asked.

"At the Dark Man with Harry, Billy, and Sara. What's up?" Roper told him, and Dillon laughed and echoed Roper: "A bit of a coincidence, isn't it? And you know what I think about those. Look, why don't you join us? Get Tony Doyle to bring you down."

"All right, I will," Roper said. "I'll be with you in half an hour."

Rasoul got a taxi and left it on Wapping High Street, pausing in the entrance to the lane with the sign that indicated Cable Wharf down by the Thames and Harry Salter's beloved pub, the Dark Man.

There were still plenty of ancient warehouses awaiting development, and he kept to the shadows, moving down toward where the cars were parked. There was music on the night air, laughter from an open window. He stayed among the vehicles, quite close for a few minutes, then approached a window and peered in. He saw them at once — Dillon, Harry Salter, and Sara — Baxter and Hall, the two minders, propping up the wall. It occurred to him that a hand grenade would have been the end of all of them, but that was not to be.

As he turned away, a van arrived, although it meant nothing to Rasoul, who eased back among the parked vehicles. He watched as the black driver in army uniform honked his horn and operated a hydraulic device, which opened the rear and deposited Roper in his wheelchair.

The door of the pub opened and the others appeared, standing in the light and laughing. Rasoul could have chosen anyone, even the woman, but what Saif had said about the Master and Billy Salter took control. Dillon and Billy were spinning Roper around in the chair, laughing uproariously. Rasoul, down on one knee, fired twice, catching Billy in the back and sending him sprawling. The cough of the silenced weapon had been drowned by the laughter.

It stopped, and they crowded in, sitting Billy up, four of the men between them. Rasoul was more excited than he had ever been, but then Billy was on his feet, someone taking off his jacket, then the shirt and the nylon-and-titanium vest was plain to see.

Rasoul was already easing back into the darkness as pistols were drawn and someone called, "He must have been close. Two rounds in the vest."

But Rasoul was already fading into the comforting darkness back to the old warehouses, until he finally reached Wapping High Street again, where he flagged down a cab.

■ ■ ■ ■

They sat in the sitting room of the Dark Man, Billy stripped to the waist while Sara attended to the two heavy bruises on his back. Dillon was holding the vest, extracting one of the two rounds embedded in it, holding it up to the light.

"Walther PPK, unmistakable, silenced version. Lucky you were wearing it, Billy."

"Dillon, I'm ashamed to say I haven't showered and changed since I put it on in Algeria at the crack of dawn this morning."

Harry was handing out drinks. "Here's to you, my son," he told Billy. "Remember the old saying: Keep your friends close and your enemies closer. Here's to the Wilkinson Sword Company. A work of genius, that vest."

"But who do you think was behind it, Sean?" Sara asked.

"I think it's all related to Emza Khan and al-Qaeda. I don't believe for a moment that Aziz was mugged. He was executed, just as somebody just tried to execute you, Billy."

"Al-Qaeda?" Sara asked.

"I'm convinced of it." Dillon tossed back his Bushmills. "And from now on, I'd say it's titanium vests at all times for everyone

274

here."

At Park Lane, George Hagen was well into his night shift when a police car drove in and an energetic man in a trench coat jumped out.

"Detective Inspector Howard, Mr. Khan's expecting me. Where's the lift?" Hagen showed him. Howard called, "Wait here, Sergeant," then departed for the penthouse.

"Can I ask what's up?" Hagen asked.

"It seems Mr. Khan was a patient at the Aziz clinic," the sergeant told him and got out of the car.

"That's right. He's only got back this afternoon."

"Aziz was mugged earlier this evening in the clinic garden on his way to his car. Whoever did it went too far. He's dead."

"That will shock Mr. Khan. Aziz was his regular doctor, in and out of here all the time. So what's the inspector after with Mr. Khan?"

"Just to see if he'd noticed anyone hanging round in the garden or the cars when he was there, that kind of thing. I think the geezer who did it is long gone and running for his life. Probably wanted a few quid for drugs, now he's facing a life sentence for murder."

"Well, there's no answer to that," Hagen said, and the lift door opened and Howard appeared. "Are you his driver?" he asked.

"No, I'm the night porter."

"Well, keep an eye on him. He's taken the death of this Dr. Aziz to heart."

"I can imagine he would," Hagen said. "They were very close."

"So it would appear. Right, Sergeant, let's get moving." Howard got in the car, and they moved out into the rain.

At Pound Street, Saif went down to the kitchen for fresh coffee and Rasoul came in through the back door, wet through and looking miserable.

"So how did you make out? Is Billy Salter dead and gone?" Saif asked.

"No, damn you," Rasoul said. "But I shot the bastard twice in the back. His friends came running, Dillon, that damn woman, but it turned out he was wearing a vest."

Saif was surprised. "Well, full marks for trying. I'd say you were lucky to get away."

He walked to the door, and Rasoul said, "Will you tell the Master?"

"He'll already know," Saif said. "This city is a sieve, we have sympathizers everywhere. That's why French Intelligence calls it Londistan. Help yourself to coffee, tea, or anything else you fancy."

He walked back whistling cheerfully. *Poor Rasoul, so near and yet so far.*

Sometime after the police had gone, Hagen checked his watch. It would be somewhere after eleven in Tehran. He was going to send a text but decided to try calling, and Declan answered at once, his voice low.

"Who's there?"

"George, Colonel. I have more news. Dr. Aziz murdered by a mugger in the garden of his clinic. Isn't that terrible?"

"But not surprising. I don't think it was a mugger," Declan said. "But to be frank, I've had a pretty extraordinary day myself, so I've got to go, George."

George closed his mobile and said softly, "Well, that's a turnup for the book. What in hell is going on?"

11

The minister of war's hair was snow white, his face tanned, and he wore the blue suit and striped tie beloved of politicians the world over. He brushed Declan's apologies to one side and shook hands with enthusiasm.

"A great honor, Colonel Rashid, as always. Let's go outside."

The windows stood open to the terrace and there was a table under an umbrella. Ali ben Levi rose to meet them. At sixty-four and still soldiering because of the national commitment, he was an imposing figure in paratroop uniform. He and Declan were old comrades.

"As you can see," the minister said. "We have coffee, sandwiches, fruit, so take what you like, but let me get down to business. As you know, General ben Levi is commander of the army's secret police. I propose to appoint you his second-in-command immediately in the rank of full colonel."

Declan was bewildered. "Naturally, I'm honored, Minister, but why?"

"Because I don't like the Security Services or the Secret Service, and I prefer to keep military business under my control."

"What kind of business?" Declan asked.

"The possibility of nuclear war, for example. Simon Husseini — you know him, I understand?"

Declan nodded. "I accompanied Emza Khan to Paris to see Simon Husseini receive the Legion of Honor."

"And did you meet him to talk to, get to know him, I mean?"

"It was only a weekend, but Khan arranged a cocktail party. We talked, but I didn't really get to know him."

Declan glanced at ben Levi, who looked solemn, then turned back to the minister. "What is it? What's happened?"

"He's disappeared."

"You mean cleared off, left everything?" Declan shook his head. "That doesn't make sense. He made it clear to me the distaste he felt for his work, but he planned to soldier on because of his mother and daughter. They're being held under house arrest."

"Yes, well, they aren't any longer," the

279

minister said and nodded to ben Levi. "Tell him."

"They are dead," the general said.

Declan frowned. "When did this happen?"

"The day he and Wali Vahidi, his body-guard, got back to Tehran, Husseini re-turned to the nuclear compound at Qazvin, while Vahidi called in on his mother and daughter. Vahidi was driving them to an ap-pointment when a truck came out of a side road without stopping." General ben Levi shrugged. "The driver was drunk and Hus-seini's mother and daughter were killed outright. Vahidi is in the military hospital and not expected to live."

Declan turned to the minister. "How did Husseini react?"

"The Security Services did not inform him that the two women were dead. To be fair, nobody knew what to do in the circum-stances."

Declan said, "Which meant he was pre-vented from attending their funerals, am I right?"

General ben Levi said, "The experiment he was engaged in was of absolute critical importance. We're close to production of the bomb the government is placing so much hope on. But now — the situation is different. There is nothing to keep Husseini from fleeing."

"Which seems to be exactly what he's done."

"How did he find out what happened?" Declan asked.

General ben Levi passed a letter across. "He sent this to the minister. It says he was lied to when he asked about Vahidi, and then he got an anonymous phone call telling him the truth."

Declan flipped through. It was all there, the anger and the anguish and the promise that he would make every effort to leave Iran and die trying if that was necessary.

Declan handed the letter back. "I can't say I blame him."

"Look, I don't like it any more than you do," the minister said. "And I'm sure I speak for the general, too, but we live in troubled times and do the best we can with the cards we're dealt."

"I am not a religious man, but the business of the funeral leaves a nasty taste. The Irish half of me is disgusted and the Bedouin is far from happy. To deny him the chance to bury his mother and daughter negated not only his Koranic rights but his duty as a Muslim." He struggled with his emotions. "What do you want me to do?"

"Find him," the minister said. "I've cut

the Security Services out of it completely."
The minister snapped his fingers at ben
Levi, who produced an envelope, which was
passed to Declan. "This is a warrant, signed
by the President, ordering anyone to help
you in any way you ask."

Declan read it. "Impressive." He put it
into his briefcase.

"Where will you start?" the minister asked.

"With Wali Vahidi. When I spoke to him
in Paris, I was impressed. He has an excellent army record, a first-class police record."

"Then I'd get moving if I were you," ben
Levi said. "My impression was that Vahidi's
not long for this world."

"Aren't we all?" Declan Rashid said.
"Good morning, gentlemen," and he walked
out.

The military hospital was a good one, which
Declan knew well from personal experience.
The doctor responsible for Vahidi's care was
a Major Hakim, who read the presidential
warrant and jumped to attention.

"A great honor to meet you, Colonel," he
said and led the way to a private room at
the end of the corridor, where a male nurse
sat outside.

The room was in half darkness. Vahidi lay
there, eyes closed, his vital signs endlessly

repeating on electronic screens, connected to tubes, drips, and oxygen that were very probably the only things keeping him alive.

Hakim said, "You know this man, Colonel?"

"Yes, I do. He had an excellent record in the Iraq war. What can you tell me?"

"That he's not got long."

Vahidi opened sunken eyes, dull with pain, stared at Declan and smiled. "Colonel Rashid," he croaked. "Where did you come from?"

"I'm sorry to see you like this." Declan turned to Hakim. "I'd like a little privacy here, Major."

"Of course." Hakim brought a chair for him. "The nurse will get me when you're ready."

Declan sat down. "A bad business."

"You can say that again. I had the Security Service bastards in here discussing me. I know they didn't inform Husseini about the accident. But what are you doing here?"

"Husseini has disappeared. They're keeping it an army matter. I've been transferred to the secret police with instructions to find him. Apparently, someone called him anonymously to tell him what happened."

Vahidi was silent for a moment. "That was me," he croaked. "One of the nurses left her mobile on the side table. I gave him a call. He didn't recognize me because my voice is so rough."

"He sent a letter to the minister saying he was leaving. That he would die trying if necessary."

"I've known him a long time, and I'm sure he means that. I felt he deserved the truth about his family. On the other hand, I'm torn. I'm sorry for him, but we're constantly presented with the threat of war. Other people have the bomb, so why not us?" Vahidi asked. "Your father died for our country, and surely you are just as much a patriot as he was."

"It's not that easy for me, I'm struggling with a split personality," Declan said. "For the moment, I'm a colonel in the Iranian Army, but if I do catch up with him, maybe I'll tell him to keep on running." There was more silence.

"Oh, what the hell," Vahidi said. "He has passports in another name. I found them one day. Both French and Lebanese. He used his mother's surname, LeBlanc. Ali LeBlanc."

Declan said, "Why didn't you confiscate these when you found them?"

"Because there was no need. They were from his past, and I thought he'd just kept them renewed. If I'd raised the issue, it would indicate I'd spent time rooting about in his private things and spoiled our friendship. If you want to find him . . . I'd look in Lebanon. He's had a place in Beirut for many years, in the Rue Rivoli."

"Thank you, Wali," Declan said.

"For some reason, I'm more worried about him than about what remains of the rest of my life. When you see him, tell him I'm sorry for everything and my part in it."

"And then what do I do?"

"The right thing, the honorable thing."

"Which is what?"

"You'll know that when the time comes," and he closed his eyes.

Declan took a small gadget called a dissembler from his pocket, pressed a button that destroyed any recording made in the room, then went outside.

He said to the nurse, "He's just going back to sleep. Thank Major Hakim."

He walked away, and Hakim, who'd been listening in the next room behind a half-open door, emerged and said to the nurse, "You're sure you've got it on the remote?"

The man opened his jacket, revealing the radio listening device. "Yes, I checked."

"All right. I'm going in."

He entered Vahidi's room, found him

sleeping again, breathing hoarsely. Hakim looked down at him and said softly, "There is one God and Osama is his Prophet." Then he adjusted some tubes and left, walking away, the nurse already gone.

Five minutes later, the alarm sounded, harsh and ugly. In a few moments, the corridor was all action, nurses first and then the crash team crowding into Wali Vahidi's room, none of which was any help at all.

Declan's next visit was to Tehran's airport. At the sight of the presidential warrant, the chief security officer put his people straight to work. They had no difficulty finding Husseini's departure on an early-morning flight to Baghdad the previous day.

Then they traced the continuing flight to Aleppo using the French passport in the name of Ali LeBlanc, and the hiring of a Citroën car for the onward journey. Some judicious computer work indicated that his entry into Lebanon had been at the border town of Wadi Khalid early that morning, after which he had taken a taxi, Declan assumed to Beirut.

It wouldn't be a good idea to go in uniform, so Declan gave his driver instructions to take him back to his apartment so he could change. While he was there, the phone rang. It was ben Levi.

"Did you hear the news from the hospital?"

"No, what?" Declan asked him.

"Apparently, Wali Vahidi died shortly after you left. I've had a Major Hakim in touch. He says that in spite of a crash team responding to Vahidi's relapse, they couldn't save him. How was he when you saw him?"

"Very weak, but our talk was worthwhile."

"So do you know where he went?"

It was at that moment that Declan Rashid surprised himself. "It's early yet. There are some things to check out, but I'll need time."

"As long as it takes," ben Levi told him. "And whatever it costs. Go anywhere you like, but find him."

"Thank you, General, that's exactly what I wanted to hear."

Ben Levi hung up.

"Now, why did I say that?" Declan asked softly.

There was no answer except that something was stirring inside him. He phoned the secret police headquarters and asked for the duty officer, who came on, full of enthusiasm.

"I've just seen your promotion, Colonel. My name is Captain Selim, and it's a

287

privilege to serve under you. How can I help?"

"My assignment is top secret. How do I get to Beirut as fast as possible?"

"By high-speed executive jet, Colonel. We fly twice a day, with general mail and private and confidential material for the embassy. There is room for a passenger or two. You could go this afternoon."

"I won't be in uniform, but it would be necessary for me to be armed."

"That will be no problem."

"Who is the military attaché in Beirut?"

"Captain Shah, a good officer, one of our own."

"Tell him to meet me, but no one else. I don't want any fuss. Get me a room at the Tropicana, and a Range Rover with a couple of AK-47s. Stress that secrecy is essential."

"As you command, Colonel."

Declan hung up, checked his large canvas holdall, slipped in a small traveling laptop for note-taking. He was wearing a black shirt now over a titanium vest, a summer suit, and ankle boots of soft leather. In the bag was a similar suit of fawn linen, a couple of extra shirts and underwear, a toiletries bag, and a holstered Glock pistol. A soldier traveling light. The final thing he took, from a locked drawer beside his bed, was a Colt

.25, which he slipped into his waistband at the small of his back. A pair of Ray-Bans meant for desert conditions and he was ready to go.

When he went out and stood waiting for the lift, he had the strangest of feelings. It was as if he was leaving something behind when it should have been that he was starting out on something new. For some reason, it made him unaccountably cheerful as he hurried out to his limousine and told the driver to take him to the airport.

As Simon Husseini was being driven to Beirut, two and a half thousand miles away in London, Sara Gideon was just finishing a late breakfast. Her grandfather was away, chairing a seminar on comparative religion at St. Hughes College, Oxford. She was hoping for some flying time, and then Roper came on the phone.

"If you're interested, Ferguson's had to do some fast packing. He'll be out of our hair for at least a week to ten days."

"Tell me," she said.

"The Cabinet Office phoned him in the middle of the night. The PM wants him to help the Foreign Secretary with some UN committee about the Middle East."

"Is he on his way?" she said.

"Already gone in the foreign minister's plane. Can't even use his own Gulfstream. He's not pleased at all."

"But you are," Sara said.

"Well, it's nice to be off the lead occasionally. You know the old saying. When the cat's away, the mice will play."

"So what are we going to do? Concentrate on Emza Khan?"

"The computer can do that," Roper said. "It's only a question of time before he comes tumbling down like Humpty Dumpty. Why don't you join me and we'll try and work something out together."

"Why not?" she said. "But give me a little while. I feel like a nice brisk walk through Hyde Park. I'll see you soon."

It had rained earlier and would again, wind stirring the trees and not too many people abroad in such brisk March weather. She wore a flying suit and boots, a black bomber jacket, in all a rather dashing figure, and was happy striding along, when her Codex trembled in her pocket with the special signal. She answered, and found Simon Husseini calling.

"You didn't block your location," she said. "I can see you're in Beirut. Did you mean to do that?"

"No, I was careless," he replied. "I didn't expect to have to use this special phone you gave me in Paris so soon. Where are you?"

They talked for several minutes, and she heard the awful news about his family. As she tried to digest it, she turned and started to walk back home. "Why Beirut?"

"I've had a place in the old quarter for years, in Rue Rivoli. Bibi, my housekeeper, lives in the place permanently. This is the first time I've been back for some years, for obvious reasons."

"And you got to Lebanon using your own name?"

"No, no, I have passports with another name. LeBlanc was my mother's maiden name, so I'm Ali LeBlanc."

"So what's your plan? I imagine the Iranians are already chasing you," she said as she went up the steps to Highfield House and opened the front door. "What comes next?"

"I haven't the slightest idea," he said. "I'd planned something like this for years, but never for these dreadful circumstances. I suppose I'm running away from that as much as anything else."

She was into her grandfather's study now and sat at the desk. "So what do you want from us?"

"I don't think your General Ferguson will be very helpful. I've no intention of carrying on with my nuclear work. I know I'm older, but I'm returning to medicine, and that hardly makes me of interest to any of the great powers."

"Never mind any of that now. The main thing is to get you safe," Sara said. "I guarantee you they'll find out about Beirut, may even be on their way already." She paused. "When we talked in Paris, you mentioned your old friend, the philosopher John Mikali, who'd had an influence on you. In old age, he has given up his professorships to serve as a priest at St. Anthony's Hospice in the Saudi Arabian desert. If you could join him, no one would suspect, and perhaps he could sort out some of your head problems."

"How would I get there?"

"During the war with Saddam Hussein, the Saudi Air Force laid down an airstrip for jet fighters needing an emergency landing. It's at al-Shaba, right next door to the hospice. It's no longer manned, but they left a communication facility in the hospital powered by solar panels, which is supposed to support a satellite phone. The trouble is that with the extreme desert weather patterns, it hardly ever works. I had our Army

Air Corps check it out for me once. But we'd have no difficulty landing a jet at al-Shaba."

"Where would such an aircraft come from?"

"The other year, the Gideon Bank was approached by an Israeli firm seeking investment to help them enter the executive jet market, with the intention of producing a quality aircraft on the same level as the Gulfstream or Falcon. We approved of their ambition, and when they suggested we call the result the Gideon, we were happy to oblige. We now have a small fleet ourselves, which we keep at Northolt. Chief pilot Don Renard has a DFC from the Gulf War. Jane Green, like me, is an old Afghan hand. I'll tell them I'll need one Gideon for hazardous duty. I'll call you when I'm in the air."

At Pound Street, one of Ali Saif's daily tasks was to make coherent sense of the mass of information passed to him and his associates by well-wishers. He was engaged in doing this at the same time Sara was leaving for the airport, when the Master called him.

"Are you sitting down, Saif?"

"That bad?" Saif said. "You'd better tell me."

The Master did — everything that had

been learned at the hospital — and Saif said at once, "What an incredibly stupid way to handle the situation. Husseini must loathe those responsible."

"I should imagine so, not that it helps."

"Forgive me for asking, Master, but is all this information sound? His false identity, Beirut, his street address?"

"The surgeon handling the bodyguard, Vahidi, in the military hospital is one of our assets. He knew a man like Rashid would wipe Vahidi's room clean of recordings, so it was a stroke of genius to have someone recording it remotely. Yes, it is all sound."

"Do you want me to go to Beirut?"

"No need. We have an excellent branch of the Army of God there run by a true believer named Jemal Nadim. I have dealt with him before."

"So this Jemal Nadim and his people, they will kidnap Husseini?"

"Exactly, and dispose of Colonel Rashid. Then Husseini will be working for *us*. Tell me, how is Rasoul doing?"

"He takes young students for physical training in the gym."

"I think we should leave him there, for now. However, Cyrus Holdings has a very sizable port unit in Beirut. I think the chairman should show his face and meet with our people. If Khan gives you the slightest problem, let him speak to me. I will also make clear to Jemal Nadim that you are my middleman on this. Any problems, he can sort them out with you. I'll also leave you with a special number with which to contact me. This is a big one and we must get it right."

"Of course, Master," Saif told him.

"I've good faith in you, Saif, you've come a long way."

He switched off. Saif said softly, "The bastard, saying things like that to make you feel warm and cozy. God dammit, it's almost sexy. Ah, well . . ." He poured a brandy, lit a cigarette, and then decided to go around to the penthouse and confront Khan, for the pleasure of being able to tell him what to do.

At the same time, Sara was driving a Mini Cooper toward Northolt Aerodrome when her mobile cut in. Roper said, "I got tired of waiting, where are you?"

He was sitting in front of his screens, Dillon enjoying a cup of tea and flipping through a newspaper, when Sara replied.

"I was walking across Hyde Park to come and join you when I had a call from Simon Husseini."

"But how could that be?" Roper demanded. "What about his bodyguard, Vahidi?"

"Vahidi's in the hospital, Giles, and Husseini's mother and daughter are dead." She explained what Husseini had told her. "He's got out of Iran and reached Beirut, and I'm riding to the rescue, just like one of those Western movies. Isn't it exciting?"

"Not when the Indians catch up with you, so be careful. Okay, I admit that Ferguson isn't likely to go berserk at your pulling off a coup that brings Simon Husseini to us."

"I'm afraid he's going to have to be disappointed. Simon isn't interested in any of that. His intention is to move back into research on medical isotopes and to renounce his nuclear work. And if that's what he wants, it's all right with me. I was never keen on our government wanting him to do the exact same thing for us as he's been doing in Iran. That's why I'm going on one of my own planes, and I don't care what Major General Charles Ferguson says or thinks."

"Oh, I think I can tell you, Captain. He'd remind you that you're a serving officer in the British Army who would certainly rate a court-martial if she persisted in such action."

"All I can say is, bring it on."

Roper exploded with anger and frustration. "It may sound corny, but you're greatly loved in this neck of the woods. Will you at least promise to stay in touch while I try to work things on this end?"

"You're a great guy, Giles Roper, and a true hero, which is why I love you, too, but I've got to do this, I've no choice."

"Okay, damn you, but stay in touch, I beg you," he implored her.

"I'll try. Over and out," she said.

Dillon had heard every word, and was already opening a cupboard and taking out a military bag, his contingency kit for jobs in a hurry, containing weapons, passport, and finance.

"Where's she going from?" he demanded of Roper, whose fingers danced over the computer keys.

"Northolt, one of the Gideon planes. Pilots are Don Renard and Jane Green. They're booked out in forty-five minutes, to Beirut."

But Dillon was already running out of the door, calling, "Tony, where are you? I need Northolt like yesterday. Where's the Alfa?"

Sergeant Doyle came down the corridor on the run. "Right outside the front door, sir."

"Then let's get the hell out of here."

In the computer room, there was sudden relief on Roper's face as the engine roared and faded away. Roper reached for the whiskey and murmured, "Sometimes you frighten me, Sara. However sound your intentions, you always need backup, because in our game, going solo is the loneliest place on the planet. Damn you, why won't you learn that?" He swallowed his whiskey and smiled wryly.

At Northolt, with Sara aboard and Don Renard at the controls, Jane Green was about to close the airstair door when the Alfa roared across the tarmac, skidded to a halt, and Dillon jumped out, bag in hand, went up the steps and smiled.

"Jane, isn't it? I'm Sean Dillon. Room for one more?"

"It's okay, Jane," Sara called. "Like all actors, he's particularly fond of the dramatic entrance."

Dillon moved up the aisle, stowed his bag, and sat across from her. "You shouldn't do it, love, not to Giles Roper. He's always been afraid you were going to come to a bad end."

"You are a bastard, Sean."

"There's no one I'd rather go to war with than you, but two is always better than one, so give me time to get my breath and find a drink and perhaps you could fill me in on what's happening."

She shook her head, produced her Codex, and called Roper. "Just to let you know that this little Irish so-and-so made it with about one minute to spare and we're now on our way. I'm sorry if I caused you any worry."

She switched off and said to Dillon, who was emptying two miniatures into a glass, "So what do you want to know?"

Ali Saif had visited the Khan's penthouse on a number of occasions and had met George Hagen in his usual role, and so was surprised on ringing the doorbell to have Hagen answer it, wearing Rasoul's green apron.

"Hello, George, this is a turnup for the books. Going up in the world, are you?"

"Not funny, Ali. With his son dead, Rasoul a mystery, and poor old Aziz murdered not fifteen minutes' walk away, Khan is depressed and reaching for the vodka bottle every five minutes. I'm still night porter, but I'm helping out. I use the staff bedroom on the landing. Go right in, I'll be in the kitchen."

Emza Khan was in his chair by the terrace window, looking terrible, in bad need of a shave, and stinking of booze. His shirt and baggy trousers looked as if they had been slept in. He glared at Saif, tried to sound belligerent, and failed completely.

"What do *you* want?"

"Is that the new perfume, urine and vodka? Most unpleasant. It will never catch on."

"How dare you?" Emza Khan tried to get up. Saif shoved him down.

"Simon Husseini has fled from Iran and reached Beirut, and Declan Rashid is hot on his trail. The whole thing's blown up."

Khan was horrified. "In the name of Allah, what's to be done?"

"We'll leave him out of it. A creature like you doesn't deserve to mention his name. So let's stick to the Master, who wants you in Beirut." Khan opened his mouth, and Saif said, "Shut up and listen."

By the time he had finished, Emza Khan had sobered considerably. "You think it's true that Colonel Rashid is still unaware of my connection with al-Qaeda?"

"So it would appear, though I wouldn't rely on it continuing, not with a man like Rashid on the job," Saif said.

"And this Jemal Nadim? His people will kidnap Husseini and dispose of Declan Rashid?" In a way, he was lively again. "This is good, I can see that. What do we do with Husseini?"

"That's why he wants you there with your executive jet. To deliver him wherever the council decides." Saif lit a cigarette, a certain contempt on his face. "It's something of a coup for you. Osama would be proud."

Emza Khan actually took it seriously and got up. "I must phone the office and get things moving at once."

"I'll leave you to it. Let me know when you're going, but I'd make it sooner rather than later, if I were you. I'd hate to see the Master disappointed." He opened the door and turned. "Don't forget the clothes. Strip and put them down the trash chute. The stink would frighten people away. And for the love of Allah, please bathe."

Emza Khan was oblivious to the scorn in Saif's voice, but George Hagan was not, for with the kitchen door ajar, he had heard every word. That Emza Khan would soon be on his way to Beirut was interesting in itself, but his reasons for going, the fact that he was involved with al-Qaeda, were so astonishing that Hagen hurried to his room, called Declan at once and found him in the backseat of the Falcon, reading a magazine.

"Thank God I've got you, Colonel," Hagen told him. "Where are you, can we talk?"

"Yes, George, I'm the sole passenger on a private jet proceeding to Beirut."

"Gawd almighty," Hagan said. "You ain't going to believe this, but you're going to have company."

"And who would that be?"

"Emza Khan."

Declan laughed out loud. "What's the joke, George?"

"No joke, Colonel, and there's worse to come. What would you say if I told you Emza Khan was involved with al-Qaeda big-time?"

A tiny smile touched Declan Rashid's mouth. "If that's so, George, tell me more."

George did, while Declan listened intently. Because of his time at the Iranian Embassy in London as military attaché, he was familiar with some of the players, had met Ali Saif, had visited the Army of God headquarters at the Pound Street Mosque. It was Emza Khan's favorite charity. One could now see why. A cloak of good works to mask the excesses of al-Qaeda. What had motivated Khan to embark on this path? Well, it was irrelevant, really. What was important was that Declan now knew pretty well all those involved in this game and could take appropriate action.

"That's about it, Colonel," Hagen said finally.

"You've no idea how grateful I am, George," Declan said. "You could well have saved my life in advance. Take the greatest care and watch your back."

"I will, Colonel, and you do the same."

Declan switched off his phone, leaned back, and opened the bar box behind him. He took out a couple of cold vodka miniatures, opened them, and poured the contents into a plastic tumbler, thinking of Emza Khan with a certain anger.

"Right, you bastard, bring it on," and he swallowed the vodka down.

So Bibi left Husseini resting at Maison Bleue and walked down through the alleys of the old quarter to the Beirut waterfront, which was busy as usual.

Café Marco had air-conditioning, but most of the locals preferred to savor the sun outside, leaving Omar Kerim on his own in a corner booth going over his books.

The waiter behind the bar reading the newspaper said, "He's busy."

"No, he isn't," Omar called. "Not for Bibi. Send her over and bring a sherbet — she loves those, don't you, darling?"

He had olive skin, a dark mustache, and black hair plaited into a pigtail. His linen suit of light brown was as creased as it was supposed to be, and his half smile and good teeth made him enormously attractive. On the marble-topped table was a Walther PPK, ready for a quick response to anyone attempting a hit on Beirut's most notorious gangsters, which had, on occasion, happened.

"So how's life, Bibi?" he asked as the waiter brought her sherbet.

"That's what I've come to tell you. It's very strange." She sucked on her straw. "You know my circumstances. Well, the man who owns my house, Ali LeBlanc, has just walked in after five years."

"That's interesting," Omar said. "Where's he been? What did he have to say?"

So she told him everything, responding readily to his careful probing, and when she'd finished he looked very thoughtful indeed.

"Bibi, my love, I smell politics here. I think we should adjourn next door and speak to my good friend Jemal Nadim."

The man in question sat at a cluttered desk in the small office, small and bearded, with round steel John Lennon spectacles. The only overtly Arab thing about him was the black-and-white-checkered head scarf, which set off dramatically his plain white shirt and khaki trousers, and yet this man controlled everything that happened concerning al-Qaeda in the entire city of Beirut.

"Bibi has a puzzle to unravel," Omar explained. "I can't help, but I thought you might, as there appears to be a political element to it."

"So tell me, Bibi," Jemal ordered.

She did, and he listened politely. When she was finished, he smiled. "Ali LeBlanc is a most important man, Bibi, you have been privileged to serve him. Now return to Café Marco, tell them Omar Kerim's order is that you can have anything you want. We will tell you later what we expect you to do."

She left at once, pure delight on her face. "A simple soul," Jemal said, "and easily pleased."

"Am I permitted to know what this is all about?" Omar inquired.

"Certainly, but first let me explain something. I knew of Bibi's situation before you brought her in. I've emphasized to you recently, al-Qaeda's tentacles reach out everywhere."

"So I accept that," Omar said. "But where

is it taking us?"

"Less than an hour ago, I had a call from a man we only know as the Master, who represents the council of our great movement, even in Western Europe. He has given me orders which I am delighted to obey, especially as I know you'll be pleased to assist me in this matter."

"For a price, of course," Omar said. "I mean, a man has to live."

"I knew I could rely on that grasping soul of yours."

"So what do we have to do?"

"Kill one man and kidnap another."

Omar laughed. "Is that all? I thought it was going to be something difficult."

"But this is more important to al-Qaeda and our future than anything I've ever been involved in, so sit back and I'll explain."

When he was finished, Omar said, "This Emza Khan who's on his way, he sounds like big stuff. Is his connection with us for real?"

"It must be. It's his plane that will fly Husseini out of Lebanon to wherever the council wants him to go. His money doesn't buy him special privileges. He must obey the call of Osama when needed, like any other supporter of a great cause."

"I take your point," Omar said. "So how

do we handle this?"

"We'll keep it simple," Jemal said. "You and your thugs deal with the colonel in some alley — make it look like a street robbery. Bibi will slip something in Husseini's drink, and we'll bundle him into a car."

"When will this be?" Omar demanded.

"Obviously, we must wait for Emza Khan, but sooner rather than later. Once we have Husseini, we get him out of Lebanon fast. Too many people, the Iranians in particular, want him back. Let's go talk to Bibi."

They moved out into the glare of the sun, turned toward Café Marco, and saw Bibi sitting with Simon Husseini, for Jemal recognized him at once.

"It's Husseini," he said. "There was a photo in *Le Monde* a week or so ago, receiving some honor."

"Shall we go and speak to them?" Omar asked.

"Why not?" Jemal said.

As they got close, Bibi was talking in an animated way to Husseini and, noticing their approach, rose to greet them. "There you are. This is my friend, Ali LeBlanc. Ali, this is Omar Kerim, the owner of Café Marco, and Jemal Nadim, who runs the Army of God charity in Beirut."

"Sit, Bibi, please," Omar said and shook

307

Husseini's hand. "Good to meet you."

"I echo that," Jemal said. "You have been long absent, I understand?"

"Business took me abroad, but I think I can say I am home for good now." Husseini's mobile rang and he answered it, listened, then said, "I'll call you back." He smiled at everyone. "Bibi, I must go. Gentlemen, I hope we meet again." He crossed the road through the crowd and went toward the breakwater.

The two men sat down. "You like him, don't you, Bibi?" Jemal said.

"He is a good man, this I know because of kindness many years ago, and he has supplied me with a wonderful home."

"Yes, but all is not what it seems," Omar said. "And he is not the man you think he is."

She looked alarmed. "Can this be so?"

"So I believe," Jemal told her. "Watch him carefully." He produced a card and gave it to her. "If new people visit, or anything different happens, phone me at once."

She was anxious to please now and nodded her head energetically. "I promise."

"Accept my blessing, Bibi. There is one God and Osama is his Prophet," and he and Omar walked away.

It had been Sara calling from the plane, and Husseini leaned on the wall above the harbor now and talked to her. "When do you expect to arrive?"

"Two and a half hours."

"I look forward to seeing you."

"Well, as it happens, you're seeing Sean Dillon, too. He joined me at the last minute, just as I was leaving. He and Roper are my main associates, and they were concerned I had no backup. You must realize I've acted on my own initiative in this matter. General Ferguson is away. God knows how he'll react when he finds out."

"With anger, I suspect," Husseini said. "But I think Dillon was right to come along. I saw some bad things on my travels."

"How is it in Beirut?"

"Lots of sunshine, and everyone seems to be having a good time, though I know, having traveled through it, that just outside the city is hell on earth. Anyway, what's the plan?"

"I thought we'd start fresh tomorrow and make for St. Anthony's."

"And tonight?"

"My pilot says that the airport is nine

kilometers from the center of Beirut. He says that some place called the Tropicana on the waterfront is the place to stay."

"I haven't been, but I've heard of it," Husseini said. "So when do I see you?"

"We'll definitely have dinner tonight, but can a taxi reach your house?"

"Oh yes, it stands in a small square."

"I'd like to see it. We'll drop by on the way to the hotel. The driver can wait for us."

"Excellent," Husseini said. "See you then."

He stayed there, thinking how grateful he was, for the prospect of meeting Father John Mikali again meant so much to him, and the chance of an answer to the way his life should go. He stared out at the shipping in the harbor, absurdly happy.

At the airport, the mail plane from Tehran nosed into the VIP section where Captain Shah waited eagerly. He wore sunglasses, and was in civilian clothes: a navy blue blazer, white shirt, and striped tie. When the airstair door opened and Declan came down the steps, Shah had to restrain the impulse to salute.

"Colonel Rashid, an honor, sir."

"Good to meet you. Is everything in order?"

"I trust so, Colonel. If you'll follow me, the Range Rover is waiting. I've driven it myself. I'll deliver you to the Tropicana and walk back to the embassy. It isn't far. Allow me to take your luggage."

They reached the Range Rover and got in. Declan took the envelope from his pocket. "The presidential warrant. You've probably never seen one, but for the sake of protocol, take a look."

Shah did as he was told, then handed it back. "Remarkable, Colonel, I feel a part of history."

"It is absolutely top secret, the reason for me being here, you'll have to take my word for it." As they drove away, Declan added, "The AK-47s? Any trouble with that?"

"Not at all."

"I'm glad to hear it," Declan told him, taking in the scenery as they drove into the city.

They seemed to reach their destination in no time. Shah parked the Range Rover, gave him the keys, and departed reluctantly, leaving the colonel to book in. A duty manager escorted him to a pleasant suite with a view of the harbor.

He stood looking at it for a moment, considering his next move. He was suddenly aware of an overwhelming tiredness, his exertions of the past twenty-four hours catching up with him, took off his jacket, lay on the bed, and was promptly asleep.

12

Jemal Nadim's sources were unmatched, information constantly flooding in from the airport, streets, and harbor. He was aware of the arrival of Colonel Declan Rashid, a hero who stirred his Arab soul and yet who refused to believe as he did. And then there was Captain Sara Gideon, who greatly intrigued him, as did her unexpected passenger, Sean Dillon. Thanks to his new friendship with Ali Saif in London, Jemal knew all about the man who had been the Provisional IRA's most feared enforcer.

The prospect of Emza Khan did not faze him in the slightest. The loud voice on the telephone, the bullying tone — a hint of insecurity there. Kerim's people hanging about the Tropicana for signs of movement from Colonel Rashid had orders to rough him up, if the opportunity arose. The news from the taxi driver who'd picked up Sara and Dillon, that she'd asked him to take them to the Rue Rivoli and wait, meant that all contingencies were covered and Jemal could sit back and enjoy developments.

The taxi driver parked at the side of the small square, Sara got out and was immediately impressed with the vivid blue of the house, which seemed to tower into the sky. The door was opened at once by Bibi, who had obviously been waiting. In her black silk dress and white chador, she looked striking but seemed shy.

"I am Bibi, I am pleased to meet you."

Her English seemed halting and strained, and Sara took a chance and said in very fluent French, "And I, you. We're a little late. This is Monsieur Dillon."

Bibi was delighted and the French flowed. "It does not matter, not at all. This way."

The lift passed through five floors to the penthouse apartment. Sara took in the blue-and-white awnings, the staggering view over the city to the harbor, and Simon Husseini himself, wearing linen slacks and a deep blue shirt, and now moving to meet Sara, arms outstretched.

"You're here." He drew her to the couch. "I can't believe it. Champagne, Bibi, I put a bottle in the icebox. Mr. Dillon, we only met briefly in Paris."

Bibi moved to the kitchen and left them alone to talk, taking her time over the champagne and listening to the conversation, which she could hear perfectly. Sara was doing the talking.

"My senior pilot, Don Renard, flew jet fighters in Desert Storm, he knows that kind of country well. He'll plot a course tomorrow for Qatar and put down at al-Shaba, using the old Saudi emergency landing strip."

"Which wasn't there when I knew it," Husseini said.

"After the end of the war, when the Saudi Air Force vacated the place, they left an energy system in the hospice powered by the sun, also a satellite phone. My Codex mobile is so advanced that it can link with it, and we managed to hunt the number down online. The trouble is it hardly ever works, due to desert weather. On the way over from London, I got my pilot to try dozens of times without success, and then we had a hit."

"And you managed to get in touch?" Husseini demanded.

"Yes, but the reception was very bad and eventually cut off, and it proved impossible to get back. However, it was with a monk emailed Father Andrew, whose English was basic, but spoke Greek, which I speak a little myself. He told me there are only fifteen of them serving the hospice these days, but they actually have a doctor, aged seventy-five. Father Mikali is at present in the infirmary with a chest infection. I don't suppose that's too good for a ninety-year-old man," Sara said. "There's always the danger of pneumonia."

"There would be if we were in dear old Ireland with the rain constantly intervening," Dillon said. "But I wouldn't have thought that would be such a problem with desert conditions."

"That's true," Husseini said. "So let me make a suggestion. Speak to the desk at the Tropicana, ask them to find a doctor who could prescribe the best drugs for the infection, and we could take them with us."

"I'll drink to that," Dillon said.

"And so we shall." Husseini reached for the champagne bottle.

Bibi made her move, found her linen shopping bag, and came in from the kitchen. "I need a few things from the market."

"Tonight my friends and I dine at the Tropicana, Bibi," Husseini said. "Tomorrow we fly out to the backcountry for a few days. You'll be all right, won't you?"

"But of course," she said, hurried out, and

they heard the lift descend.

"So where were we?" Sara asked.

Declan Rashid had come awake with a start, instantly aware, the mark of a true soldier. He lay there on the bed, thinking of the situation. There was Emza Khan to look forward to, although he had no knowledge when that would be. Of course, Khan wouldn't realize that Declan knew of his al-Qaeda link, which would make for an interesting situation. In the meantime, it seemed to him a good idea to go in search of Husseini's place in Rue Rivoli. He got up, tidied himself, slipped the Colt .25 into his waistband, and left.

Early evening, the sun going down, still crowded. An obliging doorman indicated a street on the other side of the square that climbed up through the old quarter and told him he would find Rue Rivoli at the top. Declan thanked him and walked away, and the doorman nodded to two men seated at an adjacent pavement café. They might have been twins with their sunglasses, white T-shirts, and jeans, except for the fact that one had shoulder-length hair and the other's skull was shaved.

They got up and followed him through the crowds, to the narrow alley on the left climbing up through the old quarter. The one with the shaved head said, "So Omar said to rough him up."

"That's right," the other replied. "That's a great suit he's wearing. Egyptian linen, I'd say. It might be worth stripping him."

"I know one thing," his friend said. "I smell money here." They increased their pace as Declan moved faster.

He paused at the end of the street, looking up at a sign with Rue Rivoli on it and an arrow pointing across to a small square. He saw a taxi parked in a corner and the deep blue tower that must be Husseini's.

"Isn't that a grand sight," he said to himself in English and with a pronounced Irish accent. "Sweet Jesus, but my mam would have liked that."

So they rushed him, the one with a shaven head, slightly ahead of the other because of the narrowness of the alley, reaching out. Declan grabbed the right wrist, locking the arm so that the man bent over, then ran him face-first into a nearby doorway. He bounced back, nose squashed, blood on his mouth.

His friend paused, pulled a knife from his pocket, and sprang the blade. Declan pulled the Colt .25. "If you're good, I won't shoot you in the kneecap, because I need you to help your friend down the alley."

His use of Arabic caught the men by surprise. "I thought you were a Westerner."

"You thought wrong. My father was Bedu from the Empty Quarter, and his family before him."

The man closed the blade and put the knife into his pocket. "A Bedu." He shook his head. "A bad-luck day for me indeed. What happens now?"

"You'll tell me who put you up to this, I'll let you go and you'll take this fool with you."

"And if I don't?"

"I'll cripple you," Declan said calmly. "Leave you both here to crawl."

"I guess you leave me no choice. All right — his name is Omar Kerim. He's the greatest thief in the city, and he paid us to follow you if you went for a walk and rough you up."

Declan put his Colt away, took out his wallet, and extracted an American one-hundred-dollar bill, which he held out. "Take it, and take this worthless idiot with you. Tell Omar Kerim that if he doesn't stay out of this affair, he's a dead man walking."

"Aren't we all, Colonel? But I'll tell him." He pulled his friend up, pushed him in front, and followed him down the alley.

Declan turned away, heard voices, and the

door of the house opened. Dillon stepped out and whistled to the driver. Declan was amazed to see him and stepped back as the taxi moved toward Dillon and then Husseini joined him. There was laughter, the voices clear, and then the greatest shock of all, as Sara Gideon appeared. For a wild moment, he thought he was delusional, but only for a moment.

Sara laughed again and said clearly to the driver, "You can take us to the Tropicana now."

Declan backed away, allowing the alley to swallow him up, turned, and started to walk down toward the harbor, trying to make sense of what he'd seen. Dillon and Sara together in Paris made perfect sense, because they'd both represented the Ministry of Defence, but surely if they'd had any other kind of contact, he'd have noted it.

He was thinking so hard that he almost missed Bibi sitting at a coffee table outside Café Marco with two men, neither of whom he knew. He noted a large advertisement for what was described as Omar Kerim's Special Cabaret Night, the photograph on it matched exactly one of the men sitting with Bibi. It seemed highly probable that this was the same Omar his attacker had mentioned.

He hurried on to the Tropicana, approached reception, and inquired if Sara and Dillon were staying. They confirmed it for him, and also the fact that they were expected for dinner in the main restaurant in half an hour.

He went to his suite to freshen up and give himself time to decide how to handle the situation, but decided there was only one way, which was head-on. After all, unless he was greatly mistaken, he had some extraordinary information for all of them.

They were in the bar area, he saw that at once, because to his surprise Dillon was sitting at the piano, feeling out a few chords while the maître d' looked on approvingly. Satisfied with the piano, Dillon eased into an upbeat version of "As Time Goes By" and called out, "Remember the Paradise Club, Sara? Let's see if you can still strut your stuff."

Laughing, she got up, mounted three carpeted steps, and joined in, her voice deep and rich. The regular drummer came running, and a moment later, a double bass player. People were clapping, shouting their approval, and Dillon kept it going, another chorus, and then the moment came when she saw Declan in the entrance starting to clap, hands high. The look of astonishment on her face was something to see. She stood looking at him.

Someone shouted, "Get on with it, kiss him, then let's have another chorus."

So she did, on the cheek, and ran back to Dillon, calling, "One more time, and give it all you've got."

He did, the sound echoing up to the roof, while Declan went and dropped into a chair next to Husseini and grinned. "Haven't we met before somewhere?"

Husseini smiled. "What is this, Colonel, have you come to arrest me?"

"How on earth could I?" Declan asked. "We're in a foreign country." He reached for the champagne bottle in the ice bucket. "Can I have a glass?"

"You can have two if you like," Husseini told him, and they started to laugh.

Later, the three of them listened as he explained what he was doing there. "So you see," he said to Husseini, "I have my orders, but what can I do about it? Lebanon isn't Iran. In the last few words I had with Vahidi as he lay dying, I told him that if I did catch up with you, I might well suggest you keep running. He then offered me the information that has led me here so quickly." He looked serious now. "I believe he was murdered. Pushed into the next world."

"And who do you think did it?" Sara asked. "This General ben Levi you've mentioned?"

"Oh no, but al-Qaeda would," Declan told her.

Dillon said, "To what purpose?"

"To help get their hands on that bomb of Simon's. And here's a question for you and Sean, Sara. What would you say if I told you that Emza Khan is up to his neck in al-Qaeda?"

Sara turned to Sean and smiled savagely. "I knew it, Sean, I damn well knew it. It's what I was trying to suggest to Ferguson, and he knew I was right."

"Just hang on." Dillon turned to Declan. "Where's your proof?"

"To start with, I have a spy in his household, but you can ask Khan himself. He's due to join us on the spurious excuse of visiting Cyrus Holdings in Beirut. He'll be expecting to see me, but not you." He took an envelope from his pocket. "Rather than explaining it all, I've written everything down. Read this. You'll find it very revealing."

"Give it here," Dillon said. Declan flicked it across, and Sara and Husseini squeezed in to read what was inside.

Declan waved to the wine waiter. "Another bottle of champagne. I think we're going to need it."

When they were done, Dillon said, "I never liked him, but his business success seemed to speak for itself. I mean, he's a billionaire, for God's sake."

"The epitome of the man who had everything," Sara said.

"And threw in his lot with al-Qaeda," Declan said. "The act of a maniac."

"And one of incredible stupidity," Declan said. "To put yourself in the hands of such people is an act of suicide."

"Well, I'll drink to that," Dillon said, reached for the bottle, and refilled the glasses. "So where does this leave us?"

"With the fact that Emza Khan is to arrive soon to supervise the kidnapping of Simon Husseini and arrange his onward passage to wherever the al-Qaeda council decides."

"And what about the rest of us?" Sara asked.

"Oh, the rough stuff will be carried out by gangsters, Omar Kerim and his men under the direction of Jemal Nadim."

"So they could get nasty," Sara said.

"Already have," Declan told her. "I took a walk up toward Rue Rivoli earlier and was followed all the way from the Tropicana by two of Omar's men, who attacked me."

"You don't look damaged."

"I'm a paratrooper. They were clowns. The first one broke his nose falling into a door, the second was persuaded by my suggestion that I put a bullet in the kneecap to inform on Omar."

"The kneecap? That's a ritual IRA punishment," she said.

"For God's sake, woman," Dillon told her, "his mother was Irish. Now, enough of this. What's our next move?"

"I've already been through that when we were at Simon's," Sara said. "Don Renard plots a course for Qatar. On the way, we put down in the desert on the emergency landing strip at al-Shaba and visit St. Anthony's."

"And then what?" Dillon asked. "I mean, what next for Simon Husseini? Does he decide to be a novice and end his days in the desert?" He turned to Husseini. "I hope you don't mind me raising the point."

"And don't think I'm unaware of it," Husseini told him. "To be honest, I've just taken this odyssey step by step. As you know, the beginning just happened, and I'm not sure about the ending now."

"And none of us will be until we experience it," Declan put in. He turned to Sara. "Am I right that you discussed the flight plan for the trip to St. Anthony's while you were at Husseini's?"

"That's right," Sara said. "Why do you ask?"

"Was Bibi present?"

Husseini said, "Yes, she met Sara and Dillon, served us drinks, then left to go to the market."

"Then we've got trouble. When I was walking back to meet you at the Tropicana, I saw her sitting at a table outside Café Marco, deep in conversation with two men. One of them was definitely Omar. The other had steel glasses and an Arab head cloth."

"Jemal Nadim," Husseini said.

"So it's looking as if al-Qaeda has their hooks in her," Declan told him.

Sara said, "But let's accept that's the way it is and leave it alone. Don't let Bibi know we're on to her. You can tell her we're not leaving until eleven o'clock in the morning, while I check with Don at the airport and arrange a six a.m. start, or something like that."

"That sounds good to me," Dillon said. "So Emza Khan and his crew find out we're not around for kidnapping or murder, but as they'll know our destination, thanks to Bibi, they'll simply follow us."

"We'll sort that out when it happens," Declan said. "For the moment, am I the only one who realizes we haven't eaten? Can we go in now?"

There was laughter, they went up the stairs into the dining room, and Sara half turned to him. "It seems it was right what you said to Vahidi. That if you caught up with Husseini, maybe you'd tell him to keep on running."

"Yes, it must be confusing for you."

"More so for you, I think. It must be very difficult." She took his right hand and squeezed it. "We're on your side, Declan."

"Yes, I know that."

"Well, you guys get started. I don't want a first course anyway, but I want to call Don at his airport hotel. I'll join you later."

She found Renard with no difficulty, he and Jane Green comfortable enough at the airport where they could keep an eye on preparations for the onward flight. Sara had been frank in warning Don that they could expect hazardous duty. She'd left open what that entailed, but what was developing — that was something else again.

"Is Jane there?"

"She sure is."

"Well, put this on speaker and listen well. Both of you are still serving officers on the reserve?"

"That's correct," they chorused.

"Then as an operative of the Secret Intelligence Service, I can invoke the Official Secrets Act. Do you agree to be bound by that?"

"Of course," Don said as Jane joined in with, "Absolutely."

"All right. As you've known for some time, Don, I work with Sean Dillon under the command of General Charles Ferguson directly for the Prime Minister. Anything we touch is of prime importance."

"That's what I've always understood."

"We've joined up with Colonel Declan Rashid of the Iranian Army. Our task is to get Simon Husseini in one piece to this St. Anthony's Hospice I've mentioned. The problem is, I've just heard there's a Falcon coming in from the UK carrying Emza Khan, chairman of Cyrus Holdings."

"We know him well," Don said. "Often flies out of Northolt. Just let me check, there's a screen in the room. Yes, it's due in an hour, and a couple of right bastards in the cockpit."

"Why do you say that?"

"Because they are," Jane called. "They're ex–Russian Air Force. Ivan Kerimov and Dimitri Lisin. Good pilots, but they're all hands, if you follow me, and drink like fish. It's said they're something to do with Russian intelligence, but that could be gossip."

"So, in a way, they're like you two, up for hazardous duty."

"I suppose there could be something in that," Jane agreed.

"To cut to the chase," Sara said. "What would an old Afghanistan hand say if I told her that we have positive proof that Emza Khan is seriously involved with al-Qaeda?"

"That would sound absurd coming from anyone else," Don said. "But from you, I've got to believe it. Does that hold for you, Jane?"

"Of course it does," Jane said. "Where is this going?"

"He could make a lot of trouble for us. We're making sure that people think we're flying out at eleven tomorrow. How early could we make it if we wanted to catch them napping?"

"Six o'clock is good," Don said. "We could just hang in there, with everyone on board, then suddenly decide to go."

Jane cut in. "Once they know we've gone,

though, I'm sure they'll get their act together fast. Those Russians are good, I've
got to admit that."

"Point taken. We'll see you round dawn,
then."

Next she contacted Holland Park.

"Damn you, Sara Gideon, I've never been
so worried. You drive a man mad," Roper
told her.

Sara cut in, "Shut up, Giles, time is
limited. Have you spoken to Ferguson yet?
If so, I expect he's frothing at the mouth."

"Actually, he was strangely calm. I told
him about Husseini's call, your wild decision to go, and Dillon's hot pursuit. His
actual words were 'Thank God Dillon is
there to watch her back. I suppose she'll be
in touch when she's got something to say. Is
it all right if I go back to work now?' "

"See if he's more impressed with this.
Declan Rashid turned up from Tehran with
orders from the minister of war to get his
hands on Husseini and bring him back."

"Well, he managed that pretty damn
quick."

"Declan got information from Husseini's
security man that led him straight to
Beirut."

"So it's Declan, is it? You seem to be terribly chummy with what I know Dillon

describes as the enemy."

"He's no more the enemy than I am. He's an Iranian citizen whose mother was Irish."

Roper said, "Sara, my love, it's obvious to me that you're so much on Rashid's side that the only conclusion must be that you fancy him. He's had an outstanding record with the Iranian Army, he's likely to make general one of these days. Why would he throw all that away?"

"Because he's on our *side,* Giles. And what I'm going to tell you now will have General Charles Ferguson gasping to hear more."

"So what would that be?" Roper sounded weary. "Get on with it, Sara."

"We've uncovered a plot, thanks to Declan, an al-Qaeda plot to murder him and then kidnap Simon Husseini. I'm sure you realized for what purpose: They want the bomb."

Roper stayed surprisingly calm. "And when is all this due to happen?"

"There's a Falcon out of London, flying here with a top man appointed by the council. His aircraft will transport Husseini to wherever his masters order. He's arriving here in an hour, flown in, I'm told, by a couple of very questionable Russian pilots named Ivan Kerimov and Dimitri Lisin. I'd

331

note the names in your files for future reference. I'd have thought Cyrus Holdings could have found a better class of pilot, but then, I suppose they suit their boss's purpose."

Roper said, "Hang on, where are we going with this?"

"Let me be the first to break the good news," Sara said. "Thanks to Declan, we now know that Emza Khan is up to his neck in al-Qaeda. But Emza Khan doesn't realize that Declan is here, and knows what he is."

"And presumably, he isn't aware of you and Dillon being around, either."

"I'm afraid not. Poor him."

"So what happens when the big confrontation takes place?"

"Not much, I hope. We're going to get the hell out of here tomorrow, fly down to Saudi, and drop in at a place called St. Anthony's Hospice." She explained why, and finished with, "I hope you've been recording all this, Giles."

"Of course I have. I'll knock it all into shape and get it to Ferguson as quickly as possible. It's going to make the old devil's day. It explains so much."

"Everybody else is having dinner right now, but I wanted to get it all to you to keep

Ferguson happy, if such a thing were possible."

"Take care. You never know where you are with Russians."

"I know what you mean. Now I'm going to go eat. Bye, Giles."

She went. Roper punched a button on one of his computers and watched as it transcribed his recording of the exchange with Sara into print. It was certainly going to make Ferguson sit up and take notice.

The dinner had reached the brandy and coffee stage when Sara arrived. Dillon said, "What kept you?"

"I was talking to the hotel doctor on the phone. I told him about Father Mikali, and he's having a load of special drugs sent round at once."

The maître d' approached, concerned. "Madame has missed dinner. What may I do?"

"Scrambled eggs and a tossed salad," Sara told him. "If there's any champagne left, pour me a glass; if not, find a fresh bottle."

"You haven't answered," Dillon told her. "The doctor couldn't have taken that long."

"I was also reporting in to Roper and bringing him up to date on where we are in this rather convoluted affair."

"An apt description," Declan said.

"He's spoken to Ferguson, who took the brief account of my rebellion and Dillon's pursuit with extraordinary calm. I've given Roper a full and frank account, including your situations as I see them, Declan and Simon."

Husseini said, "I would imagine the information about Emza Khan will disturb Ferguson greatly."

"Oh, not at all," Sara said. "He'll be pleased to have been proved right. He's been convinced for a long time that there was something dodgy about Khan."

At that moment the maître d' appeared in person bearing the tossed salad and scrambled eggs, followed by the wine waiter with another bottle of champagne in an ice bucket. They served them with a flourish.

"Thank you, it looks marvelous," Sara said. "Am I right, aren't you expecting Mr. Emza Khan tonight?"

"Indeed we are," the maître d' told her. "In fact, I've just had notice from the airport that they landed forty-five minutes ago. Is Madame familiar with this gentleman?"

"Yes, I think you could say that," Sara said. "But I'd better eat my eggs before they get cold," and she proceeded to do so.

"Are they good?" Dillon asked.

"Excellent."

"Well, enjoy them while you can. When you have a moment, turn around. You'll find Khan in the flesh."

The maître d' was in the act of bowing to Emza Khan, who looked transfixed as both Husseini and Declan stood up. His face was a mixture of shock and horror. The two Russians stood behind him, tough, cynical-looking individuals, sporting an unshaven look but handsome in uniform, each of them with four gold rings on his sleeve.

The maître d' moved, leading the way toward a booth at the back of the room. Sara remained seated as they approached, with Dillon, Husseini, and Declan standing behind her.

Dillon smiled cheerfully. "The top of the morning to you, Emza."

Emza paused, his voice low, as he ignored Dillon and spoke to Husseini and Declan.

"You've disgraced your family and your regiment," he hissed at Declan. "And you, Husseini, have betrayed your country. May you rot in hell for your perfidy." He glared at Sara. "You murdered my son, you whore. I'll see you burn in hell for that."

He continued to follow the maître d', and Kerimov glanced admiringly at Sara and said in Russian to his friend, "Now, there's a real woman for you. I wonder if anything is on offer?"

"Careful, you stupid idiot," she said in Russian. "Continue to keep company with a dog like Emza Khan, you're likely to catch fleas."

Both of them were startled by her fluency, and Kerimov clapped and replied in Russian, "Thank you for such excellent advice. We'll take it."

He and his partner moved to join Khan at the end of the room, and Dillon, Husseini, and Declan sat down as the wine waiter hurried over to freshen the drinks. Husseini said, "What on earth is Khan up to? He's acting as if he's in the clear. It doesn't make sense."

Sara said, "It does if you consider the spot the Iranian government is in. It's only been a little more than a week since that accident in Tehran, but the word's getting out. They've got to find a way to contain it, and the last thing they need is a scandal."

"So what are they waiting for, these people in Tehran?" Husseini demanded.

"They're desperately hoping that Declan will manage to get his hands on you," Sara said. "And the ironic thing is that he has, just not the way they expected."

"Which raises the question, what are you going to do?" Dillon said to Declan. "Where would you go?"

"As has been said, I have an Irish passport," Declan told him. "What hasn't, is that my mother inherited a country estate near Galway from an uncle on her mother's side. It came to me on her death and is managed by lawyers, who are family cousins."

"God help us, but I've difficulty in seeing you playing the squireen in a tweed cap, fishing for trout in Galway," Dillon told him.

Declan said, "So many years of war, and the possibility of death has taught me that the only way of coping is to take each day as it comes. So, enough of talking. We know what lies ahead tomorrow, so let Emza Khan see us retire for the night to grab four or five hours before sneaking out at dawn."

"Let's do it." Sara stood up, glanced at the enemy, and walked out, pausing to shake hands with the maître d'. "Lovely meal," she said loud enough to be heard at Khan's table. "We're leaving for Qatar in the morning, flying out around eleven. We'll have a late breakfast with you before we go."

"A pleasure to serve you," he said.

Dillon muttered, "Excellent performance, full marks."

She half turned, smiled at him, and led

337

the way out.

The meal was excellent, but for Emza Khan, the pilots were the problem, drinking huge amounts of vodka and talking to each other in Russian. He didn't speak the language, which was good, because their opinion of him was low. When his phone sounded it came as a relief, and he went out to the terrace and discovered it was the Master.

"I know what's going on, so just listen. I gather that Husseini has a burning need to visit this Father John Mikali at St. Anthony's Hospice. Our need, on the other hand, is to kidnap Husseini and dispose of Rashid."

"Which is why we will follow them to the hospice and confront them there," Khan said.

"I have a better idea. Leave *before* them. When they arrive and find you holding Mikali hostage, the effect on Husseini will be dramatic, especially when the threat is to blow out the old man's brains. Husseini would do an exchange on the instant, I promise you."

"But, of course, Master," Emza Khan said. "Husseini is the kind of holy fool who *would* sacrifice himself."

"No need for a gang of cutthroats. I'd take Jemal and Omar to back you up, but no more. After all, you have the Russians."

"Yes, that would do it."

"I'll speak to Jemal and order him to report to you as soon as possible with Omar, but I think speed is of the essence here, so get moving and don't take no for an answer from those Russians. I can only envy your inevitable success."

Renewed in spirit, Emza Khan bustled into the restaurant and said, "Things have changed, so follow me to my suite to discuss it."

"Discuss what?" Kerimov demanded.

"Oh, the extra money I'm putting into your worthless pockets," and suddenly he was the old Emza Khan again, and smiling as he led the way out.

■ ■ ■ ■

St. Anthony's Hospice
Saudi Arabia

■ ■ ■ ■

13

It was no problem for Kerimov to obtain a new departure slot from the Rafic Hariri Airport. The flight plan was for Qatar, eight hundred miles away and mainly over desert. The stop-off at the emergency airstrip close to the St. Anthony's Hospice at al-Shaba was technically illegal, but air traffic control was notoriously easygoing in Arab airspace. Many pilots simply vanished from the air if it suited them to switch off communication for a period.

Things had gone exactly as the Master had suggested. He had spoken to Jemal, who had accepted without a moment's argument, and Jemal had persuaded Omar that it could do him a lot of good in the council's eyes.

An approach by Kerimov to the right person, a greasing of palms, and they had taken off at three-thirty in the morning. They had an eight-hundred-mile flight ahead of them, but as Kerimov said, they were in no hurry, had already won the engagement.

They were having a small drinks party in the cabin, Emza Khan, Jemal, and Omar. Kerimov joined them, leaving Lisin in the cockpit sitting back reading a magazine while the plane flew on autopilot.

In the cabin, Khan had a martini cocktail, Kerimov vodka, and so did Omar. Only Jemal refused a drink, although he did smoke Turkish cigarettes. He was indulging in one now and examining an old *National Geographic* magazine. He passed it to Emza Khan.

"There's a five-page article on this St. Anthony's Hospice. Apparently, it's run by Greek Orthodox monks. It's at a small oasis, a well that hasn't run dry in several hundred years."

Khan examined it. "How did it start?"

Jemal said, "Food and lodging for travelers going south to the Oman. They offered medical aid as well, a tradition."

"Why Greek monks?" Emza Khan asked. "I could never see the point of that. Living at the back of beyond in total desolation. What does it prove?"

"Jesus Christ spent forty days and nights in the wilderness, we are told in the Christian Bible, and found truth when God spoke to him. The monks seek the same salvation."

"They must be soft in the head," Khan said. "And I thought this Father Mikali was supposed to be someone special."

Jemal said, "I was at the Sorbonne in Paris in my youth, studying comparative religion. He was a professor, wrote books, everybody respected him."

He suddenly recognized how much he disliked Khan, particularly when Khan said harshly, "Then why did he retire to such a godforsaken place at his age?"

"Because the search for Allah and meaning and purpose is never-ending," Jemal told him. "But enough of this, let's move on. What is our plan when we land?"

Kerimov said, "As far as I'm concerned, the important thing is making sure the Falcon is safe and secure and ready to get us out of here when we're ready to leave."

"What are you saying?" Omar demanded.

"That Lisin and I aren't here to do any shooting, we're here to guard the plane and make sure it's available for a quick departure."

"That's not good enough," Emza Khan told him. "We had an agreement."

"Lisin and I were in the military. We've seen things go wrong for the stupidest of reasons too many times, so this isn't up for argument."

Omar took over. "We've got all the right weapons, so there's no problem there. The enemy are fifteen monks, the eldest ninety and the others very probably close behind him." He turned to Jemal. "I know where I stand, I kill people for a living, but what about you, old friend?"

"I can handle it," Jemal said. "But I'm sure it won't be necessary." He glanced at Emza Khan. "What about you, have you ever fired a gun?"

"You know who I am. It's never been necessary," Khan said. "I'm perfectly content for you two to handle matters."

Jemal said, "Somehow, I thought that's what you'd say." He got up. "I don't know what the rest of you are going to do, but I'm taking one of those backseats for a couple of hours' sleep. I'd advise you to do the same."

Which they did, Ivan Kerimov taking a front one up by the cockpit, Omar on the opposite of Jemal, and Emza Khan halfway along, easing his chair back and thinking about things as someone dimmed the lights.

He was considering his problematical future. With Husseini on his hands, he had two interesting options. On the one hand,

346

he was a man desperately wanted by al-Qaeda. On the other hand, the government in Tehran would be only too willing to pardon past sins when the prize he was offering was Husseini and his bomb. So — what should he do? He lay back a little farther, closed his eyes, and started analyzing the situation again.

Earlier, at Rafic Hariri, Jane Green stirred and came half awake as she heard a plane take off, quite loud, then die away into the distance. She lay there wondering about it, made to get up, and then another plane took off, so she drifted into sleep again. An hour passed and she came awake with a jerk to a knock on the door, and when she got up and opened it, found Sara standing there.

"What's happened?" Jane asked, coming awake fast.

"They've stolen a march on us." Sara brushed past. "Got out of here around three-thirty with a flight plan for Qatar. It didn't feature on the screen until a short while ago. So much for us hoping to make a quick departure around six. We got here, went to check on our plane, and discovered their Falcon gone."

Jane was dressing hurriedly. "What are the guys doing?"

"Buying a fast takeoff on my behalf," Sara said. "There are times when owning a bank has its uses."

"I'm sure that's true." Jane grabbed her old military bag, ran around the room recovering the few things she'd unpacked, and stuffed them in. "Right, ready to go. Afghanistan was a good learning curve."

"You can say that again," Sara told her. "Now, let's go and see how our gallant lads have progressed."

They hurried to the lift, and as they got in, Sara's Codex sounded. As they descended, Dillon said, "It's taken care of. Ready to go."

"I'm with Jane now and we're on our way," she said. "Did you have enough cash to handle it?"

"You know I always keep five thousand dollars in my contingency kit. I'm taking care of it. No worries. Just get yourselves down here."

Don Renard was in the cockpit of the Gideon, turning the engines over, and Simon Husseini was already on board. Declan was standing by the steps up the airstair with Dillon. There was a doorway nearby, a light above it. A man stepped out in a porter's uniform and nodded, another in similar garb lurking behind him.

"They would appear to be waiting for you," Declan commented.

Dillon went to meet them, Declan followed him, and as they approached the doorway, Dillon said, "Congratulations on your efficiency, Abu, you've organized things damn quickly." He took a roll of bills from his pocket. "So what's the damage? You said a thousand."

The man behind Abu said, "Oh, I think you can do a lot better than that." He stepped around his friend and produced some kind of pistol. Declan moved with incredible speed, twisting it savagely out of the man's grip and at the same moment forming a Phoenix Fist with his right hand, stabbing into the temple, knocking the man out on the instant.

The first one was horrified. "Listen, there's been a mistake."

"Yes, and you made it." Dillon peeled ten one-hundred-dollar bills from his roll and dropped them fluttering down at the man's feet. "There you are, a thousand dollars. I always keep my promises."

The man was mesmerized. "Yes, I can see that."

Next, Dillon produced his Colt .25. "This holds hollow-point cartridges. If I decided to shoot you in the kneecap, it would blow it clean off."

The man was panic-stricken. "Please, tell me what I must do to atone."

"Oh, that's simple enough. How many people were on the Falcon that left earlier?"

"Two pilots and three passengers."

"And who were they?"

The man was all eagerness now. "I've never seen the pilots before, but I was told they were Russian and the boss man was Muslim, but a stranger to me."

"And the other two?"

"Omar Kerim, a dangerous man to know, and Jemal Nadim."

"And what does he do?"

"He runs the Army of God."

"I see, there is one God and his Prophet is Osama." There was instant terror on the face in the yellow light. "Oh, go on, get out of it," Dillon said. "And take your friend with you." He turned to Declan. "Nice move, Colonel, you must show me sometime."

The two women were just arriving, and Jane boarded instantly. Sara said, "Problems, Sean?"

"Not so you'd notice, but let's get out of here while the going's good. The trouble these days is the way sympathizers to Osama's message turn up at every level of society."

Jane peered out. "Come on, best we get moving."

They went up the steps, and the airstair door closed. Jane joined Don Renard in the cockpit, they started to roll even before the others had settled themselves, turned into position, roared down the runway, and lifted, climbing into the comforting darkness.

Dillon peered out and back at the lights of the airport. "So a not-so-fond farewell to Beirut. In the circumstances, I don't think we should rely on being welcomed back." He smiled wryly at Husseini. "Sorry about that."

"Don't worry, I've got more important things to think about," Husseini told him, leaned back, and closed his eyes.

Half an hour into the flight, Don Renard emerged from the cockpit to find Husseini still apparently dozing and the others enjoying a pot of black coffee. He helped himself and said, "Even if we push our speed as far as we can, we'll still be landing at least an hour and a half after the opposition. What are we going to do?"

"Tell me something," Sara said. "How

many times did you try to connect me and my Codex to their satellite phone system on the flight from London?"

"Dozens," he said. "Any kind of bad weather affects the system. I think the one time we did get through was just a fluke."

Declan, peering out, said, "You can't find fault with it tonight. Remember that I have Bedouin forefathers from the Oman and the Empty Quarter, so I have a feel for how things work round here. To start with, the moon is full and looks different from the norm, and there is a total lack of wind."

"Then let's have another go, Don," Sara said. "If we could warn them to expect unwelcome visitors, it would be good."

He vanished into the cockpit, and Husseini said, "At least I could know how Mikali is doing."

"You might even get to speak to him," Dillon said.

"Well, we'll see, shall we?" Sara said, and they sat, waiting, as the plane droned on into the night.

At St. Anthony's Hospice, the enormous moon had moved on from the west, bathing everything in harsh white light. In the oasis fed by the well, goats and camels stirred, and Brother Andrew, reading an English primer, picked up his lantern and started back toward the hospice. He was not concerned if the animals were restless, for there was nowhere for them to go in all that desolation.

At thirty, he was by far the youngest member of the order, a male nurse in Athens whose wife had died in childbirth. Having lost his way in life, the offer of a place in the order from his uncle, Abbot Joseph, had brought him to the hospice.

He entered the ancient buildings through a rear door and walked along a corridor that brought him to the infirmary. Seated at the center table, dozing, was Father Peter, so small that he seemed swallowed up by his black robes. In his mid-seventies, he had once been an army doctor. There was a row of beds, six of them empty, and Father John Mikali in the seventh, his eyes closed.

He wore a black cowl, so that only the face and silver beard showed. His skin was almost transparent, drawn tightly over the cheekbones in a noble face. His eyes suddenly opened, and he smiled and his voice was still strong.

Andrew asked in English, "How are you, Father? Any pain at the moment?"

"Not as bad as it has been."

"We still have an ample supply of morphine, thanks to the battle packs the Saudi Air Force left us."

"I can manage at the moment," Mikali said. "But I must say your English improves daily. Speak it as often as you can."

"That's due to you, Father."

"Not at all. Speak it aloud to yourself, if that's the only way. It's the road to fluency, I assure you."

Before Andrew could reply, Brother Damien came in from the kitchen. An octogenarian, with a white apron over his black robe, he was carrying a two-handed small beaker.

"Get this down you and you'll feel much better," he told Mikali.

Andrew said, "What is it, what's so special?"

"It's a tisane of honey, fruit juice, and tea. Guaranteed to bring him back to life," Damien answered. "Raise him if you can."

Andrew managed to sit Mikali up, thanks to a back support, and Damien stood beside him, clutching the beaker in both hands, pouring carefully.

He paused and said, "Is that good?"

"Excellent," Mikali told him. "I'll have a little more."

But before Damien could pour, there was the sound of a bell from outside and Andrew swung around, amazement on his face.

"Blessed Mary," he said. "It's the satellite phone system."

"Now, who can that be?" Father Mikali asked. "Better answer it before they go away again, whoever they are. It's the first call we've had in a couple of months."

Andrew ran out into the corridor, opened the black oak door to the vestry, and hurried in. The stone walls had been painted white. There were shelves stacked with manuscript registers and books and various religious vestments hanging from rails. There were also two wooden desks, one with an old-fashioned typewriter, paper stacked beside it, all very businesslike; the other contained the telephone equipment, which was also old, with a fixed microphone.

Andrew sat down and flicked a switch. "This is St. Anthony's Hospice."

He had spoken in Greek, and Sara Gideon answered in the same language. "I am receiving you loud and clear." She changed to English. "I am the woman who was asking after Father Mikali. Do you remember me?"

"Of course," Andrew said. "Who are you?"

"Tell me first, is he still with you?"

"Yes, he is, a patient in the infirmary."

"We have one of his oldest friends on

355

board my plane, Simon Husseini. It's of vital importance that he speak to Father Mikali. Will you tell him?"

"Yes, but he'll need to come to this phone, and that means the wheelchair. This is so exciting. We seldom get calls, so please be patient."

He ran back to the ward where they were all waiting, and his Uncle Joseph, the abbot, had arrived, disturbed by the bell sounding from the vestry. "What is it?" he demanded.

"A call from a plane which intends to land here," Andrew told him, running to an ancient wheelchair in the corner, swinging it around, and approaching Mikali. "Apparently, an old friend of yours is coming to see you, Father," he told Mikali. "A Simon Husseini."

There was astonishment on Mikali's face. "Simon on his way here? I can't believe it."

"But you must come now." Andrew pulled the bedcovers aside. "Let me ease you into the wheelchair. I'm afraid we may lose the connection."

Abbot Joseph said to the rest, "You must leave the vestry clear and listen from the corridor."

He waved everyone to one side to allow Andrew and Mikali free passage and followed, with the others trailing beside.

On the Gideon, the door to the cockpit stood open and, thanks to the genius who had produced the Codex, with the speaker switched on, everyone on board was able to follow the conversation that now took place. In the vestry at the hospice, it was the same, thanks to the transmitter loudspeaker. The abbot and Brother Andrew stood on either side of Mikali in his wheelchair, while, the word having spread, a dozen brothers crowded together in the corridor.

Mikali spoke into the microphone, a certain caution in his voice. "Simon Husseini, can this be you?"

"Oh yes, Father. I assure you it's me, and I can prove it. As a young lecturer at the Sorbonne, I was one of the very first to be exposed to your concept of essential goodness, because you gave me a typescript to consider before the famous book was published."

Mikali laughed in delight. "Yes, I did, and you presented me with a review within twenty-four hours. So, Simon, I have followed your career with the greatest interest and I know the predicament you have found yourself in with the Iranian government. How are your dear mother and your daughter? Well, I trust?"

"No, they were recently killed in a road accident in Tehran."

Mikali was shocked. "My dear friend, what can I say? May they rest in peace. But this changes everything for you, I think?"

"I'm running away from a situation I can't face in order to see you and find out if you can offer me a solution," Husseini carried on. "I've created in theory the possibility of a nuclear bomb four times more powerful than any at present existing. My government wants it, probably Russia and China, and certainly the UK and America. I've even got al-Qaeda wanting it."

"So what is your problem?" Mikali asked.

"What if I don't want anyone to have it? What if I destroy my own work?"

"My dear friend, that's a quixotic approach indeed which would do you little good. A scientist is like an explorer, searching for something that already exists. To destroy your case notes would be pointless. Someone else would just come along. Let me put it this way: Einstein didn't create relativity, he discovered it."

"So where does that leave your theory that essential goodness is the most important building block in life, Father?"

"Let me ask you a question," Mikali said.

"Who are these people on the plane with you?"

"Good people, and on my side."

"And you were coming to seek my advice and for no other reason?"

"That was the idea, but al-Qaeda discovered our intention, stole a march on us, and intend to land at al-Shaba to ambush us. It's me they want.

"Then why are you bothering to come?"

"Well, we can't just leave you to handle such a thing on your own."

There was a crackling over the sound system, a slight buzz, and the Gideon was buffeted by a sudden wind.

"Ah, I see now." Mikali raised his voice. "You're coming to save us. A perfect example of essential goodness in action. When may we expect these people you speak of?"

"In an hour or so. On their plane are two pilots and three passengers. There would be no profit in them harming you or your people, as long as you avoid confrontation. It's me they want, not you. We will be there, I promise you, an hour and a half after they arrive."

"And will you leave with them?" Mikali asked.

But to that, there could be no answer, for the crackling over the sound system developed into a roaring that drowned out any intelligible conversation.

Mikali said to the abbot, "It's unlikely we'll get them back. I suggest you order everyone into the infirmary, and, with your permission, I'd like to try to explain to them what's going on. I don't think we've got long before the plane that Husseini warned us against gets here."

"Of course." The abbot raised his voice. "I want you all in the infirmary as quickly as possible. Now, go."

Whispering to each other, they turned obediently and did as ordered, followed by the abbot, and Andrew pushing the wheel-chair. They crowded into the infirmary, and Mikali addressed them.

"Very soon now, a plane will land on the airstrip and some of the men on board will come to see us, particularly me. They are not good people, but do as they say and I don't think any harm will come to you. They are waiting for another plane to arrive. If they speak to you, don't mention that you know the second plane will be coming. Speak Greek between yourselves. I suspect they can't, and will tend to leave you alone. The people on the other plane *are* our friends. I can't tell you what will happen when they arrive, because I don't know. May God bless all of us."

The brothers were murmuring among themselves, and some looked anxious. The abbot said, "We are all brothers in the sight of God. He will help us get through this. Now, go about your usual work and we'll see what happens."

On the Gideon, Don Renard glanced out of the cockpit into the cabin. "I'm afraid we've lost it again."

"Don't worry, what we got was useful," Sara told him. "We know what's going on at the hospice now."

"And that's fine," Dillon said. "But it makes one thing clear. That there's nothing the brothers can do to help themselves."

"True," Declan said. "And they can't help us, either. When Emza Khan and his friends arrive, the brothers will have no option but to comply with their demands. They're only pawns in this game. Al-Qaeda only wants Husseini, and they want him alive. He's absolutely no use to them dead."

Dillon said grimly, "And he's no use to them alive if he's not willing to toe the line and produce that bomb."

There was silence for a while, Declan frowning slightly, Dillon glancing from one to another, Husseini perfectly calm, and

Sara looking troubled.

Husseini said to her, "You attended the Military Academy at Sandhurst. Didn't they have a saying: Difficult decisions are the privilege of rank?"

"Yes, they do," she said.

"Good, I must bear that in mind." He sat down in the seat opposite Dillon, reached for his bag, opened it, and produced a small black-and-silver notebook, a tiny green light throbbing in it. He also took out a pad and an envelope.

Dillon said, "Is that notebook electronic?"

"A Sonic," Husseini told him. "It can only be opened by a code word. It's very useful for preserving the important things in life."

He wrote quickly on the pad as the Gideon droned on, tore out the sheet, folded it, then put it in the envelope, sealed it, and passed it to Dillon.

"What's this?" Dillon asked.

"We live in dangerous times. The contents are self-explanatory. I give it to you because you are the great survivor. You'll know when it's right to open it."

Dillon frowned, but put it into an inside pocket. Husseini dropped the pad into his bag, slipped the Sonic into his left jacket pocket, closed his eyes, and leaned back.

■ ■ ■ ■

It was just after six a.m. when the Cyrus
Holdings Falcon came in low from the
north at four thousand feet and descending.
There was no sun, dark cloud formations
blanketing the area, a rumble of thunder in
the distance, and as they went down, it
became obvious that there was considerable
wind at ground level.

They came in at a thousand feet, but the
desert below looked uninviting, and then
they saw the oasis and palm trees. Kerimov,
who had the control column, took her right
down to St. Anthony's Hospice, looming
out of the early-morning gloom, lights at
various windows, camels and goats scattering, and Kerimov and Lisin laughing.

"That's wakened the sods up," Kerimov
said. "What a dump."

"You can say that again," Lisin agreed.

Kerimov turned and came back at six
hundred feet, and several brothers appeared
through the front door of the hospice and
stood, staring up.

"That's given them a shake," Kerimov
said. "Down we go."

Emza Khan, Jemal, and Omar had seen
all this from the cabin windows. Khan said,

"What kind of people would live in such a place?"

"Well, they've been doing it for a thousand years or more," Jemal said. "They believe in God, but in their own way."

Kerimov swung around into the wind and dropped down to an aircraft hangar, a few concrete buildings on each side and a small control tower. He kept going, as far as he could take it, halting about a hundred and fifty yards from the hospice.

When Kerimov switched off, Lisin opened the door and went down the steps. With the engine stopped, the only sound was the moaning of the wind in the thornbushes and around the derelict buildings. Kerimov emerged and stood halfway down the steps.

"There's something spooky about a decaying airfield. I'm not sure why, but it makes me feel strange."

Lisin said, "Jet fighters used it for emergency landings in Desert Storm. Probably a few good men died here." Kerimov stiffened. "There's a small welcoming committee. We'd better get back inside and prepare to receive them."

Omar was bringing out weapons, three AK-47s, four Makarovs. Jemal said to Kerimov, "During the flight, you did try that satellite number I gave you for the hospice?"

"Several times, but it didn't work. Deserts can be difficult places for reception."

Omar said, "Never mind that. There's a Makarov each for you, and you can take one of the AKs. You're still not coming with us?"

"Absolutely not. I've given you my reasons, and they're sound."

"Enough of this," Emza Khan said. "I'm perfectly content for you and Omar to take care of this," he told Jemal. "A few Greek monks can't possibly give us a problem." He peered outside. "And here they are."

Brother Andrew was standing at the bottom of the steps with the Brothers Mark and Luke. Emza Khan appeared and stared down at them, frowning.

He said, "Allah aid me, they probably don't even speak English."

"I do," Andrew said. "But you are right. We are a Greek order and most of my brothers speak only Greek. Abbot Joseph has sent me to inquire as to your purpose in visiting us."

"You have a priest here, a Father John Mikali. I want to see him. He is here, I presume?"

"Oh yes, a patient in the infirmary."

"Let's go."

"Of course."

Andrew and his brothers started off and

Emza Khan followed, Jemal and Omar walking together, each with an AK-47 at the ready.

They found Mikali in his wheelchair, a blanket over his knees, another around his shoulders. The abbot stood to one side, Father Peter the other. Jemal and Omar stood on either side of the door, rifles ready.

Andrew said, "This is Abbot Joseph, and the other, Father Peter, our doctor." Stretching the truth, he added, "I need to translate if you wish to talk to them. You wished to meet Father John Mikali. This is he, and he does speak English."

"Who are you people?" Mikali demanded. "What do you want with me?"

"My name is Emza Khan and I don't want you, I want a man named Simon Husseini, who is on his way here to see you. You and he are old friends, and don't try to deny it."

"Why should I, but what do you want him for?"

"That's nothing to do with you. He should be here in about an hour and a half."

"What do you intend to do with him?"

"Fly away to another country. Behave yourselves for the next few hours and nothing will happen to you. Don't, and I'll have the abbot shot."

"That's hard to argue with," Mikali said.

■ ■ ■ ■

On the Gideon, they were holding a council of war, and Husseini was speaking.

"I'm worried about everyone in the hospice, and not just John Mikali. It's my fault that they are all greatly at risk from these people, so what do I do about it? It's me that Emza Khan and al-Qaeda want."

"Yes, to make the bomb for them," Declan said. "Say no, and I don't think you'd last long once they got to work on you."

"So what do you suggest?"

"They will be armed to the teeth, and we'll be, too," Declan said. "There are three spare bulletproof vests on this plane available to anyone who doesn't have one. We challenge them, very close up, weapons ready. Few people can stand that, even soldiers."

Dillon said, "Lots of shouting. What do you say, Sara?"

"In Afghanistan, we called it a face-off," she told him. "I've seen it work a time or two, and I've seen it a total disaster."

Jane Green had been watching and listening by the open cockpit door. She said now, "What about our Russian chums? Are you sure they'll stick with the aircraft and not go on the prowl?"

"Absolutely, and for the same reason as you. You can't take a risk that someone might have a go at the plane, and that's the last thing we want in such a remote area."

"So how do you think the Russians will play?"

"They'll stay on their plane and wait," Dillon put in. "As long as their wages are safe, they're happy."

Jane said, "I'll discuss it with Don, we should be there in forty minutes." She returned to the cockpit.

Husseini was the only one not wearing a bulletproof vest, so Sara found one and threw it over to him. "Get it on, and that's an order."

"If you say so, but I'm leaving the gunplay to you," he said and went alone to the restroom to change.

He locked the door, sat on a stool, and considered the state of play. Possible carnage in a face-to-face gun battle, the likelihood of many deaths, and all because of him and who he was. There was something he could do about that, of course. He'd been thinking about it for some time. So he called Emza Khan on his mobile and found him in the courtyard of the hospice, inspecting the jeep.

"Who is this?" Khan asked warily.

"In your circumstances, your best friend," Husseini told him.

In a kind of reflex, Khan said, "How did you get this number?"

"This is Simon Husseini. You gave it to me in Paris."

"Where are you?"

"In the toilet on the Gideon. We're quite close to you. We'll land soon."

"So why are you calling me, what are you up to?" Khan demanded.

"Gunplay is not for me. This whole business has gone sour. What I'd like to do is get the hell out of here on your plane, but forget all this al-Qaeda nonsense. If you turn up with me in Tehran, you'll be a hero to the government. All follies wiped clean."

Emza Khan felt a flow of energy released, a kind of joy, because Husseini was so obviously right. "But what would happen to you?"

"They'll be so happy to get me back, they'll give me anything I desire, dancing girls, the works. Where are you, anyway?"

"I'm just looking over an old jeep the Saudis left here, but never mind that, how do we handle things?"

"When we land, Sara Gideon, Dillon, and the colonel will be armed to the teeth. I won't take part. Once they've gone, I'll cross to your Falcon. You must phone Kerimov and tell him to expect me."

"But what about the two pilots on your plane?"

"I'll find a way to slip out, but if not, I'll shoot them. You won't have any problem at all at the hospice. Wait for the Gideon woman and her two friends to get about two-thirds of the way on their walk from the plane to the hospice, then you and your people can jump in that jeep and drive like hell to your Falcon. I'll be ready and waiting on board, and we can get out of this damn place."

"This is brilliant," Khan said. "I think it could work."

"It will," Husseini told him. "I'll leave you to pass the good word to your two henchmen, and I'll see you later."

Dillon had found a bottle of Bushmills whiskey in the kitchen area, poured two large ones, and went and sat opposite Declan.

"Your Muslim half may say no, Colonel, but your Irish half says yes, and in the circumstances, the Irish half wins. So here's to you."

"And to you, my friend," Declan Rashid said.

Sara was across from them, a holstered Glock on her hip. She was writing in her daybook. Husseini came down the aisle, dropped the bulletproof vest on the seat opposite her, and sat next to it.

"I can't use this, so I'm returning it," he said. "As I said, I'm leaving the gunplay to you, and I'm not going to join you on your first venture into the hospice. You've got enough to do without having to protect an unarmed man."

"I understand," she said and smiled. "You're too valuable to lose, Simon."

He turned to the other two. "I'm also a terrible coward who is frightened to death of firearms."

At the same moment, Jane Green's voice echoed throughout the cabin. "Fasten your seat belts, we're going to descend."

From the hospice end of the runway, Kerimov and Lisin watched the landing, Lisin with approval. "Very nice, just what you'd expect from their military experience."

Kerimov had received a call on his mobile the moment the Gideon had started its descent, and he was listening intently. Lisin watched, puzzled. Finally, Kerimov said,

371

"Of course, Mr. Khan, we'll be ready and waiting."

He switched off and turned to Lisin. "Khan says to get ready now for a flight to Tehran."

Lisin was astounded. "When for?"

"Sometime during the next half hour."

"That's crazy," Lisin said. "What in hell is going on?"

Kerimov told him, and when he'd finished, Lisin shook his head. "Nineteen years I've been flying planes, but I've never known the likes of this. Is Emza Khan all right in the head?"

"I wouldn't know about that," Kerimov said. "But he pays top dollar, so whatever he wants, he gets. That means you better go and open the airstair door to receive Simon Husseini when he decides to join us."

The Gideon slowed down and took a position parallel to Khan's plane. Kerimov, looking across to the cockpit, recognized Jane Green, and raised a hand in salute. She returned it, and at the same time Lisin slid into the left-hand seat.

"Our door's open, but Husseini's going to find it difficult not to be seen from their cockpit when he makes his move."

At that moment, the door opened in the

other plane, the steps came down, and Sara Gideon descended, dressed for war, holding an AK-47 at port, followed by Dillon and Declan Rashid, similarly attired. They glanced across, had a brief conversation, and started to walk toward the hospice.

Jane Green and Renard were watching the progress of Sara and her companions through binoculars, so Kerimov produced his own from a locker and examined the other pilots, who were concentrating so closely on following the progress of Sara and company that they failed to notice Husseini slip out. He ducked under the Falcon and disappeared. A few moments later, he opened the door of the cockpit, smiled at the Russians, and said, "Permission to board, Captain."

In the courtyard of the hospice, standing outside the open door, Emza Khan looked out through the arched gate toward the two planes, side by side, watching the progress of Sara, Dillon, and Declan Rashid. Brother Andrew was behind Mikali in his wheelchair, Abbot Joseph and Father Peter next to him, and most of the brothers close together in the yard.

The jeep stood ready near at hand, Jemal behind the wheel and Omar sitting next to him, gripping an AK-47. Emza Khan's lips were moving, as if counting, as he stared out at the approaching figures.

Suddenly, he shook everyone around him by shouting, "Let's go," running to the jeep, and heaving himself into the rear.

Jemal gunned the motor and roared out of the entrance with plenty of wheelspin, raising a cloud of choking sand. As they neared his enemies, Khan was unable to resist a shot at Sara, gripped a rail, and stood up, trying to take aim. Dillon, immediately aware of what he was trying to do, hurled himself at Sara, knocking her out of the way. Khan fired twice, creasing the side of Dillon's left shoulder.

The jeep swerved away and rushed at full speed toward the Falcon, which already had its engines turning over. Jemal braked and leapt out, turned to help Khan mount the steps, and it was Simon Husseini who leaned out to pull him in. Jemal and Omar followed, and Lisin closed the door. Kerimov increased speed, turning in a wide circle, and started down the runway for takeoff.

Inside, Husseini led the way to a corner table close to the kitchen area. He had an ice bucket on the floor with a bottle of prime Russian vodka, and there were two tumblers in the table rack. He filled them and pushed one across to Khan, who drank it greedily. He looked terrible, sweat trickling down — his face coated with sand.

"So you were right," he gasped, clutching the arm of his seat as the Falcon started to climb. "The whole thing worked like a charm. Tehran next stop."

"Yes, they'll be delighted to get their hands on me, especially as they'll have found nothing on my computers."

Khan said, "You mean you wiped them clean?"

"No, there was nothing there in the first place. It's all in my head."

Khan was astonished. "I can't believe that."

"However, all my discoveries, the mathematics, the equations, the calculations, the key that opened everything up to a new level — all the things that I didn't want anyone to have, even the good guys — have been recorded."

"But you've got it somewhere?" Khan said. "You must have."

"Of course." Husseini produced the small black-and-silver notebook with the green light throbbing in it that he'd shown Sean Dillon. "An electronic notebook. It can only be opened by a code word. Like this, for example."

He tapped some buttons, and the green turned to red. "There we go. Do you want to know what my code word is? A six-letter word — Semtex. Czechoslovakia's gift to the world, a present from Osama, whose name be praised. It's the explosive no terrorist should be without."

The slight smile on Emza Khan's face vanished, his mouth opened to cry out, but it was too late. There was a massive explosion and the Falcon disintegrated, a ball of fire that blossomed into an enormous scarlet-and-yellow flower as it descended over the desert.

Sara, Dillon, and Declan had continued toward the hospice and were in when the explosion took place, the sight of the fire descending unforgettable.

Dillon stood there, clutching his shoulder, blood passing between his fingers. Sara turned to him, her face bleak. "What's happened? I don't understand."

Dillon said, "I've an idea we'll soon find out." He faltered, and Declan grabbed him. "I could do with a doctor. It's a good thing this Father Peter used to be in the army."

Father Peter attended him in a side room at the infirmary, aided by Brother Andrew.

Declan and Sara, the abbot and Father Mikali, in his wheelchair, were drinking strong black tea when Andrew appeared.

"Seventeen stitches and he refused chloroform. Insisted that a local anesthetic would be enough. He was unlucky. Bulletproof vests seldom cover the arms."

"We have a private hospital facility for our people called Rosedene," Sara said. "Professor Charles Bellamy runs it. Many people think him the finest general surgeon in London."

Andrew said, "Believe me, I think he will approve of Father Peter's work," and Dillon walked in behind him, leaning on a walking stick, his left arm in a sling.

"Sean, you shouldn't be up," Sara scolded him. "Sit down at once."

Which he did, and at that moment, there was the sound of the jeep arriving in the courtyard, and a moment later, Jane Green entered, her face grave.

"Don's guarding the plane." She nodded at Sean. "I can see you've suffered."

"I'll survive," Dillon told her. "It could have been worse."

"No, it couldn't, so brace yourselves," she said. "Don and I were so busy watching you advance on the hospice that we didn't notice Husseini was gone. When they roared back in the jeep, we witnessed them all scrambling into the Falcon. It was a hell of a shock when Husseini appeared from inside and pulled in Emza Khan."

"What? Simon was on their plane? But why?" Sara demanded. "It makes no sense."

"Or all the sense in the world," Dillon said. "He was always very conscious that it was his very existence that was center of all the troubles, that and the bomb. He talked to us about it. And then he wrote a note, sealed it in an envelope, and gave it to me. He said the contents were self-explanatory and that I would know when to open it." He shrugged. "As I've only got one good hand, in the circumstances, I'll hand it to you, Father," he said to Mikali.

The old priest read it, then handed it to Sara, his face sorrowful. "He says he couldn't bear the thought of more good people dying over him. So he tricked Emza Khan into believing he wanted to return to Tehran."

"He must have been planning this for some time," said Rashid. "Got hold of an explosive somehow."

"That poor, poor man," said Sara.

"He's certainly set back Iran's nuclear program," said Rashid.

"But for how long?" Dillon said. "Anyway,

I think it's time we got out of here."

Jane Green said to Andrew, "That's what Don wants me to raise with you. There was mention of a large stock of aviation fuel here somewhere?"

"Yes, that's true. It hasn't been used for a long time, but it should be fine."

"Great," she said. "I'd appreciate getting started. We'll follow you up to the hangar if you'd get your people up there. I'll take the others in the jeep. Dillon's not fit for that walk."

As they went out, Sara turned and said to Mikali, "He was a good man, Father, did we do right by him?"

"Let's just say he did what he thought was right by us, and leave it at that."

She shook her head, took a deep breath, and walked out.

■ ■ ■ ■

LONDON

■ ■ ■ ■

14

The Gideon lifted off from al-Shaba very fast and climbed up to forty thousand feet, with Don Renard at the controls while Jane Green plotted the three-thousand-mile trip northwest that would eventually end in London. Dillon had been made as comfortable as possible, lying back in a half-reclined corner seat, a blanket over his legs. Filled with morphine thanks to Saudi medical supplies, he still had his hand around a tumbler of whiskey and dozed.

Declan appeared to be asleep, but as for Sara, she made a pot of black coffee, drank two cups of it, waiting for the plane to settle in flight, then she opened her laptop and tried Roper on Skype. It was the middle of the afternoon in London, and her appearance took him by surprise.

"It's good to see you, Sara, though I must say you look as if you've been through the wringer," he told her.

"It would. It got rather nasty."

"Go on, tell me the worst."

Which she did, and Roper was astounded. "It's one of the most remarkable stories I've ever heard. And in the end, nobody gets the Husseini bomb, including our side. And the blow to al-Qaeda is beyond price."

"Let's hope Ferguson's as pleased as you are," Sara said.

Roper nodded. "No doubt about that. How are you feeling? It must have been a shock to the system, Emza Khan trying to knock you off."

"He truly hated me, Giles. I was the whore who murdered his son. He'd have never left it alone."

"What about Colonel Rashid? How is he going to come out of all this?" Roper asked.

"His superiors won't be impressed with the way he handled things, I suppose," Sara said.

"I'd say that's an understatement."

"Is there any word from Daniel? What's happening with this Timbuktu affair?" Sara carried on.

"The UN couldn't find any African countries to send troops." Roper shrugged. "Daniel and his freebooters have done a great job, but they're in the process of withdrawing under orders from Algiers."

"It's certainly made the Algerian government look good," Sara told him. "Well, I'm glad he's safe. I'm going to have a drink now and try to sleep. Bye for now."

She helped herself to brandy from the small bar, mixing it with ginger ale. Declan opened his eyes and said, "What's that?"

"A Horse's Neck," she told him. "Popular with officers in the Royal Navy since time immemorial. I thought you were asleep."

"Dozing. You were reporting in?"

"To Roper."

"After he got over his astonishment, I imagine his big question was, what about Colonel Declan Rashid?"

"Yes, you were discussed, so what *are* you going to do?"

"First of all, report in to my commanding officer in true army fashion. I'll do that now."

"Do you want me to step out?" Sara asked.

"No, I'd like you to stay, and I'm sure Mr. Dillon hasn't missed a word of everything said in the past half hour."

"God bless you for the kind word, your honor," Dillon murmured. So Declan took out his mobile, put it on speaker, and called the general.

"General ben Levi? Colonel Declan Rashid reporting."

"And where the hell have you been for the last four days?" ben Levi demanded.

"Three and a half, actually," Declan said. "I discovered where Husseini had gone on the same day you gave me my orders. That was thanks to Vahidi, just before he was murdered."

"What nonsense is this?"

"Oh, he was murdered, all right, and probably by al-Qaeda. But we won't argue. At the moment, I'm traveling on an executive jet over the Saudi Arabian desert. Four hours ago, to the south of us, Simon Husseini blew himself and some interesting companions to hell by activating an explosive charge that destroyed the Falcon in which he was traveling." Declan laughed harshly. "Do you think that's more nonsense? Do you want the full story on that, too?"

"Yes, Colonel Rashid," the general said hoarsely. "Everything."

Declan took him at his word and gave him a military-style report, omitting nothing. When he finished, there was a pause before ben Levi spoke.

"An excellent report, Colonel, I would have expected no less from you."

"You'll pass it on to the minister?"

"Of course. We'll have to figure out what

to do with this. I think I'll suggest putting a security blanket over the whole business, especially Husseini's death. You know the sort of thing? The great man must have seclusion, buries himself in his work, never gives interviews. Then we'll still seem like a threat to the world."

"Ingenious, General," Declan said drily. "I take your point."

"So when can we expect to see you report back for duty?"

"Actually, I don't think my return would be advisable," Declan said. "After all, I know what happened, I was aware what Emza Khan was, a traitor to his country, and I know why Simon Husseini did what he did. No, it's London next stop for me, General. I've always carried my Irish passport for years, even in battle, as a good-luck charm. I won't even have to seek asylum. I'm an Irish citizen."

Ali ben Levi raised his voice. "Colonel Rashid, you're a serving officer of the Iranian Army. You can't do this."

"Try me," Declan Rashid told him and switched off.

"My word, but that was the Irish half speaking," Dillon said. "Your mother would be proud of you. You can take up residence at Holland Park until you find your feet, or there's my cottage in Stable Mews and glad to have you. Now, get yourself a drink and another for me, for you've earned it."

"What kind of man is General ben Levi?" Sara asked. "Will he be all right?"

"Made his bones in the war with Iraq: Eight years of that and huge casualties made rare opportunities for dedicated men. Commissioned from the ranks and never looked back. Takes life seriously. He ought to be fine. It'll certainly be interesting to hear the Iranian spin on this in the coming days." He tapped his phone. "I also took the precaution of recording our phone call. You never know when it'll come in handy."

"And let me send it on to Roper," Sara said. "Ferguson will be very interested."

"It's all happening," Rashid said cheerfully and passed a glass of Scotch across to Dillon. "That should help to ease the pain."

Dillon tasted it. "Well, it isn't Irish whiskey, but it will do to take along."

General Ali ben Levi sat at his desk, considering what had happened and trying to take it all in, especially Declan Rashid's astonishing act of defiance. From any soldier, it was an action completely unacceptable. In other circumstances, he would have reached for the phone to inform the minister. That was not possible, and there were reasons.

He was a man of the people who genuinely loved his country. It was the army which had made him, supported him on the long climb to the top, given him prestige and position at the highest levels of society. And yet he hated what he had found there. The rapacious oil billionaires whose vast wealth made it so easy to corrupt those around them at every level. And then Osama bin Laden had descended on the world of Islam to astonish Muslims around the globe in a manner none had experienced before, offering a life of sacrifice. Ali ben Levi had embraced it completely, had served al-Qaeda with all his heart, so he phoned Dr. Ali Saif at Pound Street Mosque in London.

Saif was at his desk when his phone went. He'd gotten into the habit of screening all calls and discarding those he didn't want, but when Ali ben Levi spoke, he jumped to attention.

"We seem to have been here before, Saif."

"Ah, is it that bad, Master? Tell me the worst," Saif said.

So Ali ben Levi did, and in detail. When he was finished, Saif said, "Emza Khan and Husseini dead, and not a word on television or in the press. You're sitting tight on this for a moment?"

"I hope I can afford to. After all, they were killed in a plane blown to smithereens over one of the most desolate deserts in the world. There could be a substantial delay before it's reported. I'm not sure what I'm doing. I must consider what's best for al-Qaeda, and I haven't had a chance to inform the council yet."

"It's a difficult one, particularly this new problem with Colonel Rashid," Saif said. "A pity you aren't here to handle it yourself."

"That's true, but it's all sudden and needs careful thinking about. We'll speak again."

He sat there considering, particularly Saif's point that it was a pity he wasn't there. He could do something about that. Filled with sudden energy, he picked up his desk phone and contacted the secret police HQ.

"Embassy, please," he said to the officer in charge. "Is there anything going to London today?"

"Yes, General, we have a Falcon with confidential dispatches and two junior ministers from the Diplomatic Service."

"How long does it take?"

"Between ten and eleven hours, depending on weather. It leaves in fifty minutes."

"No, it doesn't. You'll hold it until I get there."

Ali ben Levi went through the outer office without stopping, saying to the duty aide, "If the minister needs me, I'll be away for three days on a high-priority project and you don't know where."

He was gone, the door banging behind him before the aide could reply.

It was obviously going to be evening before the Gideon got in, and Roper was going through all the information he had on the business and nodded to himself. One thing was missing: a face-to-face with Dr. Ali Saif. Considering it now, he realized he'd been leaving him alone to see what he would do and Saif had responded by not doing very much. Roper pressed his buzzer, and Tony Doyle appeared wearing the full uniform of a staff sergeant in the Royal Military Police, including the red cap.

"Sorry, Major, I've only just got back from court duty at the Ministry of Defence," he said. "If you can give me a minute, I'll go and change."

"No, you won't," Roper said. "You look very impressive, and I love the medals. I'd like you to take me on a fishing trip."

"Sir?"

"At Pound Street, and the Army of God. When you push me in there, that uniform will scare the hell out of them."

"My pleasure, Major." Doyle smiled. "It sounds like fun."

"Yes, but remember I need you suitably severe, if not menacing."

"My pleasure, sir," Tony Doyle said. "Shall we proceed?"

At Pound Street, Doyle lowered the wheelchair on the hydraulic lift. They ventured inside, ignoring the astonished scores of Muslim students, and found a receptionist, who asked what they wanted and insisted on showing the way, to the point of opening Saif's door and ushering them inside.

Saif, a cigarette in his mouth and editing a typescript, glanced up, totally thrown. Tony Doyle stood to one side, and Roper took charge of his chair and eased up to the desk.

"Dr. Saif, a great pleasure. My name is Roper and I work for Charles Ferguson. I read your book *The Later Years,* about what happened when the Romans left Britain, with great pleasure. How nice to find someone who still smokes. Do you think I could have one?"

Ali Saif was bemused and offered a cigarette automatically. "Of course."

Roper accepted a light and smiled. "I've been looking forward to meeting you for quite some time."

Saif blanched, face turning very pale, choked for a moment on his cigarette smoke, coughed several times. "It's nice to meet you," he managed to say.

"No, it isn't, it's awful to meet me, because it means the game's up and the thought of sharing a cell with some hulk with the hots for you, or venturing into the showers on D landing, is flashing before your eyes."

Ali Saif looked ghastly and Roper carried on. "But I'm here to tell you it doesn't need to be like that, to show you a better way."

Ali looked dazed, but suddenly opened a drawer, took out a bottle of whiskey and a tumbler, poured a large one, and poured it down. He shivered, took another tumbler from the drawer, poured, then pushed it across to Roper.

"Very civil of you." Roper drank, and Saif joined him in another. He was calmer now. "So what are we talking about?"

"Your personal achievements as a scholar, historian, and author are a matter of record. The educational facilities for the charity side of this institution are excellent, and your fundraising abilities legendary."

Saif smiled painfully. "Don't overdo it, Major."

Roper ignored him. "All this while working ceaselessly under the direction of a member of the al-Qaeda council who is known only as the Master."

Saif tried to conceal his alarm by taking another drink. "I don't know where you've got all that from."

Roper said, "I notice your desk phone, as I would expect from a clever chap like you, has a recording device which means that all your calls are on it. Would I be right?"

There was real desperation on Saif's face now, and he grabbed at the phone, and Roper snapped his fingers. "Sergeant."

Tony Doyle was around the desk in a second, one arm about the neck, pushing the phone across to Roper with his free hand. "Now, you be a nice gentleman and calm down," he told Saif.

Roper said, "You *are* getting upset. I'd say it's because you and the Master have had words recently. Shall we have a look?" He ran things back, and within a very short time, there it was.

"Damn you," Saif said.

"Taken care of a long time ago. Now, shut up and we'll listen." Which he did, fascinated. "My goodness," he said when it was finished. "What unlooked-for treasure."

"So what happens now, the Tower of London?" Saif asked bitterly.

"Actually, that was where we shot spies in the Second World War," Roper said. "But I've a feeling that if you are a very good boy, you might emerge from all this with a smile on your face. General Charles Ferguson can be a very forgiving man in the right circumstances, especially to those who can be useful to him."

Dr. Ali Saif brightened considerably. "You really think so?"

"I don't see why not. We'll discuss the details later. Just be smart, Saif." He took out a card and flicked it across the desk. "My number if you need me."

"You mean you're not going to charge me or anything?"

"Oh, I don't think so, and you're not going to do a runner, are you? We'll be watching you, and anyway, where would you go? Let's get back now, Tony," he said to Doyle, switched on his chair and led the way out.

Saif sat there bewildered, and yet by some miracle a door had been opened for him. He was grateful for that. What he needed now was a real drink to celebrate, preferably at the pub across the street. He got up, found his raincoat, and left, switching off the light.

It wasn't full darkness, that would come later, but it was gloomy enough, as a door creaked and light leaked in from the book stockroom. It was a shortcut to Saif's office from the gymnasium and teaching areas. Rasoul habitually used it when he needed to see Saif. It had been a few inches ajar when he'd arrived, and it was the sight of Tony Doyle's military police uniform that had brought him up short. He had held back and listened, had heard everything.

The news of Emza Khan's death was the worst shock he'd had to endure in his entire life. It was that he now faced the loss of a life of privilege, money, and power. The truth was that Khan had been his mentor, a man so powerful that the connection itself had made Rasoul a somebody, a man to be feared by other people.

He went to Saif's desk, switched on a lamp, sat down, and found the whiskey. He poured a large one, drinking it slowly. He was alive, and yet to others he was a dead man, a ghost. And he planned to return the favor. Roper, Dillon, Ferguson, perhaps even the Jewish whore who had murdered Yousef Khan would all be targets. He had his Walther PPK in his locker with a silencer and several clips of cartridges. He nodded slowly and poured another whiskey. All debts would be paid.

Iran's courier aircraft had a contract that allowed them to use the Northolt airfield when it suited. Ali ben Levi had been treated like royalty during the trip, had made it clear to the crew and other passengers that he was on a top-secret mission. The fact that he was who he was meant that he was accepted without query, including the offer of a lift in the embassy limousine. He simply asked for a taxi and left for central London.

He was wearing a polo-neck sweater and gabardine suit and a Burberry trench coat. He carried a small military bag that he'd been allowed to bring through without a search. Sitting there in the back of the taxi, he checked inside the bag surreptitiously, feeling the bulk of the Walther PPK for a moment. Compact and smaller than some, but devastating in the hands of an expert. He looked out into the falling darkness, the constant traffic. He'd enjoyed happy times here in the past, loved London, but that was then; *now* was Saif at Pound Street and any information he could give on Declan Rashid's whereabouts.

Sara, Dillon, and Declan were enjoying a drink in the computer room at Holland Park when Roper rolled in.

"Thank God you're back in one piece," he said. "Except for you, Dillon. You know our policy with any kind of damage. You report to Professor Bellamy at Rosedene and let him assess the situation. You'd be a fool not to take advantage of his skills."

"I will, Giles, I swear it. I just want to hear exactly where we are with things, then I'll be up to Rosedene like a shot."

Sara turned to Roper. "You think you've come across something. Tell us."

"I have a recording I'd like to play to you, of a telephone conversation between Dr. Ali Saif and his al-Qaeda asset, the man known to him as the Master. Just listen."

They all did. When it was finished, Sara said, "What's the point?"

"All right. Now listen to the conversation between General Ali ben Levi and Colonel Rashid here.

Even before it finished, Sara said, "Oh my God, it's the same man."

"Of course it is," Roper said. "Condemned by his own voice."

"I've known him for years," Declan said. "It's hard to take in, hard to explain how wrong one could be about somebody, but it has to be faced."

"And there's even more to consider, you know. My computers are programmed to send me any interesting information. It appears that General Ali ben Levi has just arrived at Northolt an hour ago on an Iranian Embassy courier run. He hailed a taxi and is headed for downtown London."

Dillon said, "So why's he here? Do you think he's doing a runner, Colonel?"

"I was going to say, not the man I knew," Declan said. "But now I wonder if I ever knew him at all."

Saif had spent close to an hour in the pub considering his predicament, and his final conclusion was definitely that it could have been a lot worse. A pragmatist at heart, he realized that one chapter in his life had closed, but if he behaved himself, something worthwhile could be on offer, especially if he played his cards right.

So he was cheerful enough as he opened the door of his office and turned on the light, and there was Rasoul sitting behind the desk, the Browning in his right hand and the whiskey tumbler in his left.

"So there you are, you bastard," he said. "I've been waiting. Get in here and close the door."

Saif knew fear, real fear at the angry and drink-sodden face, but desperately forced a smile. "Why, Rasoul, what's this?"

"Don't try to make a fool out of me. I was in the book room when the major in the wheelchair was turning you inside out. I heard all of that phone conversation, what the Master said to you about what Ferguson's people had done to Emza Khan. I should kill you right now, except I'd rather it was Ferguson or that Jewish whore."

Ali ben Levi had arrived at Pound Street to find no one on the desk, but an obliging student had pointed the way to Saif's office. He'd paused, aware of voices inside, had taken the Walther from his bag, was holding it at his side when he opened the door with his left and stepped in. For a moment, it was a tableau frozen in time. Himself, Saif, and Rasoul at the desk with the Browning in his hand.

It was the sight of the gun that did it. Ali ben Levi started to raise his too late, and Rasoul shot him in the heart, knocking him back against the door, and he slid to the floor.

Saif was terrified, expecting to be next at

any moment, but Rasoul came around the desk, dropped to one knee, fished in the dead man's pockets, and found a passport. "Iranian and a general. Some sort of military police. Do you know this man?"

"I swear to you, I've never seen him before in my life."

"Well, the way I see it, he must have something to do with this whole bloody business. We'll hide him in the storeroom, so do that now."

Saif did as he was told, dragging the dead man across the floor and into the storeroom, turning the key in the door.

"That's good," Rasoul said. "I remember Roper giving you his number, so you can call him now and tell him you know where this General Ali ben Levi is. If it doesn't mean anything to them, it won't matter. On the other hand, it might."

"Is that all?"

"No. I'm interested in pulling Ferguson or some of his people in."

"And how do I do that?"

"Tell Roper and his friends that if they want to see a dead man walking, Rasoul is back, and he's shot someone dead at your office. He'll be waiting for them himself at Emza Khan's penthouse in Park Lane."

He was drunk, sweating, eyes glittering,

and obviously quite mad. Saif said, "You're going to kill me, aren't you?"

"Of course not. I want you to be there and see me in action with those swine." He laughed harshly and stroked Saif's face with the barrel of the Walther. "Then I might kill you. So make the call and then we'll get out of here in that Citroën van of yours and try for Park Lane before they get there."

At Holland Park, there was the briefest of discussions. "No time to call in more troops," Roper said.

"You can count on me, my friend," Declan Rashid said. "Just provide a weapon."

"There you are," Sara told Roper firmly. "We've got plenty of those here."

"And don't try to keep me out of it," Dillon said. "It's my left arm in a sling, and the right's in perfect working order, so let's get on with it."

"Damn you, Sean," Roper told him. "But I don't have much choice and time is of the essence, so why aren't you roaring out of the front gate now? Only, for God's sake, take care."

"I always knew you were a big softie at heart," Dillon said and led the way out.

Seconds later, the Alfa Romeo's engine burst into life and faded into the night.

Suddenly, Roper was alone. This was always the worst time, the waiting. For something to do, he phoned Mr. Teague. "Major Roper here. I need a disposal unit at the Army of God headquarters at Pound Street, the storeroom in Dr. Ali Saif's office. Grade A security, this one. I'd appreciate your most urgent attention."

"I'm sure there will be no problem, Major. I'll keep you informed."

And Teague did. It seemed like only minutes later that he called Roper and asked, "Do you know anybody named ben Levi?"

Absorbing the information, Roper poured a large whiskey to settle his nerves and lit a cigarette, for his bomb-battered body needed any relief he could find, and now he sat there wondering what was happening at Park Lane.

The penthouse was in darkness as Saif turned off Park Lane into the underground garage. Rasoul said, "That's no good. I need the lights on to make them think I'm up there." He passed Saif a key. "Jump in that lift, press express, and you're there in no time. Put all the lights on."

"Do I come back?"

"You'd only be in the way, so stay out of

it. I'm going to surprise them. Now, clear off."

Which Saif did, and as he stepped into the lift, in the bravest act of his life he shouted, "I don't know if you're there, but he's going to ambush you!"

"You bastard," Rasoul cried and fired at the door as it closed.

Sara, crouched down in the Alfa, kicked the door open, followed by Declan, both of them gun in hand. Rasoul pivoted, firing wildly; she fired back, clipping his left arm, and then she slipped on an oil patch.

"I've got you now, whore." As Declan bent over her protectively, Rasoul shot him in the back twice, then advanced, Walther raised, his left arm hanging.

The rear door of a station wagon opposite was kicked open, and Sean Dillon sat up, one arm still in a sling, a Glock in the other hand, and shot Rasoul in the center of the forehead, lifting him off his feet to fall on his back.

There had been little noise, just the dull thud of silenced weapons exchanging fire, then the whirring of the lift descending. Saif appeared cautiously and then ran forward, paused to look down at Rasoul, then approached Declan on the ground, leaning against the Alfa, Sara crouching beside him, trying to stem blood with her scarf.

Saif said, "Is it bad?"

"We'll have to see," Sara told him. "But you were great. Thanks for having the guts to stand up to that bastard."

Dillon, on his Codex, was calling in to Roper. "Declan Rashid's taken one bullet at least. Sara and I each got a piece of Rasoul, so we'll need disposal. You'll be pleased to know Dr. Ali Saif came through for us big-time."

"Thanks, Sean, I'll see you back at the ranch."

"Probably Rosedene," Dillon said. "I could do with Bellamy myself."

"And when you all do get back here? I might have some news for you." And he hung up.

Roper sat there, thinking about it, poured himself a whiskey, then phoned Ferguson to tell him the good news. Then he sent for Tony Doyle to come and take him to the wet room for the total treatment, steam, shower, fresh clothes, and was back in the computer room when Sara called him from Rosedene.

"One bullet was stopped by Declan's vest, but another was lower down and on the hip below the vest. Bellamy says it's going to take time and therapy. Apparently, he's been wounded several times over the years. Can I ask you what's going to happen to him, Giles? Have you discussed it with Ferguson?"

"There's no need, Sara. Declan Rashid has Irish citizenship through his mother, so he doesn't need to ask permission to live in Ireland or London or any other part of the United Kingdom. He is here by right."

"And I can tell him that?"

"Of course, although I fear it may complicate your love life."

"Oh, I'll take that as it comes," she said and rang off.

Roper sat there, wondering whether to talk to Ferguson again and deciding not to. Dr. Ali Saif was going to be a useful asset in spite of, or because of, his past. One had to be a pragmatist. This war on terrorism seemed never-ending, and he thought of what Sara had said about Declan. That he'd been wounded several times over the years.

"Haven't we all?" he said softly and poured himself another drink.

ABOUT THE AUTHOR

Since *The Eagle Has Landed* — one of the biggest-selling thrillers of all time — every novel **Jack Higgins** has written, including his most recent works, *A Devil Is Waiting, The Judas Gate, The Wolf at the Door, A Darker Place* and *Rough Justice*, has become an international bestseller. He has had simultaneous number-one bestsellers in hardcover and paperback, and many of his books have been made into successful movies, including *The Eagle Has Landed, To Catch a King, On Dangerous Ground, Eye of the Storm,* and *Thunder Point.*

Higgins, who lived in Belfast until he was twelve, had several close calls with bombs and gunfire at an early age. After leaving school at fifteen, he served three years with the Royal Horse Guards in Eastern Europe during the cold war. Subsequently, he was a circus roustabout, a factory worker, a truck driver, and a laborer, before entering college at age twenty-seven. He has degrees in sociology, social psychology, and economics from the University of London, and a doctorate in media from Leeds Metropolitan University.

A fellow of the Royal Society of Arts, and an expert scuba diver and marksman, Higgins lives on Jersey in the Channel Islands.

The employees of Thorndike Press hope you have enjoyed this Large Print book. All our Thorndike, Wheeler, and Kennebec Large Print titles are designed for easy reading, and all our books are made to last. Other Thorndike Press Large Print books are available at your library, through selected bookstores, or directly from us.

For information about titles, please call:
(800) 223-1244

or visit our Web site at:
http://gale.cengage.com/thorndike

To share your comments, please write:
Publisher
Thorndike Press
10 Water St., Suite 310
Waterville, ME 04901